FALSE START

Virginia Valley University

JESSICA RUDDICK

Peake Ink PRESS

Content edits provided by Marnee Blake.
Line editing suggestions provided by Red Adept Editing.

ISBN 978-1-946164-22-3

CHAPTER 1

Becca

I RAISED MY Diet Coke with a wry grin and clinked it against my friends' glasses. The noise was barely discernible in the crowded bar.

Nicole shot me a sympathetic look. "Just a few more months, right?"

"Less than four. Not that I'm counting." My brother and I were Irish twins, meaning his birthday was in January and mine was in December of the same year. My parents had forgotten the Irish part and raised us like we were actual twins, enrolling us in school at the same time. So I was always the last of my friends to reach new milestones, sometimes by over a year.

"Look on the bright side, Becca," Evan said. "My twenty-first was lame because no one else could drink. You won't have that problem."

"Instead, people will be mourning the loss of their designated driver." I was joking, but it was sort of true. However, the crowd I ran with wasn't exactly wild and crazy. Case in point? It was nearly ten on a Saturday night, and Jian and Joey were already closing out their tabs. No doubt Chris would be close behind.

The six of us—Nicole, Evan, Jian, Joey, Chris, and me—were all that was left of our freshman-year engineering cohort. We'd started with fifteen, but the major was notorious for its high dropout and transfer rate. Some people referred to it as survival of the smartest, but more than likely, it was survival of the most stubborn. At least that was how I'd made it to my senior year.

A commotion toward the front of the bar caught my attention. When towering figures made of pure muscle filtered in, making the already crowded space seem instantly smaller, I cursed. I'd chosen this venue specifically to avoid this.

To avoid him.

I could turn away, but that wouldn't make a difference. My sixth sense always knew when the guy I'd been in love with half my life was nearby.

Nicole nudged me. "Carson is over there."

My friend had a grade-school-style crush on Carson, so I tried to keep her as far away from him as possible. She had no idea about my feelings for him, but that wasn't why I kept her away. Nicole wasn't his type. He preferred easy girls, ones who were satisfied with a one-night stand. If for some odd reason he did go for Nicole, he would chew her up, spit her out, and leave me to pick up the pieces. *No, thank you.*

I wouldn't wish that on anyone—not my friend and not myself. Carson was firmly in the friend zone. If I had any intent on keeping my already compromised heart intact, that was where he needed to stay.

"Trust me," I told her. "You want no part of that."

Evan shot me a puzzled look. "Isn't he your friend from home?"

While I sometimes joined Carson's crowd, he rarely joined mine, so Evan had only met him a few times in the past three years. I caught the gist of what he was saying, though—he was wondering why I would talk smack about a friend. Maybe it was bad form, but I called them as I saw them.

"My brother's best friend, yeah."

During his teen years, Carson had spent more time at our house than his own, which didn't make sense on the surface. His house was practically a mansion, complete with a media room, swimming pool, and home gym. Though once I'd met his parents, his desire to spend his time elsewhere became understandable. They were nice enough people, but the sheer intensity they radiated was enough to make the most secure person nervous.

Nicole flipped her hair over her shoulder. "What she's trying to say is he's way too hot for a nerd like me."

I gasped. "That's not what I meant." Nicole *was* on the nerdy side, but then again, so was I. It came with the territory of being in the engineering program.

She put her hand up. "Let me revise. He's way more than a nerd like me can handle. I know he's out of my league, but a girl can dream, can't she?"

"He's not out of your league," I corrected. "He's a player."

"Eh." Nicole chewed on her straw as she watched him and his friends, who were most likely all football players for Virginia Valley University. "It might be nice to be played."

I didn't know how to respond to that. It had never occurred to me that Nicole might want to dip her toe in the water of one-night stands. *To each her own.* Still, I didn't know if my heart could handle Carson and Nicole hooking up. It was bad enough watching him with girls I didn't know.

Evan drank the last swallow of his water. "On that note, I'm heading out."

Nicole laughed. "We can talk about girls you want to play with if it makes you more comfortable. We're equal opportunity."

Evan balked. "I'm not uncomfortable. I'm just..." His mouth kept moving, but no words came out. "I got nothing. I'll see you tomorrow."

As soon as Evan left, Nicole put a hand on my arm. "Don't worry. I'm not going to throw myself at Carson or anything."

"I'm not worried." All it would take was one word from me for Nicole to put Carson on her never-ever list, but not a soul knew about my feelings for him, and it was going to stay that way.

"With that expression, you're either worried or constipated."

My eyes widened, and my cheeks flushed. "Jesus, Nic." I looked around to see if anyone had overheard her. Her lack of a filter was usually one of the things I liked about her, but at the moment, it had lost its appeal.

Laughing, she leaned forward on the table. "We're seniors. Soon we'll have to be responsible adults. Like *real* ones. Our window for random hookups is closing."

"I don't think we're missing out on anything." Plus, I didn't believe there was a limited window for making mistakes. There were plenty of screwed-up adults who made questionable choices, not that that was something to aspire to.

Shrugging, Nicole looked longingly at Carson and his friends. "Maybe. Maybe not." She patted my arm again. "But don't worry. I would never hook up with Carson. I know that would be weird for you."

"Thanks," I mumbled. I could have told her it wouldn't be weird for me, but that would've been a bold-faced lie. So I let her think it would be weird because he and I were old friends and not because I had my own eye on him.

"Come on." Nicole drained the last of her drink and pushed it back on the table. "The boy nerds are gone. Let's go mingle."

Mingle? It was supposed to be a quiet night out to reconnect with our engineering friends whom we hadn't seen all summer. Now all of a sudden, I was Nicole's wing woman on her quest for a random hookup. *Lord help me.* I silently cursed my December birthday. I needed a drink.

I watched for a moment as Carson flashed a roguish grin at a girl who had sidled up to him. She was pretty and dressed appropriately for a night out, meaning her dress was tight and short, and her heels were high. In contrast, my outfit was geared more toward Sunday afternoon grocery shopping—shorts, a T-shirt, and sandals.

Carson was wearing the guy equivalent of my outfit, but it worked. Everything he wore worked because of his muscular physique. The bottom of his tattoo peeked out of the sleeve of his gray T-shirt, giving him a slight bad-boy appearance. Only slight, though, because that night, he was clean-shaven and had that all-American look nailed. But once he let his face get scruffy, he would leave all-American behind and claim badass status. He looked good no matter what persona he was trying to pull off, and the trouble was he knew it.

He must have felt me staring at him because he glanced my way. His face lit up, his grin meeting his green eyes. One look from him, and my carefully constructed wall turned to cellophane—I felt exposed, as if he saw my darkest secret.

But he'd never given any indication that he saw me as anything more than a pseudo-little sister. Our relationship was complicated. One minute, he was my best friend, and the next, he was irritating me so badly that I wanted to throttle him. For instance, he took his promise to my brother to watch out for me way too seriously and scared off any guy who dared to talk to me. That was a big reason why I'd never had a serious relationship. Well, that and the fact that no one could ever be Carson.

I gave him a little finger wave, and he jerked his chin up, still smiling. The girl who'd been trying to claim his attention followed his line of sight, and when her gaze landed on me, she shot me a dirty look. Her eyes gave me a once-over, and the dirty look dropped off her face as she dismissed me. *Bitch.*

"Becca, you coming?" Nicole asked.

I shifted my gaze back to Carson and his lopsided smile. What was left of my cellophane shriveled into nothing. The girl put her hand on his shoulder, staking her claim, just in case I actually was a threat. I definitely was, but not in the way she thought.

My lips stretched into a slow smile. Perhaps it was time I repaid Carson and saved him from himself. I might not be intimidating like he was, but there was more than one way to get the job done.

"Coming." I threw my shoulders back and ran my hands through my hair.

This was going to be fun.

***

Carson

"ZIZZO!"

Shit yeah! My night just got a million times better. Ziz was my best friend, Roman's, little sister and the only person at VVU from home that I'd kept in touch with. It had been almost a month since I'd seen her. *Way too long.*

She tossed her hair over her shoulder as she sauntered toward me, swinging her hips and attracting the attention of several guys she passed. I scowled and instinctively cracked my knuckles. Those dudes better tuck their eyeballs back into their skulls before I was forced to knock their teeth out.

Beside me, Demarcus grinned. "Damn. Who's that fine thing?"

Before I could set him straight, Jimmy shook his head. "Do yourself a favor and don't even look at her, man." *Damn straight.* I'd taught my teammates years ago that Ziz was off limits. I knew better than anyone that no VVU football player would ever be good enough for her.

Ziz came in for a hug and wrapped her arms around my neck, which surprised the shit out of me. Her tits pressed against my chest, making my pants suddenly feel too tight. *What the hell?* Ziz and I were close—she knew me better than anyone else at VVU—but we didn't hug on the regular.

As she pulled away, she trailed one arm across my shoulder and down my arm, leaving the other arm wrapped around me. She cozied up against me, practically purring.

Fucking shit all to hell. Not much took me off guard, but her behavior was throwing me for a loop. The upper half of my body stiffened, and the lower half... Well, let's just say the lower half stiffened as well. *Fuck.*

Ziz was like my sister, but times like these made me remember that she was very much *not* my sister. She was the prettiest girl I'd ever laid eyes on. Her hair was gorgeous—long, wavy, and golden blond. She had big brown eyes and thick lashes that, as a kid, she'd used to get her way with her parents. Lord knew she could bring any guy to his knees with just a bat of her eyelashes. But my favorite part about her face was her mouth. She had lips that were made for sin—full, plump, and pink.

I pitied the man who ever tried to tempt her to sin, though. *His funeral.*

I looked at Ziz out of the corner of my eye, confused all to hell. She wasn't even looking at me, though. Instead, she was smugly gazing at the chick that had come up to me a few minutes ago. Kayla? Carly? I couldn't remember. In fact, I'd forgotten she was still there.

Despite my alcohol-fueled haze, the reality of the situation finally clicked. I burst out laughing, wrapped my arm around Ziz's waist, and pulled her closer. The skimpily dressed girl's eyes widened and then narrowed in anger. She turned on her heel and walked off without a word.

"You know," Ziz said in my ear, her breath warm against my skin. "I just did you a favor. She isn't nearly good enough for you."

I laughed harder. I'd said almost those exact words to her before. The difference was that when I said them, they were true.

The girl who'd walked over with Zizzo cleared her throat and shifted her weight from one foot to the other. I'd met her before, but I couldn't remember her name. *Damn.* I was sensing a trend.

"Carson, you remember Nicole, right?" Ziz asked.

"Of course," I said smoothly, silently thanking Ziz for her good social graces. Most of the guys I'd come in with had wandered off, but I introduced Jimmy and Demarcus. They started chatting up Ziz's friend, who was cute for guys interested in nerdy scientist types.

Zizzo extracted her arm from around my shoulders, and I stifled the urge to stick out my lower lip like a petulant child. I could have gotten used to having her tight little body pressed against me. *Better me than some other guy.* At least she would be safe with me.

She nodded toward the drink in my hand. "Shouldn't you be eating clean, going to bed early, and all that other stuff?"

I shook my head. "Not until Monday." Classes started then, and our first game was the following weekend. Some of the guys didn't bother altering their routines during the season, but football was one of the few things I took seriously because it was one of the few things I was good at. Hell, it might have been the *only* thing I was good at.

Nah. I was good at drinking too.

"What's your schedule look like this semester?" Ziz asked.

Talking about the classes I was taking was enough to kill my buzz, but I owed it to her to give her a heads-up. A semester hadn't gone by that Ziz hadn't helped me with something. Not only was she the most beautiful woman on campus, but she was also smart as fuck. She fit in with my family better than I did. I didn't hold that against her, though.

I took out my phone and pulled up my schedule. "There. I sent it to you."

"You could have just told me."

"I don't even remember what I'm taking."

Ziz probably had her schedule memorized, including the full course titles, numbers, and locations, but I was the quintessential jock. My major was interdisciplinary studies, which basically meant I was getting three minors. Best-case scenario, I would enter the draft and be playing pro football at this time next year. Worst-case scenario, I would wind up a college dropout, embarrass my family, and be forced to take a position in the mail room at my dad's company. The thought made me want to get shit-faced.

I drained the last of my beer then looked at Ziz. "What are you drinking?"

"Diet Coke."

I made a face. "Coke? Why are—" *That's right.* I was a moron. Since she'd always been in the same year as me at school, I often forgot she was a year younger. She wasn't a big drinker anyway, so it didn't usually matter. But tonight, I wanted her to be able to cut loose. "Hey," I said to my friends to get their attention. "Let's move the party back to my place."

Ziz put a hand on my arm. "I'm fine, really. I'm about ready to head home anyway."

"No way. As you pointed out, this is the last weekend to get crazy for a while." Unlike me, she didn't have football, but her engineering course load was grueling. And again, unlike me, she actually gave a shit about getting A's in her classes.

Tucking her hair behind her ears, she appeared guilty as she looked toward my friends. "I don't want to ruin anyone's time."

"Ziz, knock that shit off. The only way you'll ruin my time is if you won't hang out." Running into her had been a stroke of luck. I always had a good time, but now I could have a *great* time.

"What about your friends?"

I shrugged. "If they want to stay, then fine. The two of us can have fun." I spent plenty of time with my teammates. But I hadn't seen enough of Zizzo recently. We used to hang out way more. I didn't know why that had changed.

I tapped Jimmy on the shoulder. "Are you okay with going back to my place? Or do you want to say here?"

He shrugged. "I'm up for whatever."

I looked at... *shit...* Nicole. *Nicole, Nicole, Nicole.* I needed to remember that. "How about you?"

She cast a sly look at Jimmy before responding. "Sure."

I grinned. "See, Ziz? It's settled." I draped my arm around her shoulders. "Who looks out for you?" *Even when you think you don't need it.* It didn't matter, though. I would always have Ziz's back, whether it meant kicking some guy's ass for ogling her or forcing her to unwind.

She sighed. Her exasperation was just a show, though, because she was fighting a smile. "You."

"Damn straight."

CHAPTER 2

Becca

"TELL ME ABOUT Jimmy," I said.

Ignoring or not hearing my question, Carson frowned while he surveyed the spread on his kitchen counter. "Do you think this is enough?" He'd insisted on stopping at Kroger on the way home, and he'd picked up every kind of mixer imaginable—orange juice, soda, cranberry juice, sweet and sour mix, and even grenadine. He'd also bought snacks—fruit and cheese platters, chips and dip, and cheesecake, of all things. I'd waited in the car, and the sight of him strutting out of the store with a shopping cart full of groceries was comical.

"This is a ridiculous amount of food," I told him. "There are only four of us. And it's not like it's mealtime."

"Yeah, but at the bar, they had a full menu. If anyone is hungry, I want to make sure there's something they like." That was Carson logic.

"I don't think cheesecake is on the bar menu," I pointed out.

He grinned. "Upgrade, right?"

He was so pleased with himself, I couldn't help but smile and agree. "Upgrade. Back to my earlier question— tell me about Jimmy."

Carson picked at the plastic seal on the cheese platter. "What do you want to know?"

"Well..." I leaned around the wall so I could see into the living room, where Jimmy and Nicole were sitting. Carson's place was a townhouse instead of an apartment. His dad had bought it, saying it made more financial sense to own rather than rent while Carson was at school. His roommate had moved out at the end of last year, so now it was just him. "Nicole seems into him, so I was just wondering about him."

"He's an okay guy."

That told me nothing. I pursed my lips. "Would you be okay if I dated him?"

"Hell no." His response was immediate and firm.

I crossed my arms. "If he's not acceptable for me, then he's not acceptable for Nicole."

Carson leaned against the counter and crossed his arms. "He's acceptable."

"You just said he wasn't."

"For you. But for her, he's probably fine."

"Probably fine?" I gaped at him. "Don't be an ass. Nicole is my friend."

"I don't know him all that well, but I don't have anything bad to say about him."

"Then why wouldn't he be acceptable for me to date?"

Carson's jaw clenched. "Are you saying you want to date him?"

I threw my hands up. "No! Haven't you been paying attention? *Nicole* seems into him. I don't understand your standards. If I shouldn't date him, then neither should my friend."

He looked at me like I was the one talking in circles and being asinine. "He's an okay guy, so I won't cockblock him. But I won't let you date him because I don't know him well enough."

Closing my eyes, I rubbed my fingertips in circular motions over my temples. "You don't get to *let* me date or not date someone."

"Uh, yeah, I do."

My eyes snapped open. "No, you don't."

"Remember Brody?"

"Oh... my... God." I rolled my shoulders and let my head fall back so I was staring at the ceiling. "That was junior year of *high school.*" Besides the fact that he was referring to something that had happened nearly five years ago, it wasn't some horrible experience. Brody had been a senior in my calculus class. When his girlfriend broke up with him a week before prom, I agreed to go with him. At the dance, he made up with his ex-girlfriend and ended up leaving with her, stranding me at the hotel. It wasn't that big of a deal—more annoying than anything. I should have known better than to call Roman to pick me up. He and Carson had swooped into the Marriott to save me like my life had been in peril. I was pretty sure they had words with Brody afterward because he'd moved his seat away from mine in calculus after that.

"No one ever mistreated you again."

"Yeah, because you and Roman scared away any guy that got within five feet of me." Even back in high school, Carson had been intimidating. Well over six feet tall, he'd already had biceps bigger than my head. Though my brother wasn't as bulky as Carson, he was no slouch either. The two of them made a formidable pair.

"I don't see the problem."

Of course he doesn't. To be fair, I'd never complained. For the most part, I hadn't minded. Even in high school, my studies had taken up most of my time, not to mention all the extracurriculars I'd been involved in. It had all paid off, though, in the form of scholarships. And that was a good thing because out-of-state tuition wasn't cheap. Anyway, I hadn't bothered to develop my own extensive social networks. It was easier—and more fun—to hang out with Carson and Roman.

"Forget it," I muttered.

"Are you?" Carson countered. "What's going on with you, Ziz?"

"It's Becca." I didn't know why I bothered correcting him because I'd long ago stopped trying to change that. He'd started calling me by my last name freshman year. I guessed since my brother wasn't there, I'd become the Zizzo of VVU.

"Hey." Carson's voice was soft as he stepped closer. "What's wrong?"

I smiled tightly. "Nothing that a drink won't fix."

Unfortunately, there wasn't a drink in the world strong enough to make me forget Carson. What Nicole had said about us being seniors resonated with me but not in the way she'd intended. I had wasted the first three years of college watching Carson hook up with random girls while I secretly pined for him. He loved me—I knew he did—but I couldn't wait around forever for him to see me as more than a little sister. To quote the wise words of my father, it was time to shit or get off the pot.

Carson clapped his hands together and rubbed them. "What can I make you? Rum and Coke? Screwdriver? Sex on the Beach?" He wriggled his eyebrows suggestively.

Uh, yes, please. That was the thing with Carson—most of the time, he treated me like a little sister, but every once in a while, he made flirtatious comments. "Do you even know how to make that?"

"No, but Google does."

"Sure, I'll take one, then."

"Coming right up." Carson started tapping on his phone, and I stared at the muscles in his tanned forearms as they flexed from the minute movement. As he read the recipe, he chewed on his lip, something he'd done as long as I'd known him. It was a good thing he wasn't an avid reader, or his lips would be shredded.

But God, it was a sexy habit, and I couldn't help but wonder if maybe he did it at other times as well.

"Better make it a double," I said.

***

Carson

I EYED ZIZ as she held her cards close to her face. "Bullshit."

She grinned. "Nope."

"Shit." I flipped over the discard pile, and sure enough, she'd laid down three queens. I grumbled as I picked up nearly the whole damn deck and added the cards to my hand. "Since when did you become a good liar?" It was just my luck she'd developed a poker face in time to hose me.

She giggled. "Since wouldn't you like to know?"

Jesus. She's wasted. I'd been keeping pace with her, but I was barely buzzed. Maybe I shouldn't have made her drinks doubles. *Eh.* She was safe there with me, and besides, it was nice to see her cut loose. Hopefully, she wouldn't be sorry the next morning.

"I would," I said evenly. "That's why I asked."

"I'll never tell..." she sang in an eerie tone that sent shivers down my spine. I seemed to remember that line from an old thriller movie.

Beside her, Nicole shuddered. "Stop it. You're giving me the creeps."

Ziz leaned closer and sang the line in her friend's ear.

Nicole pushed her away. "I'm serious! You're going to give me nightmares."

"That's right," Ziz said, not sounding sorry. "I forgot you can't watch scary movies."

Jimmy shot Nicole a pitying look. "You're missing out."

Nicole shook her head. "Oh, trust me. I'm not. The only thing I'll miss out on if I watch those movies is sleep."

"She's a scaredy-cat," Ziz said matter-of-factly.

"One hundred percent, yes. I'll own that. Is it my turn?" Once we nodded, Nicole laid down a card. "One king."

"Hang on." I shuffled through the dozens of cards I was holding. "I'm going to call bullshit on that one."

Nicole scooped up the card. "Damn."

"You can't bullshit a bullshitter," I told her. Although holding half the deck in my hand helped.

Ziz snorted. "Didn't I just do that?"

I shook my head. "No. You actually told the truth."

She scrunched up her nose, causing cute little wrinkles to form on her forehead. But I was smart enough never to call attention to a woman's wrinkles. "So I truthed you?"

I grinned. "Even I know 'truth' isn't a verb."

"Then what's it called?"

Nicole's mouth twisted to one side. "Hon, I don't think that's a thing."

"Well, it should be. I'm good at truthing."

Nicole patted Ziz's knee. "Again, it's not a thing."

"It's not like 'fetch.' I'm so going to make this happen. For real." The girls convulsed into a giggle fit.

Jimmy looked at me with a question in his eyes.

I shook my head. "Yeah, I don't know what they're talking about."

"*Mean Girls*!" Ziz exclaimed. "Obviously."

"Okay," I said, still clueless. Ziz was all about the movie references tonight.

Ziz slapped a hand on my knee, gripping it with her fingers. "Oh... my... God. You've never seen *Mean Girls*?"

"Isn't that a chick movie?" Jimmy chimed in.

"Movies are genderless," Zizzo said.

"*Rambo*," I challenged.

Nicole pointed at me. "Dude movie. He's got you there, Bec."

Zizzo cocked her head to the side. "Isn't it actually called *First Blood*?"

"Yeah," I confirmed, surprised she knew that. Then again, Becca seemed to know everything and not in a bad way. The girl had a curious mind. She always had. It was how she'd ended up getting a full scholarship. Of course, being female in a male-dominated major helped.

It didn't take long for me to lose that round of Bullshit. I didn't care, though. The only thing I was really competitive about was football. No sense getting your panties in a twist unless you knew you could win. Either way, Bullshit had gotten old.

"Let's switch it up," I suggested. "How about Spades?"

Beside me, Zizzo swayed. "Is that the one with books?" She dragged out the *s* in books, making it sound like she was hissing the word.

I leaned close. "Are you okay?" *Damn.* I really shouldn't have made her those doubles.

She turned her head in slow motion. Her eyes were wide. "I'm fine. Are *you* okay?"

"I'm always okay," I replied. It was more or less true. Not much rattled me. But at the moment, I was a little worried about Zizzo and glad we were at my place instead of at a bar. However, if we'd stayed at a bar, she would be sober. Actually, she would be at home because she'd been getting ready to leave.

Nicole stood. "Does anyone need a refill?"

Zizzo raised her hand. I wanted to nix her request, but I didn't want to be *that* guy.

Jimmy got to his feet. "I'll help you."

Once they'd gone to the kitchen, Ziz leaned her head on my shoulder. "I really did save you, you know. And I'm going to keep saving you every time I see you with a random girl."

I bit back a laugh. "Oh, really?" Ziz had saved my ass countless times when it came to writing papers, but it was comical to think of her saving me from a girl. If anything, they needed to be saved from me. I wasn't a bad guy, but I definitely wasn't relationship material. At least I never led anyone on.

"Yeah. You deserve someone nice."

"She might have been nice. But I guess I'll never know." Except I'd seen that girl out before, so chances were our paths would cross again. It didn't matter, though. I'd much rather hang out with Ziz than hook up with a random chick.

Her face lit up. "Hey, let's call Roman." She had her phone out before I could comment and held it out so we could video-chat with him.

He answered after the third ring, and his face broke into an easy smile when he saw us. "Hey."

Roman was the dude version of Zizzo. Though they weren't actual twins—and couldn't be identical even if they were because of the whole guy-girl thing—they looked a hell of a lot alike in the face. But the similarities ended there. Roman was more like me—not stupid but definitely not academic. He'd been a running back on our high school football team, but he'd never had any shot at playing in college. So while Ziz and I had gone off to VVU, he'd enlisted in the navy and was currently stationed in Norfolk.

"Roman!" Becca exclaimed.

He frowned. "Are you drunk?"

She nodded emphatically. "Yes. Yes, I am. Carson has been making me drinks."

I grimaced as Roman gave me a cold stare. "Dude."

"Oh, knock it off," Zizzo said. "I'm twenty, a grown-ass woman."

I hated to break it to her, but she would always have little-sister status, including all the rights and privileges that came with the territory. Roman's protective streak was ridiculous when it came to her. For that matter, mine was too. Zizzo had always been this cute little thing. Looking out for her was as instinctual as breathing.

"Okay, grown-ass woman," Roman said. "Are you behaving yourself?"

Zizzo grinned. "Always. But Carson isn't. Carson never does. Tell him he needs to stop hooking up with random girls."

So we'd circled back to this again. She seemed fixated on it, which was weird because she'd never said anything about it before.

"Uh... stop hooking up with random girls?" Roman said it as a question, which didn't make a convincing argument. He had no room to talk anyway.

"Zizzo," I started, and both of them looked at me expectantly. "Shit," I muttered.

"Ha!" Zizzo exclaimed. "This is why you should call me Becca. My name is Becca. Say it with me. *Bec-cah.*"

A smile stretched across my face. "Maybe I'll start calling you Little Zizzo to differentiate."

Roman laughed. "I've got people over, so I should go."

"Aww." Zizzo—*Little Zizzo*—pouted. "I miss you."

"Miss you too. Be good. Don't do anything I would do."

"Ha." Zizzo blew her brother a kiss and put the phone facedown on the table.

Nicole came back with a drink in one hand and a plate holding a slice of cheesecake in the other. Jimmy followed, carrying a bag of chips and a tub of dip.

"Ooh." Zizzo's eyes locked on the cheesecake. "I forgot we had that."

Her friend grinned. "I got two forks."

Zizzo happily took the fork Nicole offered. "And that's why I love you."

"What about me?" I asked. "You laughed at me when I bought the cheesecake."

She swiped her finger through the creamy confection and dabbed a glob of it on my nose. "I love you too, Carson. You should know that by now."

"Thanks, LZ." I wiped the cheesecake off my nose and licked it off my finger.

She stared at me with a dazed expression, like it was taking her brain extra time to figure out what LZ stood for. "Um, that's a negative. I told you—*Bec-cah.* If you want to be fancy, you can call me *Re-bec-cah.*"

"Okay, *Re-bec-cah*," Nicole said. "Is it you and me for Spades?"

She nodded. "Deal 'em."

Before Nicole could finish dealing the cards, Zizzo muttered an excuse and shut herself in the hall bathroom. When she didn't return in five minutes, Nicole went to check on her.

I heard her knock on the bathroom door. "Hey, Bec, are you okay?" Silence followed. "Bec?" She jiggled the doorknob.

A moment later, she returned to the living room. "The door is locked, and she isn't responding."

Jimmy laughed. "She's probably passed out in there."

I frowned at him. He was probably right, and while it might have been funny with some other girl, this was Zizzo.

I went to the bathroom door and repeated exactly what Nicole had done, which was idiotic. I took a credit card out of my wallet and slipped it between the door and the frame. After two jiggles, the lock clicked.

"Damn," Nicole commented. "That was fast."

It wasn't a skill I was necessarily proud of, but it came in handy every once in a while.

I slowly opened the door, and when I caught sight of Ziz on the floor, I swung it open. My heart pounded wildly. Her little body was curled around the bottom of the toilet, and she rested her head on the seat. Her eyes were closed, and she breathed deeply.

I exhaled. *I definitely shouldn't have made her doubles.*

Behind me, Nicole chuckled softly. "Guess we're not playing Spades."

"Nope," I confirmed.

Ziz's neck was at a jaunty angle. I didn't know how she'd managed to fall asleep like that.

"Let me get our stuff together," Nicole said. "I'll call an Uber and get her home."

I shook my head. "She can stay here. No sense trying to get her home like this."

Nicole looked uneasy about leaving Ziz, but I wasn't insulted. Instead, I was glad she had such a good friend. But in the end, Nicole and Jimmy shared an Uber, since it turned out they lived in neighboring apartment complexes.

When I returned to the bathroom, Ziz was awake and moaning. *Fuck.* I should have paid more attention to how much she was drinking. Her cup had never been empty, but that hadn't been all my doing. She'd helped herself to several refills.

"I'm dying," she said.

I knelt next to her. "No, you're not."

She tried lifting her head but gave up and laid it back on the toilet seat, whimpering. The sound was so pathetic, I couldn't hide my smile. It wasn't funny, but it kind of was.

Yes, I was an asshole. Zizzo rarely had moments of weakness, but God knew she'd seen me at my worst too many times to count.

She met my gaze, and I quickly wiped the smile off my face. "I'm going to sleep here."

"Yes, you are."

She nodded and closed her eyes.

"Wait," I said. "You're sleeping here at my place but not in the bathroom."

"I'm comfortable. I'm good here. Don't worry."

"No way. I'm not letting you sleep on the bathroom floor." I stood and held my hand out. "Come on."

Not opening her eyes, she shook her head. "Nuh-uh."

I scooped her up into my arms and tucked her small body against my chest. Moaning, she wrapped her arms around my neck and clung to me.

Something stirred within me, something I had no business feeling. This was Ziz—Becca. She might as well be my little sister. But I couldn't stop myself from bringing my face to her hair and inhaling. *Flowers.* Her hair always smelled like some kind of flower, but for the life of me, I'd never been able to figure out which one.

Her fingers trailed along my shoulders, and she suddenly lifted her head up, peering at them. "Your delts are so firm and big."

My body became paralyzed. "Uh... thanks."

"But not as big as these." She cupped my biceps, or tried to anyway. Her small hand didn't fit over the whole thing.

A dirty joke about what else on my body was big came to mind, but I managed to keep my mouth shut. *Barely.*

When Zizzo had her hands on me, it was difficult to keep my thoughts clean.

She ran her hands back up to my shoulders then rested her head in the crook of my neck.

Guess she's done with her inspection. I rolled my neck and shook off my temporary paralysis. I exited the bathroom, stopping abruptly at the bottom of the stairs when her hands traveled down to my chest.

Then she pinched my nipples. *Hard.*

"Shit!" I yelped.

She giggled. "I've always wanted to do that. Your nipples are so cute."

Cute? What in the actual fuck?

She lifted her head again and peered at me expectantly, as if she were waiting for me to say something.

I attempted to gather my wits. "I think you meant manly and rugged."

She giggled again. "No, I didn't. I meant cute. They're small and round and perfect, like peppermints. I want to—"

"Hold that thought." *Jesus fucking Christ.* If she said what I thought she was going to say, I might very well lose my shit. I might call her Zizzo, like I called her brother, but I was very much aware that she was a woman, especially when her breast was pressed against me.

Her fingers circled my nipples, and damn if it didn't make me hard.

"Uh..." I cleared my throat. "Could you please stop?"

"Why? I like it."

So do I. Too much.

"It's distracting," I said instead. "I don't want to drop you down the stairs." I would *never* drop her down the stairs, but in this situation, it was better if she didn't know that.

She sighed like I was asking her a huge favor. "Fine."

I carried her upstairs, keeping a close eye on her to make sure I wasn't startled by another nipple grope. But was it a grope if I kind of liked it too? I looked down at her, and that thing inside me stirred again. *Shit.* For the first time, I was glad Roman was hundreds of miles away. He would kick my ass if he could see how I was looking at his sister.

So don't look at her, dumbass. That was easier said than done. Ever since I'd walked into her and her brother's lives, I could never *not* look at her.

I hung a left into my bedroom. When I laid her down on my bed, she didn't unlock her arms. Closing my eyes, I let myself imagine she was clinging to me because she wanted to and not because she was so drunk, she didn't know what the hell she was doing.

"Why don't you see me?" she mumbled.

I gently released her hold on me. "What?"

She opened her eyes, but they had trouble focusing, so she closed them again. "I'm right here. I've always been right here."

I had no clue how to respond to her because I wasn't sure what the hell she was talking about, but it might not even matter. Chances were she either wouldn't remember this conversation, or she was speaking nonsense anyway. Even though she was drunk, though, she wouldn't make a comment like that unless something about our relationship was bothering her. That thought felt like a punch to the throat.

I sat on the edge of the bed and brushed her hair out of her face. "I'm here too," I said finally, but it was too late—she was asleep. I stretched out beside her so she wouldn't be alone when she woke.

CHAPTER 3

Becca

SOMEONE IS GOING to die. Because why the hell was a flashlight shining in my face? I peeled open one eyelid and immediately regretted it. Trying to find the source of the light, I turned my head and winced as it pounded. There— a crack in the blind. Why couldn't Carson ever remember to close the blinds at night? Beside me, he lightly snored, making me irrationally pissed that he was still sleeping while I wasn't.

I sat up, thinking I would close the blind then try to get some more sleep, but the motion made me dizzy. My stomach lurched. *Don't puke. Don't puke.* Oh God, how much had I had to drink? I lay back down and settled for turning my body away from the window. The pressure in my throat produced a burp but no vomit. *Thank God.* But the burp left a sour taste in my mouth, and I tried to remember if Carson kept mints lying around.

Mints... shit. Please tell me I didn't try to suck on his nipples like they were peppermints. I distinctly remembered them tightening as I pinched them, but had I left it at that? I was pretty sure I had, but my head ached so badly, I couldn't think straight.

I peered at Carson and cringed. *He* hadn't been wasted last night, so no doubt he remembered everything. Heat rushed to my cheeks. My opinion about him being asleep suddenly shifted, and I was grateful he slept like a hibernating bear. It gave me a few minutes to pull myself together before I had to live down my humiliation. Carson was going to be merciless with his teasing.

Taking several deep breaths, I tried to psych myself up for the trek to the bathroom, which was all of ten feet. Gripping the edge of the bed, I sat up slowly, but when I stood, I immediately became dizzy and plopped my ass right back down again.

But I didn't have a choice. Now that I was fully awake, my bladder screamed at me. I slid down off the bed and onto the floor. Crawling toward the bathroom, I prayed Carson would not wake up. He didn't need any more ammo against me.

When I made it to the bathroom, I closed the door behind me and breathed a sigh of relief. Before attempting to stand again, I pressed my cheek against the cool veneer of the toilet seat. That was the position that had gotten me into this mess. I dragged myself upright and took care of business. Then I rifled through Carson's cabinets, looking for a spare toothbrush. *Bingo.* I brushed my teeth and scrubbed my tongue so hard, I gagged. I stuck my mouth under the faucet and sucked in mouthfuls of water. I should have done that first, but I wouldn't have been able to stand swallowing with the sour taste in my mouth. More rifling through the cabinet turned up Advil. I popped four.

Bracing my arms on the sink, I gazed into my bloodshot eyes. Suddenly, my twenty-first birthday lost its appeal. Luckily, it wasn't for a few more months. Hopefully by then, I would be ready to drink again. At the moment, the proposition wasn't appealing.

I sank down onto the toilet seat. Maybe I could sneak out before Carson woke up. I normally gave as good as I got, but I didn't have it in me, especially when the humiliation was so fresh. I was no stranger to embarrassing myself in front of Carson since he and my brother had been inseparable since they were twelve, but what I'd done last night went beyond embarrassing. It was downright shameful. I had felt him up and *pinched his nipples*.

He probably thought I had some weird nipple fetish. I didn't—not in the slightest—but I would have been lying if I said I'd never noticed Carson's chest. Heck, I'd noticed his *everything*.

The longer I hid in the bathroom, the shorter my window got for sneaking away. It was cowardly, and I wouldn't be able to avoid him forever, but I didn't know if I had it in me now.

I cracked the door open and peeked out.

Carson propped himself up on one arm and grinned at me. "Good morning, sunshine."

I winced. *So much for sneaking out.* "Good morning." I walked over to the bed, each step reverberating up my body and rattling my brain. I sank down onto the bed, grateful not to have to move for a few seconds. Who was I kidding? I wouldn't have been able to sneak out anyway because I was in no shape to drive.

"How are you feeling?"

I eyed Carson warily, waiting for the punchline. When none came, I answered honestly. "Not so good."

"Sorry. I should have known better than to make you doubles."

"I asked for them."

"Yeah, but still, I shouldn't have made them."

I didn't have the energy to argue with him about how it wasn't his responsibility to be the Becca police. *Wait.* The *Zizzo* police. I appreciated having someone who wanted to look out for me, but sometimes it was simply tiring.

"I'm sorry I passed out," I said.

"It's okay. It happens to the best of us." He paused. "Well, not me, but—"

I chucked a pillow at him then groaned as my head reminded me that quick motions weren't a good idea. It was pointless anyway. He had easily deflected.

"Do you remember everything?" he asked.

"I think so." I wasn't a black-out kind of drunk. When my body was ready to cut me off, I simply fell asleep. It was actually kind of a nice failsafe. And though I sometimes wished I could puke, I'd never done that either.

"I don't think anyone filmed your striptease on the back deck, but you might want to check social media just to be sure."

My eyes widened. "*What?* That did *not* happen."

He laughed. "Just checking."

I picked at the comforter. "I'm sure I embarrassed myself enough without you embellishing."

"What's the last thing you remember?"

"Well, I went to the bathroom." I tried to read him, but his expression was neutral. I crossed my fingers behind my back. "And that's it, really. I guess you carried me up here?"

His eyes scanned my face. "That about sums it up."

My heartbeat quickened. I hadn't imagined the whole nipple thing. So why was he acting like it hadn't happened? *Oh shit.* Had I crossed the line so badly that he wasn't even going to tease me about it? Maybe it would have been better to fess up. But that wasn't a conversation I wanted to have while I felt like shit. I could always miraculously recover my memory later.

Carson stretched out, putting both hands behind his head. "What's on tap for today?"

"Getting ready for the first day of classes tomorrow, I guess. And shit, I have a WIE board meeting later."

"A wee board meeting? That shouldn't take long, then."

I shook my head at Carson's corny pun. He never tired of making it despite the fact that it had never been funny. WIE stood for Women in Engineering, and I was president of the organization.

"I wish," I said. "It's the first one, so it might take a while."

"Aren't you in charge this year? That should mean you can make the meetings as short as you want them."

"I can't slack off just because I'm president. In fact, that's a reason I *shouldn't* slack off." I believed in the mission of the organization, but at the moment, I was regretting getting talked into taking the role of president. I had been secretary for the past two years, and the quiet role in the background had suited me just fine. Regardless, I hadn't planned on starting my tenure as president with a hangover.

"What time is your meeting?"

"Three."

"Good. You can hang out until then."

I looked down at the rumpled clothes I was still wearing from last night and wrinkled my nose. "I'm disgusting."

Though Carson was also still wearing yesterday's clothes, he didn't look like he'd made out with a cheesecake. The amount of cheesecake on my shirt was impressive considering I'd only had one bite.

He sat up. "Get in the shower. I'll make breakfast."

I snorted. "Since when do you cook?"

He raised an eyebrow. "I'm an expert cereal-pourer, thank you very much."

I shook my head. "My stomach can't handle Lucky Charms." The boy had a sweet tooth when it came to cereal, and I'd seen him polish off an entire box in one sitting.

"That's not the only thing I have. I'll make oatmeal. That should be bland enough."

"If you say so." I doubted I would be able to eat anything, though.

The hot water in his townhouse lasted a heck of a lot longer than in my apartment, and I planned to take full advantage. I stayed in the shower so long, I half expected Carson to come looking for me like he'd done when I'd fallen asleep in the bathroom last night. After wrapping myself in a towel, I peeked out into his bedroom to make sure he was downstairs. Then I rummaged through his drawers to find something to borrow. The only trouble was he was way bigger than me, so all of his clothes were huge. There was no way I was putting my dirty clothes on my clean body, though. I pulled on a T-shirt and a pair of athletic shorts then rolled the waist three times. It didn't really matter if they fell off, though, because the shirt nearly came to my knees.

This was one of the nice things about hanging out with Carson—I had no problem stealing a toothbrush, using his fluffiest towel, and rifling through his stuff. It was comfortable. If he ever found out how I felt about him and things got weird, I had a lot to lose. I'd had this argument with myself countless times over the years every time I got the harebrained idea to confess my feelings—or apparently got so drunk that I fondled his nipples.

Carson was like family to me, especially now when our real families were hundreds of miles away. It would be foolish to jeopardize that.

In full stealth mode, I crept downstairs. The sound of my footsteps on the stairs was masked by the sound of

ESPN, which was the soundtrack of Carson's life. Just as I'd hoped, even though he had the TV on, he was in the kitchen.

Sorry, Carson, no ESPN today. I located the remote and quickly found the movie I wanted to rent. I only hesitated for a moment before shrugging and charging it to Carson's account. I didn't know how to switch to mine without screwing up all his settings. Besides, he wouldn't care. His family had money, and he'd always been generous when it came to stuff like this.

"Hey, Ziz, breakfast is ready!" he called from the kitchen.

I padded in there, keeping one hand on the waistband of the shorts. Even though I'd said it wouldn't matter if they fell down, I didn't want to test that theory, especially since I was going commando. I'd met my embarrassment quota for the weekend.

Carson was spooning tan glop into two bowls. I'd never been a fan of oatmeal, but he was probably right in that it was good hangover food. If anyone would know about that, he would.

I took the bowl he offered. "Thanks." Though I was tempted to add brown sugar to it, I refrained since that would defeat the purpose.

"Wait," he said before I could return to the living room. He took a huge tumbler out of the cabinet and filled it with water. "Take this. And when you finish it, refill it. You gotta hydrate."

He followed me in the living room and stopped in his tracks when he saw what was on the television in place of his beloved ESPN. "What is this?"

"You can thank me later. I'm filling a major hole in your pop culture education." I settled onto the couch and crossed my legs. "You don't know what you're missing."

He sat on the other side of the sofa. "You're right. And I'd kind of like to keep it that way."

"Oh, shut up." I hit play. "I still can't believe you've never seen *Mean Girls*. It's a classic."

"You're taking liberties with that term."

I gave him the evil eye as I blew on my oatmeal to cool it. "Be nice, or I'll make you listen to the entire *Hamilton* soundtrack." I'd been threatening that one for years, but one of these days, I was going to follow through. Though really, it shouldn't be considered a threat—more like a privilege. If Carson weren't so fond of my brother and me, I would seriously question his taste.

After a few minutes, Carson asked, "How's the oatmeal? Is it sitting okay in your stomach?"

I nodded. "I'm already feeling much better, actually. Maybe I wasn't as hung over as I thought."

He arched a brow. "Don't count your chickens. Drink your water."

"Sir, yes, sir." I saluted him the way my brother had taught me. Even after several years, it was still wild to think that my punk of a brother was a soldier. He and Carson had done some stupid stuff when they were younger. They'd figured out exactly how far they could push my parents and usually went right up to that line. On the rare occasion they'd crossed it, they were both so damn charming, they could talk their way out of trouble, especially with my mom. I, of course, had never gotten into a lick of trouble unless I was with them. I'd been too busy filling my time with every extracurricular activity that might look good on a college application. It had been exhausting but worth it in the end.

After we finished eating, I stacked up our dirty dishes.

"I'll take care of it," Carson said.

I shook my head. "I've seen this movie a thousand times. I don't want you to miss a minute of it."

"How kind of you," he said dryly.

I smiled wide. "You are very welcome."

When I returned from the kitchen, I curled up on the couch. Despite my love for the movie, it didn't take me long to doze off. I woke up in the last few minutes of the movie to find that Carson had tucked a blanket around me and lowered the volume of the TV so it wouldn't wake me.

It wasn't the first time he'd done something like that. He was always so good to me, which reaffirmed how much I didn't want to mess things up between us.

But a small part of me couldn't help wondering that if things were this good as just friends, how much better could they be if we were more?

***

Carson

AFTER ZIZ LEFT, I went over to Jake's. While Roman was my best friend from home, Jake was my best friend at school. He'd been crazy busy since taking custody of his three younger siblings, though, so I hadn't seen much of him recently. That seemed to be a theme with the people in my life lately.

Jake's brother, Ben, answered the door and looked around me. "Is that your Jeep?"

I was surprised to see him out of his room. He was a computer geek who spent most of his time engrossed in online role-playing games. Then again, he'd just turned fifteen, so it was about time for him to start showing an interest in cars.

I glanced over my shoulder at the Jeep Wrangler parked at the curb. Up until a few weeks ago, I'd driven a

Camaro, but I'd gotten tired of it. It was fast but too cramped for a guy my size. My dad had his fingers in so many business endeavors, I couldn't keep track, but the one part of Fleck Holdings, Incorporated that had always interested me was the car dealership. My dad frequently traded out his cars, and I'd taken to doing the same thing. It was one of the few perks I got as a Fleck that I appreciated.

"Sure is," I said. "Want to drive it?"

Ben's eyes lit up, but before he could respond, Jake stepped up behind him. "Maybe if he'd actually bother studying for his driver's permit test."

That was the one test in my life I hadn't minded studying for, probably because I'd already known everything anyway. It was also the one test on which I'd outscored my sister. Being a know-it-all, she hadn't studied and had failed the first time around. She was book smart but clueless when it came to practical knowledge.

Ben scowled. "It'll only take five minutes to memorize everything."

"So do it," Jake said pointedly.

Ben stalked to his room, and I stepped into the foyer. "Bad time?" I asked. Who was I kidding? In Jake's crazy new life, there was never a good time.

My friend shook his head. "I don't get it. I'm fully prepared to buy him a car once he gets his license, but he's dragging his feet with his permit."

Yeah, I didn't understand that either. "Let me know when you're ready to get the car." I followed him into the living room. "My dad's dealership might be able to hook you up."

"Thanks. I just hope he gets his ass in gear. I'd like him to be able to take on some of the driving duties as soon as possible." He settled onto the couch.

"Is Rachel here?"

"No. She took the girls to get pedicures."

"Is everything okay in that department?" Jake and Rachel hadn't been together very long, and they'd had some missteps because Jake had gotten his siblings right when they started dating. Rachel was amazing, though. There weren't many college girls who would be willing to step into the big-sister role like she had.

Jake smiled. "Things are great, man. Thanks for asking."

"Good. I'm happy for you." I might come across as a dumb jock sometimes, but if nothing else, I was a loyal friend. A black cat sashayed out of the kitchen and jumped onto the top of the couch. It was followed shortly by a white one. "When did you get cats?"

"Last week. I only agreed to one, but the girls suckered me into getting two." He didn't sound too broken up by it.

The front door opened, and a few moments later, Jake's sister Ashley wrapped herself around the door frame and batted her eyes at me. "Oh, hi, Carson. I didn't know you were here."

"Uh, hi. I just got here."

Ashley scared the piss out of me. Maybe scared wasn't the right term. But she freaked me out because she had a crush on me that was glaringly obvious and even more awkward because she was twelve. Rachel thought it was cute and told me it was harmless, but as an elementary ed major, she spent a lot of time in schools. She probably had a whole slew of little boys with crushes on her, so Ashley's fixation on me was nothing out of the ordinary. But for me, it was super weird.

"Don't you have somewhere to be?" Jake asked. He tried to save me from the awkwardness when he could.

"Nope."

Rachel came in, followed by Emily, Jake's youngest sister. "Actually, she does have somewhere to be because guess who let it slip that she didn't do all the required summer reading?"

Jake shot his sister a look that would rival any pissed-off parent's. "Are you kidding me?"

"Summer reading is stupid," Ashley whined.

Poor kid. I agreed with her, but I wisely kept my mouth shut.

"You didn't think it was stupid when you begged for us to put you in honors classes," Jake said. "You knew summer reading was part of the deal."

I scooted to the edge of the couch. "I'm gonna go."

"You don't have to," Rachel said. "Stay."

Emily tugged at Jake's sleeve. "Look at my toes." She shoved them under his nose and wriggled them. "The color is petunia, which doesn't make sense because petunias can be a lot of different colors, not just pink."

Yeah... Jake had more important things to do than entertain my bored ass. I stood. "I'll catch you later."

Jake apologized and told me to stay, but I waved him off. It was my dumb fault for showing up without calling first. I normally didn't, but I was restless.

I drove through downtown on the way back to my apartment, and everything was dead. Even the biggest partiers tended to take a break the night before classes started. Of course, it would only take about a week before the downtown scene started hopping every night. The start of a new semester was kind of like New Year's in that way—it didn't take long for good intentions to wear off.

As soon I as parked in front of my townhouse, the phone rang. It was Stacey, my mother's assistant.

"Hi, Stacey," I answered. I talked more to her than I ever talked to my mother. I couldn't remember the last time I'd gotten a direct call from my mom. *Everything* went through Stacey first. "How's your ankle?"

"Much better since I started the physical therapy. Thanks. I'm calling about Chelsea's engagement party."

My brow furrowed. "What?" Chelsea was my older sister and in her last year at Harvard Law. I had no idea she even had a boyfriend.

"As of last week, she's engaged to John Henneman."

"Why does that name sound familiar?" I muttered.

"Chelsea's fiancé is actually John Henneman III. His father is John Henneman Jr., the senator from Rhode Island."

"Right," I said slowly. Everything made much more sense now. My mother was a state senator for Maryland and had her eye on the governor's office. She must be doing backflips about her daughter being engaged to the heir of the Henneman political dynasty.

Stacey continued. "So anyway, your parents are throwing an engagement party the first weekend in November."

Of course they were, because that was the weekend of the VVU football team's family-appreciation game. And to think I'd actually invited them this year since it was my senior year. I supposed this phone call served as the RSVP that they wouldn't be in attendance.

I ran a hand through my hair and fisted the strands. "Thanks for letting me know, I guess, but you know I can't go."

Stacey sighed. "I figured as much. Your mother is not going to be happy."

"Does she seriously expect me to blow off a game for an engagement party?" I was blaming the messenger, but it was difficult to stay neutral when this happy horseshit was being shoveled in my direction. If Chelsea were engaged to John Nobody from down the street, my mother wouldn't give a damn. Instead, she was using it to further her political career. I wondered what Chelsea thought about the whole thing. She and I weren't close, but we got along well enough at family events, which was the only time we saw each other.

Stacey stayed silent, which was an answer in and of itself. *Un-fucking-believable.* My parents hadn't supported my playing football because it was a "common thug's game." When I'd earned a starting position at VVU, then it had become a little more respectable because it gave them bragging rights, though they would rather I was rubbing elbows with American royalty at an Ivy League school. I'd been nothing but a disappointment to them from the time I was a kid, and it was apparent that I was never going to excel at anything intellectual. Playing football didn't exactly further the family's business and political interests.

Cheer up, Dad. Maybe if I make it to the pros, I can be a celebrity endorser for your business.

My mother came from a wealthy family, but my father was a self-made man, something he liked to remind me of every chance he got. He'd started with nothing, and his highest education was a degree from a local community college. Fleck Holdings was now a multimillion-dollar company with business interests up and down the East Coast. Though my dad prided himself on being self-made, he sure as hell didn't like to remember where he'd come from. My grandparents had been good blue-collar people who'd worked hard to eke out a meager living. But Charles Fleck would have never been satisfied with that. He had wanted more. It was always *more* with him. Nothing—including me—was ever enough.

Except maybe Chelsea. My older sister could do no wrong in his eyes. I tried not to hold that against her.

"You'll be receiving a formal invitation shortly," Stacey said finally.

"Thanks, Stacey," I replied. "I'll handle it from there." I didn't want to put her in the middle of family drama. She'd always been good to me. Besides that, I didn't need any help disappointing my parents.

I could do that very well on my own.

CHAPTER 4

Becca

THE FOUR WIE board members lounged in Nicole's living room, munching on popcorn and sipping boxed wine. *High class.* Of course, I was sticking to water.

I nudged Nicole. "Are you taking notes?"

She looked between her two hands, one of which was full of popcorn while the other held a wine glass. "Um, no."

I sighed. Nicole hadn't wanted to take over as secretary, but we'd had a shortage of candidates this year, so I'd begged her to step up. She had only agreed after I'd promised her the position was easy. It was, but I hadn't promised her it wasn't tedious.

"Well, could you? We have to document our meetings for the Student Activities Board."

She shoved the popcorn into her mouth then wiped her fingers on a napkin before opening her laptop and saluting me.

I looked at the agenda I had pulled up on my phone. "Courtney, did you reserve space for the welcome pizza party?"

The vice president nodded. "I got a room in the student center. I'll email the invitations this evening."

"Great." Membership in WIE had dwindled over the past few years, and we didn't understand why because the number of females enrolled in engineering hadn't decreased. Our focus for this semester was building our membership.

"I bought a few cases of water last week," Hanima, our treasurer, said. "I wanted to beat the freshman rush."

"Good idea," I said. Several thousand freshmen and their parents had invaded Bleaksburg over the weekend, which meant stores were a nightmare. "Make sure you fill out the reimbursement form, and I'll sign it. Are we good on funds?"

Hanima scrolled through her tablet for a moment then read off the financial report. I didn't like how low our balance was, but it was still worth spending the money to make the incoming freshmen feel welcome. Engineering was a hard enough major without being outnumbered five to one by males. Most guys in the major were okay, but there were some who were demeaning toward the girls.

"What do you think about my idea for a weekly study hall?" Courtney asked.

"I like it." I tapped a pen on the table. "But that would require the commitment of a lot of juniors and seniors. I'm willing to do my part, but I don't want it to fall completely on us." I hoped our members would step up, but I knew how busy they were, how busy we *all* were.

"Good point." Courtney made a note. "I'll touch base with our members and see what they're willing to do. We'll need to get moving on it soon."

Hanima leaned over to see that we'd come to the end of my agenda. "Can I bring in some new business?"

"Sure." I looked up from the agenda. "What do you have?"

She slapped a pink flyer on the table in front of me. "This."

I squinted at the flyer. *VVU Homecoming Court—Apply Now!*

"Okay…" I'd gone to VVU's homecoming football games for the past three years, but I'd never paid much attention to the homecoming court presentation. I didn't understand why she was showing me the flyer because it had nothing to do with WIE.

"I want to nominate you," Hanima said.

"What? Why?" My face puckered like I'd tasted something sour. "That's for sorority girls." I had nothing against the Greek community, but that wasn't my scene.

"Most of the court *is* made up of sorority girls and frat boys, but that's not a requirement," Hanima said, and I had no doubt she'd thoroughly researched it. "You just have to have an organization sponsor you."

"She's right," Courtney said, and I knew with certainty that they'd conspired before mentioning this to me. "Last year, the girl who won was sponsored by the Christian Student Association."

"That's great and all, but I don't know why you think I would want to do it." The thought of putting myself on display and trying to convince people to vote for me made me itchy, as if I were already breaking out in anxiety-caused hives.

"Hear me out," Hanima said. "Part of being on the court is promoting a platform. You've got a platform."

"Like a charity?" I shook my head. "No, I don't."

Hanima sighed, like she was talking to a petulant toddler. "Yes, you do. Technology education for girls."

Last spring, I'd won a grant to speak at an education conference about the importance of encouraging girls to pursue studies in science and technology. It was a subject I was passionate about, but I didn't have a lot of time to devote to it because I was too busy making sure my grades were high enough to keep my scholarship. I wouldn't be a very good role model if I had to drop out of the program.

"I still don't see the point of my being on the homecoming court, though."

"Have you ever voted?" Nicole chimed in.

I shook my head. I vaguely remembered seeing tables set up around campus during homecoming week, but like the homecoming game, I'd never paid them much attention.

"You vote by adding change to each candidate's jar," Nicole explained. "Whoever gets the most money wins, but win or lose, the money raised by the candidate goes to their cause."

"Oh." That made a lot of sense. Otherwise, what was the point of each candidate having a platform?

"I already called Bleaksburg Middle School, and they have a summer program specifically for girls in STEM," Hanima said. "The money you raise could pay the tuition for an underprivileged girl who otherwise wouldn't be able to attend."

That definitely sweetened the deal, but people would actually have to vote for me for it to make any difference. My friends were forgetting that small but important detail. I couldn't pull in the votes like a sorority girl.

"I'm not going to get a lot of votes," I said. "It would be easier to throw a couple of twenties to the middle school and call it a day."

Hanima scoffed. "Engineering is one of the biggest majors on campus. You'll get votes."

"Another bonus is that having you on the homecoming court would give a lot of visibility to WIE," Courtney added. "It would be something the organization could showcase for years."

Groaning, I rested my face in my hands. I felt like I'd been ambushed. The girls knew exactly which of my buttons to push.

"Stop looking like they're asking you to punch a kitten," Nicole said. "It could be fun."

Fun? She had to be kidding me. I couldn't think of anything fun about putting myself on display for the entire student body to judge me. *No, thank you.*

"Then why don't you do it?" I shot back.

"I would never make it past the interview." She pointed at her mouth. "No filter, remember?"

"Don't look at me," Hanima said. "I'm too awkward."

"No, you're not," I said automatically. But she kind of was, which only made me like her more. What could I say? Aside from Carson, my most favorite people were awkward. It was nice not to be the weirdest one in the room... except now.

Hanima brushed her hair back. "It's okay. There's a reason I spend all of my time with computers and not people."

"My resumé isn't strong enough," Courtney said before I could point my finger at her. "I'm going to be a badass mechanical engineer, but that's about all I have going for me. I wouldn't get past the application phase."

I tapped my fingernail against my front teeth, which was an annoying habit. "What makes you think I would? It's basically just a popularity contest."

"Not to get on the court," Hanima corrected. "Faculty and alumni choose. It's not like high school, where people are rewarded for being shallow nitwits."

I raised my eyebrows and exchanged a look with Nicole. Hanima obviously had some unresolved feelings about her time in high school. I understood that. I hadn't been popular in high school, but I'd experienced most of the perks that went with the territory because of Carson and Roman, who had been immensely popular. Neither of them had been on homecoming court because they hadn't wanted the complication since they played football, but Carson had won prom king. It hadn't been a big deal because he hadn't made it one. While he always made the most of being the center of attention, he hadn't actually cared about winning.

"We can announce that you're running at the pizza party," Courtney said. "It'll be a good way for the freshmen to get involved with the organization and the school."

"I haven't agreed to it," I said, exasperated.

"Yet," Nicole said. "You know you're going to, so you might as well get it over with."

"Applications are due Friday," Hanima added. "So don't take too long to decide."

As tempting as it was to do it solely for the sake of raising money for the middle school girls STEM program, I didn't think I had it in me. It was touching that the other WIE board members thought I would be a good candidate, though. So at the very least, I would pretend to think it over for a few days before breaking the news to them. And I would try to get involved in the summer program in another way, like volunteering. In fact, that would be a good initiative for all WIE members.

Maybe that was the problem with WIE. Our focus was mainly on our own members, but students who couldn't hack it in the engineering program usually dropped out after freshman year. So aside from mentoring the incoming freshmen, we didn't have much of a mission. Perhaps we needed to turn our focus outside of ourselves. I felt like an idiot for never considering that, but in a way, it was understandable. The engineering program was so demanding that it was easy to forget about everything else.

Hanima and Courtney left, but I stayed to help Nicole clean up. Her two roommates were neat freaks, and I didn't want them to get angry with Nicole if we left behind a stray popcorn kernel.

"How did things go with Jimmy?" I asked. I obviously hadn't seen the end of that flirtation.

"They didn't," Nicole said. "I guess he wasn't interested."

"Are you sure?"

"Don't insult me by insinuating that I don't know when a guy is into me... or not, in this case."

"That's not what I was insinuating at all. It just seemed that he liked you. That's all."

"I'm surprised you remember anything. That might be the drunkest I've ever seen you."

"Yeah, well," I muttered. "Don't get used to it."

Laughing, Nicole carried the wine glasses into the kitchen. "You were fun."

I followed her. "Are you saying I'm normally not fun?"

"You were a different kind of fun. But I honestly couldn't tell if that was because you were drunk or because Carson was there."

I stuffed the empty wine box into the trash can. "What do you mean by that?"

She shrugged. "You're normally kind of uptight."

"Hey!" I might describe myself that way, but it grated on my nerves for someone else to do it.

She put her hands up. "It goes with the territory of being an engineer. But you're different around him. More relaxed."

"I've known him forever, so that's probably it." I definitely felt more relaxed around him, but I hadn't realized the change in my demeanor was so drastic that others noticed it.

"Maybe. Or maybe it's something else."

I stilled. "Like what?"

She grinned. "I don't know. Why don't you tell me?"

Shit. I'd definitely made a fool of myself after Nicole and Jimmy left, but now I racked my brain, trying to remember if I'd done or said anything to give the impression that I thought of Carson as more than a friend.

"There's nothing to tell," I said.

Nicole studied me, and for a moment, I thought she wasn't going to let it go. When she got her mind set on something, she could be relentless. "Sure. If you say so," she said finally.

***

Carson

"I SHOULD JUST drop this stupid class." What kind of psycho professor assigned a paper due the first week of class? I tried to avoid classes that required a lot of writing, but I'd missed the mark with this one.

"Don't be stupid." Zizzo held her hand out for the assignment. "Let me see it."

I handed it over. "Sorry, Ziz. Being stupid is my natural state."

She rolled her eyes before returning her gaze to the paper. "Shut up. You're not stupid."

Debatable. But I only had to make it through one more semester, then I would declare myself eligible for the draft. If a team didn't pick me up, then I didn't know what I would do. I seriously did not want to take a job with my father's company. I wasn't terribly worried, though. I might not go in the first round like FM4, but I would be surprised if I didn't get selected in the second or third round.

The team had tutors to help players with assignments, but I preferred to have Ziz help me. She'd been doing it since high school, and we were used to each other. Besides that, I trusted her. If she told me to do something on an assignment, I did it without question.

"It's not like it matters," I said. "I can take another class to fill the eligibility requirements."

She narrowed her eyes at me through her tortoise-shell glasses. Those combined with her hair in a messy bun gave her the whole hot-librarian look. I doubted she realized the effect she was creating, though. She hated drawing attention to herself. *Thank God.* If she ever decided to flaunt her assets, I would need an army to help fend off all her admirers.

"But this class fills a requirement for your major, so you need to take it now. There might not be a better option in the spring."

I opened my mouth but clamped it shut before I could tell her that graduating wasn't part of my plan. I thought she already knew that. For me, college was the means necessary to play pro football.

"Sure, okay," I said instead, not wanting to earn a look of disappointment. I should say *to hell with what she thinks* like I did with everyone else, but Ziz's opinion was one of the few that mattered to me.

She slid the paper across the table. "It's not that hard. It's only five hundred words. That's like two pages."

"Easy for you to say," I muttered. Her major wasn't writing intensive, but she was so damn smart, she was good at it anyway. If she had one flaw, it was that she didn't understand that academics didn't come easily for some of us.

"Do a page tonight and a page tomorrow. If you send it to me by nine tomorrow, I can proof it for you."

I opened my laptop and flexed my fingers over my keyboard. I held them there, but as expected, words didn't fly out of them and onto the screen. *Writing sucks.*

Ziz took off her glasses and rubbed her eyes, then she rooted around in her backpack. "Damn," she said. "Do you have any eye drops?"

I shook my head. "Are your eyes bothering you?"

"It's the dry air in the engineering building. This happens at the start of every semester. I almost had to come home halfway through the day to take my contacts out."

"Then why didn't you just wear your glasses? Or take your contact stuff?"

"It was fine the first two days," she grumbled. "I was hoping it would be okay this semester but nope."

I turned my attention back to my laptop, but the blinking cursor didn't do me any favors. "What should I write?"

Ziz chuckled. "I can't tell you that. It's a personal narrative, so that means you have to come up with it." At times like these when she was showing me tough love, I had to remind myself that one of the things I loved about Ziz was that she didn't put up with my bullshit. In some ways, it might be easier to work with a tutor because I might be able to manipulate them into helping me more, especially if it was a chick. *Slacker.*

I sighed. The class was sociology of education, and the assignment was supposed to be a reflection of our experience in education so far. The professor was going to save the essays for us to read at the end of the class after we'd been enlightened or some hippy-dippy bullshit.

Ziz took pity on me. "Here." She pointed at some bullet points on the assignment. "Start with these questions and go from there."

While I wasn't the best student, I wasn't illiterate. I could read the paper myself. I ground my teeth and mentally told myself to snap out of it. It wasn't her fault I was short on brain cells. I'd known she wouldn't help me much with the assignment, but when I had mentioned it to her and she'd offered to stop by, I hadn't declined. Any excuse to hang out with Ziz was good enough for me. Besides, we'd been doing homework side by side for the better part of a decade. I knew I was more likely to actually do the work when she was there.

She took a notebook out of her bag, and a pink paper fluttered to the floor. I picked it up, but she snatched it out of my hand before I saw what was on it. So of course I grabbed it back and held it out of her reach so I could read it. She should have known that was coming. I'd been pulling that move forever.

"VVU homecoming court." I grinned at her. "What's this about?"

I let her take back the paper, and she immediately shoved it in her bag. "It's nothing."

Oh, Ziz. Sometimes for as smart as she was, she could be dumb. If her dismissive retort hadn't given her away, her pink cheeks would have.

I laughed. "Aw, is my little Ziz going to be a princess?"

Her nostrils flared, a sure sign I'd struck a nerve. *Interesting.* She was easygoing about almost everything. As much as she'd hung around Roman and me growing up, she'd quickly developed a thick skin.

"It's homecoming *queen*, not princess. And why is that funny?"

I shrugged. "You're not a homecoming court kind of girl."

"What's that supposed to mean?"

Shit. She was still flaring her nostrils. I'd done it now. *Abort! Abort!*

"It's super girly."

If looks could kill, I would be six feet under. *So much for aborting.* But what I'd said was true. She'd played field hockey in high school and was the type of person who would much rather be playing on the field than strutting across it.

"In case you hadn't noticed, I *am* a girl."

I'd definitely noticed. *Too much.* I shouldn't appreciate how sexy she looked in those glasses, and I really shouldn't have gotten a hard-on the other night when her tits rubbed against me while she was drunk. This was *Zizzo*, Roman's little sister. My job was to scare off other guys. The trouble was I was the one who needed a good ass-kicking for the thoughts I'd had recently. But hell, she'd played with my nipples. I wasn't necessarily into that, but any red-blooded male would react.

She was still glaring at me.

"Yes, you are," I agreed. It seemed like the safest response.

She ripped her hair tie free, and her hair cascaded over her shoulders. If this weren't Zizzo, I would think she was pulling a cheap move to show just how feminine she could be. But it was Zizzo, and it pained me to say the move worked. She tossed her head to throw her hair over her shoulder, creating a scene that would fulfill any adolescent boy's naughty librarian fantasy.

Christ. I hoped they fixed the dry air problem in the engineering building soon so she could get back to wearing contacts. If she pulled that move around all those engineering nerds, one of them was bound to jizz in their pants. *Hell. Who am I kidding?* I was liable to as well.

"The other WIE girls want me to represent us on the court."

"Why?"

"Why not?"

"It just doesn't seem like your thing." Ziz had never been into traditionally girly stuff. She'd been happy to hang out with Roman and me throughout high school. While she'd had some girlfriends, she'd never been particularly close to any of them.

She met my gaze, and I couldn't figure out what was going through her head. I knew Ziz better than anyone else at VVU, and the Ziz I knew would never want to be on homecoming court. I didn't understand what was going on here.

"I'm going to do it."

"Okay," I said slowly.

"I'm going to do it," she repeated, nodding like she was still talking herself into it. *What the hell? Just why?* The experience would probably be miserable for her. But from the expression on her face, I knew it was something I wouldn't be able to talk her out of. Ziz was stubborn once she made up her mind.

"Okay," I said again. "Let me know if there's anything I can do to help."

"Tell your friends to vote for me, I guess."

"I'll tell everyone I know."

"On second thought, just tell guys. Not girls."

"Why?"

"Do you have any friends who are girls?"

I frowned. "Besides you?" I had to think. I considered Rachel my friend, but she'd only gained that status because she was dating Jake. I also considered Katie a friend for the same reason. But there was no one else. I wasn't the type of guy who was friends with girls. I was too busy sleeping with them.

God, I'm a dick. At least I was an honest dick, though.

"Just stick to your friends," she instructed. "Usually the girls you associate with aren't too fond of me."

My frown deepened. "What do you mean?"

She stared at me like I should be able to figure it out on my own. "It's just a vibe I get."

It was true that whenever I was with a girl and Ziz was around, the girls seemed to get annoyed. But that was their problem, not mine. I wouldn't apologize for my friendship with Zizzo.

I grinned. "Is it okay if I call you Queen Ziz?"

"It very much is not."

Damn.

CHAPTER 5

Becca

I USHERED THE last of the freshman girls out of the room, declining their offer to help clean up after the pizza party. There wasn't much to do, but besides that, I was done peopling. I was introverted to my core, and meeting new people—even ones cut from the same cloth as me—wore me out.

Given how tired I was after this one event, I was seriously second-guessing my decision to apply for homecoming court. I didn't know exactly what it entailed, but I imagined it involved meeting lots of people and maybe campaigning. I couldn't back out now, though. Hanima had already announced it to the incoming freshman WIE members, and I had to admit that it *had* been gratifying to see how excited they were. More than that, though, it made me happy that I would be raising money for a good cause.

Hanima was gathering the used paper plates. "Are there any more trash bags?"

"Here." Nicole handed her one then peeked inside a pizza box. "Man, we have an entire pizza left. Cold pizza for breakfast. Yum."

I wrinkled my nose. *Gross.* If pizza was meant to be eaten cold, the pizza places would deliver it that way.

Courtney tossed the paper towel she'd been using to wipe the tables into the trash. "I hate to leave you with the mess, but is it okay if I go? I have an assignment due tomorrow." She had arrived an hour before us to get everything set up.

"We got this," I told her. "See you later."

"Don't forget the court application is due tomorrow." Throwing her bag over her shoulder, Courtney gave me a stern look.

"I already said I'd do it."

"I know." She sounded skeptical, which was probably why she and Hanima had made the announcement only seconds after I confirmed I would do it—they didn't want to leave me any time to back out. They should know me better than that. Once I said I would do something, I followed through.

Though I could understand my friends' surprise when I'd agreed. Being on the homecoming court would put me way out of my comfort zone. The thought of walking on the field in front of thousands of people made my palms slick. But there was no point worrying yet. Chances were I wouldn't make it past the application phase. Part of me was hoping for that. It would only be a mild embarrassment since the only people who knew I was applying were my friends, the freshman WIE girls, and Carson.

Ugh, Carson.

His reaction had been the final push I'd needed. It was the equivalent of a dare. He didn't think I could or should do it, so I wanted to prove him wrong. I might not play sports anymore, but I was still competitive.

It irked me that he found it so unfathomable that I could be on the homecoming court. It shouldn't, though, because he'd been right—I normally wasn't into girly things like that. Maybe if I were, he wouldn't see me as one of the guys. That wasn't the reason I'd decided to give it a go, though. *Nope.* I simply wanted to prove him wrong.

Oh, and I wanted to raise money for girls in STEM. That was important too.

I was still thinking about everything when I got home an hour later. My roommate, Lucy, was in the living room when I walked in. She and I were total opposites, which was why we worked. The musical theater major was a refreshing departure from the engineering majors I spent most of my time with. On the flip side, she probably enjoyed coming home to someone who wasn't as *extra* as most of the drama students were.

She dramatically threw a stapled booklet onto the floor. "*Othello*! Can you believe it? It's finally my senior year, and the stupid director chooses *Othello* of all things."

Every fall, the drama department put on a Shakespearean play for local high schools.

"What's wrong with *Othello*?" I vaguely remembered it from my senior year of high school, and I didn't see any reason for her to be disappointed. Besides, all the tragedies were more or less the same—there were long speeches in which the characters contemplated the meaning of life, and then everyone died at the end. I knew better than to share that helpful bit of analysis with Lucy, though.

"Give me a character with some agency, for eff's sake. Desdemona just lets herself be killed," Lucy huffed. "I'd much rather be Lady Macbeth. Now she's a badass. Crazy but a badass."

"You'd make a good Lady Macbeth." Lucy would be good in whatever part she played, but she had a particular knack for playing characters that were off their rockers. Again, I knew better than to say that last bit out loud.

"I know, right? Thank you. I knew you would understand."

"Hopefully, the spring show will be better."

"It will be a musical, so there's that at least."

I hadn't been a huge fan of musicals until I met Lucy, but now I was hooked. I'd been to every one of her plays and had even gone with her to Roanoke to see *Wicked.*

"So..." I said slowly. "I'm putting in an application for the homecoming court."

Lucy squealed. "That's awesome! Is WIE sponsoring you?"

I nodded. Her unfiltered excitement was just the energy I needed. Maybe it wasn't such a crazy idea after all. Maybe it would be fun. If nothing else, it was a new experience, and that was what college was all about. Or at least that was what my mother said every time I went home. She had never gone to college, so it seemed like she might be living vicariously through me a bit. Too bad for her I was tame.

"My freshman year, the STA had someone on the court. It was cool to actually know someone on it for once." The STA was the Student Theater Association, which was separate from the drama department. Students didn't have to be drama majors to participate. Lucy had tried to get me to audition once, and it had taken forever for her to accept that I preferred being in the audience. She didn't seem to have remembered that tidbit, and I wasn't going to remind her.

"I might not get in," I cautioned. I didn't know how many people applied compared with how many spots there were.

She waved a hand dismissively. "You'll get in."

I beamed at her. Her confidence in me was just what I needed. Carson could shove his whole "you're not girly" rhetoric straight up his ass—his toned, wonderfully squeeze-worthy ass.

***

IT WAS SATURDAY—game day. I applied VVU logos to my cheeks and nodded at my reflection. *War paint? Check.* It was silly, but I'd worn the temporary tattoos to every game except one. The time I'd forgotten, Carson had had a helmet-to-helmet collision with another player and was taken out of the game for medical observation. He'd turned out to be fine other than being super pissed. After that, I'd bought a lifetime supply of the logos.

Holding the dreaded *Othello* script in her hands, Lucy was stretched out on the couch, still in her pajamas. While I'd attended every game, she had yet to go to one. She was one of the few people at VVU who didn't care about football. Even if I weren't friends with Carson, I would still go. There was something magical about the camaraderie of college football fans.

"Ugh!" she whined. "Desdemona makes me want to barf."

I chuckled. "She's not that bad. Didn't she stand up to her father?"

"Yeah, but she just went from being controlled by one man to another one."

I couldn't remember the play well enough to agree or disagree, so I simply murmured my sympathy. I wasn't meeting Evan and Nicole for another thirty minutes, so I plopped on the couch next to her. No sooner had I done so than there was a knock at the door. I shot Lucy a quizzical look. "Expecting someone?"

"Nope."

I looked through the peephole then flung the door open. "Roman! What are you doing here?" I squeezed my brother tightly, still not used to his muscular physique. The navy had made him buff. Roman had always been a bit of a slacker, so it had surprised me when he'd enlisted in the navy. He'd proven me and everyone else who'd doubted him wrong when he'd excelled. My dad had done four years before becoming a cop, but Roman was planning to be a career soldier.

"Surprise," he said wryly. "I came to watch Carson's first game of the season."

"That's awesome! Does he know?"

"Maybe. I asked him to send me tickets a while ago, but I never confirmed if I was coming. So it might be a surprise."

I pulled him into my apartment. "I'm so freaking excited you're here." Roman and I might not have been actual twins, but sometimes it felt like we were. Our connection ran as deep as if we'd shared a womb. Military life suited him, but I hated that it took him away for such long stretches.

"Lucy, do you remember Roman?" I realized my mistake half a second too late. *Of course* she remembered him. I was pretty sure they'd hooked up on one of his previous visits. Or if they hadn't, they'd come close. I didn't even want to know.

She smiled at him. "Hi, Roman. Becca didn't tell me you were coming."

"Hey, Lucy." He rubbed the back of his neck. "It was a surprise."

Lucy ran her tongue across her top lip and looked him up and down. "What a nice surprise it is."

I averted my eyes. I'd long ago accepted the fact that my brother was a player, but that didn't mean I wanted to witness it, especially with my roommate. Luckily, though, Lucy was drama queen and not in the figurative meaning of the term. She was capable of having a one-night stand and leaving it at that, even if it did look like she wouldn't mind a second taste.

"You must have hit the road early," I said. Norfolk was at least a five-hour drive, and it was just after ten.

"Yeah. Speaking of that, can you make me some coffee?" he asked. "I had duty last night, so I'm running on no sleep."

"Aww, Roman, you shouldn't drive when you're tired."

"I'll be fine after I get some caffeine. I don't know if I'll be able to make another game, so I didn't want to miss this chance."

I led him into the kitchen. "I'm glad you're here. Carson is going to be excited too." Roman's ship had been out for the last two football seasons, so he hadn't been to a game since freshman year. "Do you want something to eat?"

"That would be great."

Thirty minutes later, we were on our way to campus for some tailgating before the game. Evan's parents and grandparents were alumni and had a parking space right next to the stadium, so we usually hung out there. Some people may have thought it was lame to tailgate with parents and grandparents, but I didn't think of it like that. On game days, we were all just VVU fans. Besides that, the spread they put out was ridiculous. One year, they had an actual pig with an apple in its mouth. *No joke.* Evan's family took tailgating to a whole new level.

Though Roman had almost nothing in common with our crowd, he managed to integrate himself just fine. He and Carson had that in common—they could both maneuver through any social situation with ease. It didn't take long for Roman to have charmed Evan's grandmother into laughing at all his jokes.

Evan nudged me. "Should I be concerned that your brother is hitting on my sixty-five-year-old grandmother?"

"I mean, maybe. I don't know. How's her relationship with your grandfather?"

His eyes widened for a split second before he rolled his eyes and laughed. Evan was fun to tease because he was so gullible.

"Seriously, I think she likes your brother better than she likes me. She never laughs at my jokes like that."

I nudged him with my elbow. "Maybe because you aren't funny."

His face fell. "I'm plenty funny."

"Okay. Tell me a joke."

"Um..."

"Quick. Don't overthink it. Quick!" I snapped my fingers.

"Why don't they play poker in the jungle?"

I shook my head. "I don't know. Why?"

"Too many cheetahs." He grinned. "Get it?"

I burst out laughing. "Yeah, I get it."

His smile turned smug. "See? You're laughing. I'm funny."

"That was seriously one of the cheesiest jokes I've ever heard. It was a total dad joke." He blanched, which made me laugh harder. "You got it from your dad, didn't you?"

"So?" he muttered. "It's funny."

"Oh, Evan," I said. "I love you."

Roman walked over just in time to hear those words. His eyebrows shot up, and he scowled, going into total guard-dog mode. Just what I needed—another alpha male defending my honor. Though he wasn't as bad as Carson. *Go figure.*

"Knock it off, Fido," I told him. "I don't need to be protected."

Roman's mouth stretched into a grin. He'd just been messing with me because he knew Evan was one of my best friends.

"Especially from me," Evan said.

"Hey." Now it was my turn to scowl. Evan and I had only ever been friends, but his answer came too quickly for my liking. What was up with all of my guy friends seeing me as undateable?

"You know what I mean, Bec," Evan said. "But even if we weren't just friends, you're way out of my league."

"No, I'm not."

"Have you seen yourself lately? Yeah, you are." Looking away, he took a swig of beer. "It's good to see you, Roman. Becca didn't tell me you'd be here."

"It was kind of last minute. Luckily, Carson was able to get tickets."

Evan raised his beer bottle. "Here's to him having a great game." Roman clinked his bottle against Evan's, and I added my water bottle to the mix, which made a squishing sound instead of the satisfying clinking sound like their bottles. Besides the fact that I was underage and wouldn't want to put Evan's family in the uncomfortable—and illegal—position of supplying alcohol to a minor, the sun was already blazing, and there was little breeze. It was going to be boiling in those stands. Staying hydrated on game days like this one was crucial.

I had wanted to wait for Nicole, but she was running late. I wouldn't be sitting in my normal seat with her anyway since Roman was there, so we went into the stadium. Even though I'd told Roman we had plenty of time, he didn't want to risk missing a single second of seeing Carson on the field.

I couldn't blame him. Even though I should have been used to it by now, my chest swelled with pride every time I saw Carson run out onto the field. He was a confident guy, but being on the field took his swagger to another level. He was more than just confident—he was proud of himself. It was a good look for him and one I wished he would display more often.

"Holy shit, I'm nervous," Roman said once we'd found our seats, which were way better than my normal ones up in the nosebleeds. Carson could usually get good seats, but only a couple. Though the view was better here, it was more fun sitting with a big group of friends.

"You watch the games on TV, right?" Not all of them were televised, but a fair number were.

Roman wiped the sweat off his brow with the back of his hand. "Yeah, but it's not the same as being here."

He had that right. I had to watch the away games on TV, and it paled in comparison.

Two girls caught Roman's eye as they passed on the way to their seats. They wore tiny shorts and sports bras, and their bodies were painted in school colors.

He grinned. "The view is definitely much better here." Then suddenly he frowned and looked down at me in alarm. "You don't dress like that for games, do you?"

Some things never changed.

CHAPTER 6

Carson

THE LOCKER ROOM chatter faded into the background as I slipped my earbuds in and hit play. The beat of hardcore rap filled my ears, calming me. I was normally a rock-and-roll guy, except on game days. Something about the intensity of the music simultaneously pumped me up and helped me focus. I continued to listen as I donned my pads and double-checked the fit of my mouth guard. Around me, the other guys were tense. I couldn't hear what they were saying, but I could see it in their faces.

Our former coach, Coach Gurgin, had been a legend in college football. Under his leadership, we'd won the national title last year. But he'd unexpectedly retired, and the university had replaced him with Coach Coyle. Other players had their doubts about him because he was a high school coach from Texas, but I liked the guy. I was one of the few people I knew who didn't mind change. Sometimes it could be the best thing to happen to a person.

Coach Coyle walked in, followed by several members of the coaching staff. "Gentlemen." He didn't have to yell to get our attention. That was one thing he and Gurgin had in common—their commanding presence. "I'm not big on pregame speeches," he drawled in his Texas accent. "Y'all know what you can do. I've seen what you can do. Now it's time to show the world who you are, who *we* are. So who are you?"

"VVU!"

"Who are you?"

"VVU!"

"As long as you remember that on the field, y'all be just fine. It's business as usual, gentlemen." He nodded to the coaching staff, who started to filter out of the locker room. "Five minutes."

His pep talk was underwhelming, but I kind of liked it. He didn't bullshit or try to rile us up. We shouldn't need that. Like he said, it was business as usual. For us, that meant kicking ass and taking names. I grinned. This season was going to be epic.

Beside me, Jake's brow was creased and covered in sweat.

"Hey, man, you okay?" I asked. Jake had better pull his shit together. He was the best receiver we had.

He swallowed. "A lot is riding on this game, you know?" After his parents died last season, Jake had lost his starting position. Though he'd gained it back this season, his confidence had taken a hit. Besides that, it was his last chance to make an impression on pro scouts. Like me, he was hoping to get drafted.

"Yeah, but you got this. Just play. That's all you got to do." My words intentionally echoed Coach Coyle's.

Jake wiped his forehead with the back of his hand and grabbed his helmet. "I'm already sweating balls, and we're not even on the field yet."

"It's supposed to be in the nineties."

"Fuck."

Wyatt passed us, looking cool as a fucking cucumber. "Ready to kick some ass?"

I'd never seen him look nervous. But this had to be bittersweet—it was his first game without FM4. Good thing Jake and I were ready to pick up the slack. *Jake better be ready.* He had me worried, but I wouldn't let him know that.

I grinned. "Always."

Jake managed a nod, looking like he wanted to puke.

Wyatt eyed him. "Truitt, relax."

Exhaling, he rolled his neck. "Totally relaxed."

Jake was anything but relaxed. As we walked through the tunnel on the way to the field, the cheers of the fans echoed off the walls. A guard at the entrance handed Wyatt and me the state and American flags, which we were going to carry onto the field. Then came the sound I'd been waiting for since last season—the opening notes of Metallica's "Enter Sandman" could barely be heard over the crowd. *Fuck yeah.* That might've seemed like an odd entrance song to some, but the school had been using it forever, and there was nothing like rushing out onto the field and feeling the music in my chest.

Right before we ran out of the tunnel, I caught Jake's eye. His mouth stretched into a smile as he hung his head back and closed his eyes. *"Yessssss."*

I held out my fist, and he bumped it. Then I tore onto the field, flag waving.

***

AFTER THE POSTGAME activities, I was pleased to see I had a text from Zizzo.

Zizzo: *Meet at your place?*

That surprised me. We didn't normally hang out after games, but any time was a good time to see Ziz. I checked the time of the text. She'd sent it an hour ago. Hopefully she hadn't given up on me and made other plans.

Carson: *On my way.*

Ziz had a key to my place out of necessity. There wasn't a good place to hide a key outside, and I'd wanted someone reliable to have one in case my drunk ass got locked out. Sober me had learned early on to plan for contingencies for drunk me, who could be a complete moron. A smarter person might try to change his habits but not me—I just planned for the inevitable idiocy.

"Ziz!" I called when I walked in the front door. "I'm starving. You want to eat?" I stopped in my tracks when I saw Roman rummaging through my pantry. *Fuck yeah!* He'd asked me to get him tickets for this game a few weeks ago, which I had. But when he hadn't said anything about it, I'd figured he couldn't make it. I'd told him to give the tickets away if he couldn't use them.

It had been nearly four years, and I still wasn't used to Ziz's—*shit*—Roman's military haircut. Good thing Becca couldn't read my mind, or she would be giving me an "I told you so" lecture on why I shouldn't call her Ziz. The nickname thing was going to cause a confusing weekend but whatever. I had a good reason for calling her Ziz— several, in fact—but sharing them with her would defeat the purpose.

Roman pulled me in for a bro hug. "Damn, dude. You've gotten bigger."

I looked down at my pecs and biceps and flexed. Then I grinned. "You think so?" Though I was playing at being modest, I knew it was true. I hadn't punished myself in the gym all summer for no gain.

"Yeah, man. Don't let it go to your head, though. I can still take you."

I only hesitated a split second before tackling him and dragging his ass to the ground. What he lacked in muscle, he made up for in technique, though, and it didn't take long for our positions to be reversed as we wrestled on the kitchen floor.

"Are you two ever going to grow up?"

I looked up to see Becca leaning against the doorframe, and that second of distraction was enough for Roman to pin my shoulders down. If I weren't worn out from my game, I would have been able to prevent the pin. *Maybe.* But I didn't care. Roman could have the victory. He'd spent the last nine months out to sea in the Middle East, and it was so damn good to see him.

Roman picked himself up off the floor and offered a hand to pull me up, which I took. He grinned at his sister. "Nope."

She wrinkled her nose. "You couldn't pay me to roll around on the kitchen floor."

I was no Betty Homemaker, but my floor wasn't disgusting. I sneaked a peek to confirm. Okay... it could use a good mopping.

Roman lunged toward Becca like he was going to take her down, but her fist shot out and caught him in the throat.

Coughing, he clutched his neck. "Damn, Bec. What the hell?"

She shrugged. "You taught me that move, remember?"

"No, I didn't."

"I believe your exact words were 'if a guy is trying to grab you, fight dirty.'"

"You aren't supposed to fight dirty against me!"

She grinned. "You're lucky I didn't punch you in the balls."

Roman shook his head. "That's uncalled for."

I shook my head, chuckling. "While I'm enjoying this sibling love or rivalry or whatever the hell this is, I'm starving. Do you want to eat somewhere? I'll buy."

Roman grinned. "In that case, I'd love a steak."

"Outback?"

"You know it."

I turned to Becca. "Is that okay?"

She shook her head. "You two can go. You probably want some time to catch up."

Roman's expression mirrored mine. *What the hell?* Sure, maybe Roman and I had a bit of a bromance going on, but Becca was always included. That went without question.

"You're coming." I jerked my thumb in Roman's direction. "Otherwise, I'll be forced to stare at this ugly mug, which will ruin my appetite."

"I've never had any complaints," Roman said. "In fact, I've had nothing but rave reviews."

Becca put her hand up. "I still don't want to hear about your sex life. That still hasn't changed."

Half an hour later, we were seated at Outback. There was an hour wait, but the hostess let us skip the line. Maybe it was wrong, but I was going to take advantage of being a local football hero for as long as I could. Unlike Archer, I didn't anticipate getting picked up in the first round. I was a damn good college tight end, but once I got to the pros, I would be middle of the road.

If I'd learned nothing else from my parents, I'd learned not to overestimate myself.

When the server took our drink orders, Becca ordered water and sighed. "Drink up, boys. I'm the DD by default."

Roman and I didn't need to be told twice. I slipped the server a twenty and told him to keep the drinks coming. I normally didn't throw down during the season, but this was a special occasion. By the fourth beer, Roman let it slip that he'd re-upped his commitment to the navy and was being considered for SEAL training.

Becca's eyes widened. "Isn't that dangerous?"

Roman gave her a dismissive look. "It's the military. It's all dangerous."

"I know that, but that's more dangerous than being a regular seaman, right?"

"Technically," Roman allowed.

"There's no 'technical' about it," Becca said. "Does Mom know?"

The badass SEAL-to-be shifted uncomfortably and wouldn't meet his sister's gaze. "I'm twenty-one. I don't have to ask permission."

I laughed. "So that's a *no.*"

Their mother, Lydia, was a tiny but formidable woman. Growing up, we were always more afraid of her than their father, who carried a gun for his job as a police officer. Lydia had been a second mother to me. Hell, if I were honest, she was more of a mother to me than my own had been.

That reminded me that the invitation to my sister's engagement party was sitting on my counter at home. Since I knew what it was, I hadn't bothered opening the envelope, but I would have to deal with it eventually. When I sent my RSVP, my mother might actually take time out of her busy schedule to talk to me personally. *Lucky me.*

"I'm working up to it," Roman muttered. "I didn't want to drop that bombshell on my first visit home." He downed the last of his beer and leaned back in the booth, crossing his arms. Though he was probably just as buzzed as I was, his calculating eyes scanned the room.

It hit me that my best friend was deadly—a trained killer—and he was about to become even more trained. Roman's job was to protect our country, and what was mine? Playing football and trying not to flunk out of school so I could keep playing. It wasn't that I ever thought football was important in the grand scheme of things, but it suddenly seemed even more trivial.

Becca was on her way to bettering mankind as well. As a biomedical engineer, she planned to develop artificial organs that would save lives.

All I did was catch a damn ball.

Becca's foot nudged mine. "Are you okay?" she asked softly.

I realized I'd been staring into my beer as if I were contemplating world peace. *Not world peace, just the insignificance of my existence.*

Shit. I wasn't normally an emotional drunk. Not that I was being emotional exactly. It was more like I was having an existential crisis.

Fuck. How had I gone from the high of playing well in the game to this? I didn't like it. I didn't consider myself shallow, but I wouldn't call myself a deep person either. It was easier not to take life too seriously.

"I'm fine." *Very convincing, Fleck.*

Becca's beautiful mouth twisted into a frown. "Are you sure?"

I forced a smile onto my face and relaxed my shoulders. "Of course. I kicked ass in the game, and now I'm here with my two favorite people. What else could I ask for?"

My answer seemed to satisfy her because her mouth tilted upward again. *God, she's beautiful.* She'd always been cute, even when we were kids, but somewhere along the line, cuteness gave way to beauty. I shouldn't appreciate it as much as I did, especially with her brother sitting right next to her.

All of a sudden, I was extra glad he was there. His presence was just what I needed to remember that Becca might as well be my kid sister.

Except deep in my gut, I was shamefully thankful she wasn't.

CHAPTER 7

Becca

CARSON GOT A text from Jake. Wyatt and a bunch of the players were at Bleakers in a private room.

"Bleakers?" I questioned. "Are you sure that's right?" The last I'd heard, the bar was on the verge of closing.

True to my word, I was driving Carson's and Roman's drunk asses downtown. Had I thought ahead, I would have insisted on taking my car to the restaurant. Instead, I was forced to drive Carson's new Jeep, which made me nervous as hell. He wouldn't care if I dinged it, but I would. He'd always been spoiled when it came to material things, so he could be careless with his possessions. I, on the other hand, noticed every new little scratch on my eight-year-old Kia. It had been my parents' gift to me when I left for college. My family wasn't poor, but compared to Carson's, we were downright destitute. They'd had to save to afford the car.

"Yeah," Carson said. "They're letting us use the room after home games. It's a smart business move on their part. We get a little privacy, but once people figure out we're there, the bar will get flooded."

Downtown Bleaksburg wasn't very big, so it was difficult for more than a handful of players to go out together. It always turned into a spectacle, and a lot of them avoided it altogether.

In the back seat, Roman laughed. "Listen to Mr. Fleck spout off his business knowledge."

"Can't grow up in the Fleck house without picking up something." It might have been my imagination, but Carson's voice had a note of bitterness. I knew he didn't get along with his family very well, but he didn't usually let that affect him.

"I thought players couldn't accept gifts," I said.

"We can't," Carson confirmed. "But this is a gray area. As long as they're not giving us free drinks, letting us use the room should be fine."

I adjusted the rearview mirror. "I hope they renovated since the last time I was there."

The bar was dingy and outdated, which wasn't a deal breaker, but the women's bathroom was a wreck. Out of the three stalls, only one had a door, which wasn't saying much because it had been hanging on by a solitary hinge. I didn't have business knowledge like Carson, but even I knew that females were more likely to patronize a bar if it had a nice bathroom. And the guys would go wherever the girls were. It wasn't rocket science.

Carson fiddled with the radio. "If it sucks, we'll leave."

Word must have already gotten around that the players were hanging out at Bleakers because by the time we arrived, it was packed. Most of the players were in the private room, but a few were in the public area, which was no doubt what the manager had been angling for.

As we made our way through the throngs of people, a girl grabbed Carson's arm and pulled him toward her. "Carson! I was hoping you'd be here!"

I glanced back to see an easy smile was on his face. Though it probably wasn't obvious to anyone else, I could tell he didn't remember this girl from whenever they had met. *Probably a random hookup.* Jealousy pulsed through my veins, and I did my best to shake it off. I had no claim to Carson.

"I'm going to the bar!" Roman yelled to be heard above the music and chatter.

I pointed to the back room, and my brother nodded. But without my two guys clearing a path for me, it took me several minutes to make it the last few yards there.

A bouncer sat on a stool next to the door, and as I tried to enter, he put an arm out, blocking me. "Players only."

Well, shit. Now what? I didn't bother telling him that I was with the players because he had no reason to believe me. Plus, I was sure he'd heard that line more than once already tonight. I stepped aside to wait for Carson, feeling very much like a loser who wasn't allowed to sit with the cool kids. *Story of my life.*

Using the oldest trick in the book, I pulled out my phone and scrolled through it so that I wouldn't appear quite so lame. Though I tried not to watch the clock, I knew that it took Carson exactly eight minutes to find me. When he walked up, I couldn't help but notice he smelled like ladies' perfume. Or maybe my jealous mind was simply imagining it. People were packed so tightly in the small space, it was hard to tell where the scent was coming from.

"What are you doing?" Carson yelled to be heard over the music.

I gestured to the bouncer.

Carson's brow wrinkled as a look of annoyance crossed his face. "What's your name, man?"

"Greg."

"Nice to meet you, Greg. This is Becca. Becca, meet Greg."

I nodded to the man, who seemed to have no idea why Carson was spending so much time talking to him.

"I want you to memorize my girl, Becca's, face, okay?" Carson said. "She goes where I go."

I fought the urge to roll my eyes at Carson's big-man-on-campus routine. Though it annoyed me, it did come in handy sometimes. Back home, no one cared that he played for VVU, but his last name had the same effect. While he didn't hesitate to use his pull in Bleaksburg, I'd never seen him play the Fleck card. It was a touchy subject.

Nodding, the bouncer stepped aside. "You got it."

"Thanks." Carson clapped him on the back and slipped him a bill like he'd done with our server at Outback. I guessed one lesson he'd learned from his father was that when money talked, people listened. "Oh, and you see that guy at the bar there? In the navy shirt? He's with me too."

I was on the shorter side to begin with, but walking into a room full of football players made me feel like I was a Chihuahua in a pack of Saint Bernards—I would need to be careful not to get stepped on. It was a relief that the music was much quieter in the private room so that we could actually hear one another without having to yell.

"Do you want a drink?" Carson asked.

I pursed my lips, wondering why he'd even asked. "Underage, remember?"

"Yeah, but I could still get you something."

"Um, no. Water is fine." While my age obviously didn't stop me from indulging in the privacy of my own—or Carson's—home, I sure as hell wasn't going to drink in public. That was asking for trouble. As a cop's daughter, I knew that better than most.

When he went in search of the cocktail waitress who was supposed to be serving the room, I exhaled. While it felt kind of awkward to be standing alone in the middle of the room, I was grateful to have a moment to collect myself. I'd never liked watching Carson flirt with girls, but it didn't usually stir the thick jealousy that was still coating my insides. It was an uncomfortable feeling and one that I hoped was an anomaly. At least I could be fairly certain Carson wouldn't be accosted by anyone in the back room since everyone had to be escorted by a player. While that was a good solution for that evening, it was only putting a Band-Aid on what could turn out to be a much bigger problem.

Someone laid a hand on my arm, and I turned to see Jake's girlfriend, Rachel. *Thank God—a distraction.*

"Hi!" Her cheeks were slightly flushed, and her eyes were glassy. "Becca, right?"

We'd only met briefly over the summer, so I was pleased she remembered my name. "Yes. It's good to see you again, Rachel."

She jerked her thumb over her shoulder. "I've got a table over there if you want to come sit with me."

I nodded gratefully and followed her to the table. "Where's Jake?"

Rachel gestured to the crowd of players. "Somewhere in there, I guess."

"He played a great game." Both he and Carson had scored. Wyatt had made the third and last touchdown, giving a final score of twenty-one to seventeen. The win wasn't as impressive as most of last season's had been, but it was a rebuilding year, and a win was a win.

"I'm sooo glad he scored. I mean, I wasn't worried he'd fumble or anything, but he was so nervous." She covered her mouth with her hand. "Oops. I probably shouldn't tell you that, should I?"

I grinned. "It's okay."

She waved her hand in agreement. "That's right. We're both WAGs, so we can talk about this stuff."

"WAGs?" I felt like I should know what that meant, but I couldn't place the term.

"Wives and girlfriends. You know, like wives and girlfriends of the players. Freddie's Angie is an official WAG now that he's pro, but we're college WAGs, right? It counts." Rachel sucked up some of a fruity beverage from a straw.

I chuckled. "You're definitely a WAG, but Carson and I are just friends." I craned my neck, looking for Roman. "My brother, Roman, is around here somewhere. He and Carson have been best friends since fifth grade. They're like brothers."

"That's awesome! So if you and Carson get married, he and Roman can really be brothers. Well, brothers-in-law, anyway."

I shook my head. "I don't think you heard me. Carson and I aren't together."

Rachel peered at me for a moment before sighing. "That's too bad. After I saw the two of you at the river, I could have sworn it would only be a matter of time before you were in each other's pants." She laughed, and I tried to think back to when we'd all gone tubing at the New River to figure out what might have led her to think that. I came up blank. "Sorry," she continued. "I've been drinking, which means I pretty much won't shut up. Tell me to stop talking if I'm annoying you. I can't promise I will, though."

I felt rather than heard someone standing behind me. "You're annoying me." I turned to see Katie, Rachel's best friend and Wyatt Archer's girlfriend. I had met Katie at the river as well.

Rachel made a face at her friend. "I don't care if I annoy you. You're stuck with me."

A moment of longing hit me. I had girlfriends, but I wasn't nearly as close with any of them as these two were. It had never bothered me before, but now I wondered what it would be like to have someone to confide in. Maybe if I'd had someone to talk sense into me years ago, I would have forgotten all about Carson by now.

Katie crossed her arms and narrowed her eyes at Rachel. "We just got here. How are you drunk already?"

Rachel stuck her pointer finger in the air. "We've been here almost an hour," she corrected. "And I am indeed drunk. Do you remember Becca? She's Carson's 'friend.'" Her pointer finger made air quotes, which looked strange since she only used the one finger on one hand. I considered correcting her, but maybe if I didn't feed into it, Rachel would stop talking about it.

Katie took the empty chair on the other side of Rachel. "Just let me know if she's bothering you," she said in a mock whisper. "She might not be able to shut herself up, but I can shut her up."

"Boo!" Rachel said. "You're no fun."

Looking affectionately at her, Kate smiled. Then she noticed my lack of beverage. "So you're not drinking tonight, either, huh?"

"I won't be twenty-one until December," I explained. My underage status had come up more in the last week than it had all of last year, probably because there weren't many seniors as young as I was.

Katie nodded in understanding. "I'm still interning with the athletic department, and I have to go in early tomorrow. So I'm being responsible."

"And I am not!" Rachel declared, lifting her drink in a toast. "My student teaching starts Tuesday, so I'm drowning my sorrows in this Bahama Mama."

Jake and Carson appeared, and Jake placed another drink in front of Rachel. She hopped up so he could sit then plopped herself onto his lap. Carson took the last chair and put a chocolate milkshake in front of me with a flourish of his hand.

"What's this?" I asked.

He grinned mischievously. "You might not be able to have alcohol, but that doesn't mean you can't have a special drink." Looking at the thick beverage in its fancy glass brought back summer memories when Carson, Roman, and I would ride our bikes up to Sonic for milkshakes. *Damn him.* I was doing my best to convince myself to forget about Carson, but actions like this made it hard.

I took a sip. "Thanks." The word came out clipped, and I hoped he didn't notice. I didn't want to seem ungrateful.

"That... is... so... sweet!" Rachel squealed, her mouth dangerously close to Jake's ear.

He winced.

"Sorry, babe," she said. "I'm a little drunk."

"I noticed," Jake commented, but he didn't seem bothered by it. In fact, he looked at her adoringly. *Total boyfriend goals.*

Rachel leaned on the table. "Carson, isn't Becca pretty?" She winked at me.

Oh God. I rested my forehead in my hand, suddenly feeling the need to study my milkshake. I'd thought she would let this go. Eying me, Katie's brow furrowed, like she was thinking she should put a stop to Rachel's antics but didn't know how to do it without embarrassing me further. This was one of those *I wish the floor would swallow me* moments because I was suddenly petrified that I was wearing my feelings on my face. All I needed was for Carson to figure out that I was in love with him in the middle of a crowded bar and with my brother just yards away.

Carson didn't miss a beat, though. "She's the prettiest girl in the room."

"Just in the room?" Rachel prompted.

"Knock it off," Katie said under her breath.

I felt Carson's gaze slide over to me, and I couldn't stop myself from meeting it. "Becca is the prettiest girl in whatever room she's in. No offense to the present company."

The compliment would have meant a lot more if I hadn't just noticed a smear of lipstick on Carson's collar. *Guess I didn't imagine the perfume smell after all.*

Rachel smiled smugly. "None taken." She mouthed *you're welcome* to me, and I smiled meagerly. Though I was annoyed, I wasn't annoyed with Rachel. Yes, she was being kind of obnoxious, but I got it—she was in love, so she wanted everyone else to be in love.

I had a news flash for her—my love for Carson was never in question. It was him who didn't see me that way. I'd accepted that a long time ago and made peace with it. But all of a sudden, I wasn't nearly as okay with it as I thought I was.

***

Carson

ZIZ—*SHIT*—BECCA was having a terrible time. I would like to say it was because she couldn't drink like the rest of us, but that wasn't it. She was used to having a good time without drinking.

"Do you want something to eat?" I asked.

She did a double take, like she hadn't heard me correctly. "Are you kidding me? I'm still stuffed from dinner, and I also have this milkshake." She took a long sip of the thick liquid, and I'd never wanted to be a straw so much in my life.

Holy fuck, I'm drunk. That was one of the stupidest thoughts I'd had in a while, which was saying something. *A straw?* Thank God I wasn't one of those drunks who couldn't keep their mouths shut. *Looking at you, Rachel.*

But the main reason the thought was stupid was because this was Ziz. I shouldn't want anything to do with her mouth unless she needed resuscitation. *In that case, sign me up.* Too bad I didn't actually know CPR.

"Where's Roman?" she asked.

"Hitting on some girl at the bar."

She frowned. "Oh."

Maybe she was bummed because Roman wasn't hanging out with us. "I can go get him," I offered. I normally wasn't into cockblocking my friends, but I would do anything to cheer up Ziz. Something was off with her, and trying to figure it out was driving me crazy. Seeing her sad stabbed my heart.

She shook her head. "He's been on a ship for nine months. Let him have some fun."

"He's been on the water so long, he probably lost his touch." I grinned and leaned in conspiratorially. "Should I go be his wingman?"

"If you want," she said lightly, but her tight expression didn't match her tone. I'd said the wrong thing. *Fuck.* I'd thought she was getting along well with Rachel, Jake, and Katie, but maybe she didn't want me to leave her alone with them. She could be shy sometimes.

"Nah," I said. "He can sink or swim on his own." I elbowed her. "Get it? You know... because he's a sailor."

Ziz was normally a sucker for cheesy jokes, but she barely cracked a smile.

Rachel snagged her hand. "Come with me."

Ziz didn't bother asking where they were going. Anytime a drunk girl wanted another girl to go somewhere in a bar, there was a ninety-nine percent chance it was the bathroom.

When Rachel tried to grab Katie's hand, she evaded. "I want to find Wyatt."

After the girls left, I turned to Jake. "Does Ziz seem weird to you?"

Jake's expression was clueless. "I don't think so, but I don't know her well enough to say."

I nodded. Maybe it was all in my head, which was stupid. I didn't know why I was obsessing. She was fine because she was always fine. That was one of the things I loved about her—she didn't get caught up in the bullshit drama that some girls were so fond of.

When Rachel returned a few minutes later without her, I straightened. "Where's Ziz?"

Rachel frowned. "Who? *Oh...* Becca. Honestly, Carson, you should call her by her name."

"Ziz is her name."

Rachel rolled her eyes. "You should call her by her first name. She's not some guy in the locker room."

I liked Rachel, but at the moment, she was pissing me off. I'd known Ziz half my life. What the hell did Rachel know?

I ground my teeth. "Where is she?"

Rachel pointed. "There."

I looked where she was pointing to see her chatting with Taylor Stossel, a sophomore linebacker. She laughed at something he'd said and leaned in to touch his arm. When he took hold of her hand and brought it to his lips, I stood up so fast, my chair toppled over.

Oh, hell no.

"Carson!" Jake called after me as I stormed over. I barely heard him say "shit" through the roaring in my ears as he scrambled after me.

I inserted myself between Stossel and Ziz, forcing him to drop her hand and take a step back. As a linebacker,

Stossel was bigger than me, but he didn't intimidate me. No one could intimidate me where Ziz was concerned. "You better back the fuck off."

Stossel's eyes widened, and he put his hands up in a *no harm, no foul* gesture. "Sorry, man. I didn't know she was with you."

The whole fucking team knew she was with me. I'd made it absolutely clear that Ziz was off limits. Stossel was a transfer this year, so he might not have gotten the memo. That was the only thing keeping me from tearing his damn head off. I was reasonable like that.

Jake laid a hand on my shoulder. "Carson, cool it, man."

I shrugged his hand away, not taking my gaze off Stossel. "Are we clear?"

"Yeah, we're good." Stossel put his hand out, but I ignored it. Despite his apology, I could have rammed my fist into his nose and not lost any sleep over it. His goddamn mouth had been on Zizzo's skin.

Jake wisely led him away.

Behind me, Ziz practically growled. "I cannot believe you."

I turned, and she shoved me with both hands. I outweighed her by at least double, so it barely registered. "What was that for?"

Fire burned in her eyes, and her chest heaved. "I cannot believe you," she repeated.

What couldn't she believe? That I'd stopped a guy from pawing at her in the middle of a bar? Part of me was tempted to give her a sarcastic "you're welcome."

"He touched you," I said instead, which took admirable restraint.

"With my consent," she said, suddenly eerily calm. She peered at me like she was looking at a stranger. It was an expression I'd never seen on her before. "We were joking around."

"He—"

"Save it. I'm leaving. Find your own way home." She brushed past me and went to our table to retrieve her purse.

Not thinking twice about it, I followed.

When she turned, she nearly ran into me. "I'm taking your Jeep."

She pushed past me, and I continued to follow her as she left the bar. I didn't give a shit that she was taking my Jeep, but we'd parked a few blocks away in a dark lot. It wasn't safe for her to walk alone. If she hadn't worked herself up, she would realize that.

"You can't keep doing that, Carson." Though she addressed me, she didn't turn to face me as she continued the trek to the Jeep.

"He—"

Spinning, she laughed bitterly, cutting me off. "Let me guess. He showed interest in me. He talked to me. He touched me. Which one is it?"

All of the above, actually. But she wasn't in the right frame of mind to listen to reason.

She laughed again. "Or how about this one? He's not good enough for me."

"He's not." I didn't know the guy since he was new, but Ziz didn't need to date a football player. I'd yet to meet one who wasn't beneath her. She was this exquisite, beautiful being, and if that weren't enough, she was supremely intelligent. We were just thugs who played with a ball and knocked each other around.

Her anger dissipated, and her shoulders slumped, leaving her looking worn down and tired. I wanted to gather her into my arms, but even though I was drunk, I still realized that she wouldn't want that. And why would she? Hell, I was one of the thugs she needed to stay away from. Still, I would do anything to make her not look so sad, so broken.

"You can't keep doing that to me, not when you... when I..." She swallowed, and I would have done anything to take that look off her face. "You have to stop."

Except I couldn't do that. "I'll never stop protecting you."

She was kind, smart, and accomplished, not to mention gorgeous. Basically, she was perfect in every way. But she was small. The thought of someone putting his hands on her, *hurting* her, filled me with rage. I could never let that happen.

She shook her head. "That's not what you're doing. You're preventing me from living."

I recoiled. "I'm *protecting* you."

"From what? From meeting a nice guy who wants to date me?"

"Guys aren't nice."

"Some of them are. Roman is. My dad is. Evan is." She put her hand up. "Before you go all caveman on him, Evan and I are still just friends. And anyway, it doesn't matter. I have the right to figure that out on my own."

"I don't want you to get hurt."

She stepped closer until we were only inches apart. "You're the one who's hurting me, Carson." Her words penetrated my skin, my muscles, and my bones, going straight to pierce my heart.

I inhaled sharply, which only intensified the pain. "No..."

But the sad look in her eyes told me her words were true, or at least she believed them to be. I only wanted what was best for her—she had to be able to see that.

"I need a break from it, from you. I'm sorry. But it's more than just this. It hurts too much to be around you when..." She covered her eyes with her hand for a moment. Then without finishing her sentence, she turned and continued walking.

I waited a few seconds before following at a distance, only leaving to return to Bleakers once she was safely driving away in my Jeep.

CHAPTER 8

Becca

THE NEXT MORNING, I drove Carson's Jeep to his apartment and picked up my car. I needed to return his key, but I'd purposely set out on this errand early so I wouldn't have to see him. *Hope he has a spare.* I couldn't avoid him forever. He would get his key back eventually but not right then.

When I returned to my apartment, I found that Lucy had emerged from her room only to fall back asleep on the couch with the TV blaring. She did that a lot.

Even though I closed the door softly, she sat up with a start, her eyes wild. "Who? What?"

This wasn't the first time that had happened. I once joked that she had premature mom hearing. She didn't talk to me for two days after that. *Lesson learned.*

"Sorry," I said. "Go back to sleep."

She wiped the side of her mouth, probably checking for drool. "I'm awake now. Did you have a good night?" I hadn't seen her last night when I'd come home, which was good. Tears had blurred my sight so badly, I probably shouldn't have driven.

Damn Carson. I hadn't intended to blow up at him last night, but I'd hit my boiling point. And maybe—God willing—I'd finally hit the point where I was willing to let go of the idiotic dream that he would one day confess that his feelings mirrored mine. He'd never led me on—not exactly. He just did things like call me the prettiest girl in the room and buy me a milkshake. In short, he made me feel special in a way that he obviously wasn't intending. Although I'd ruined his chances of going home with that girl last week at TOTS, that wasn't normally how things went. He usually ended up leaving with someone. It was a punch to the gut every single time, but it was also a good reminder that Carson wasn't on my dating menu. Or to be more accurate, I wasn't on his.

That was what pissed me off the most. He didn't want me like that, but he didn't want anyone else to have me either. It was maddening. Even more maddening was the fact that I didn't even want the guys I flirted with—I wanted him.

I had always wanted him.

I realized Lucy was still waiting for an answer to her question. "I was tired, so I came home early." *Not exactly a lie.*

Not wanting to talk, I went into my room and shut the door. Then I texted my brother to see if he wanted to have lunch before he had to leave for home. I was glad I'd gotten to spend all yesterday afternoon with him at the game, but I wished he could stay longer. It was too bad Carson was the one with the spare bedroom and not me. *If Roman even slept there.* For all I knew, he'd gone home with the girl he'd been chatting up at the bar.

I wondered what Carson had told him about why I'd disappeared last night. Leaving without saying bye to Roman was a shitty thing to do, but I hadn't been thinking straight. I shook my head as I remembered how I'd almost spilled my feelings to Carson. I *really* hadn't been thinking straight. I couldn't believe I'd come so close to making that mistake while he'd had some girl's lipstick on his collar. *Talk about bad timing.*

But would there ever be a good time? I used to think there would, but maybe it was time to fully accept that there never would be, that there would never be a *Carson and me.*

Time to grow up and face reality, Becca.

My phone chimed with an incoming email, and I opened it, grateful for the distraction. It was from the homecoming court committee. My interview was set for Wednesday of the coming week. *Shit.* That was fast. I guessed it would have to be, though, since the event was the first week of October. That gave me three days to stress about it. *Ugh.* The interview itself didn't bother me. I was actually great at those. What stressed me out was that after the interview, I might actually be on the homecoming court.

That's the whole point of applying, stupid.

I never should have let Hanima and Courtney talk me into it.

No, that wasn't right. I never should have let Carson's incredulousness at the idea of me being on the court push me to go against my better judgment.

It all came back to Carson. *Always had, always would.*

***

Carson

"BECCA WANTS TO get together for lunch," Roman said. "How soon can you be ready?"

I hadn't told him the real reason Becca had left last night. Instead, I'd lied and said she wasn't feeling well. Roman hadn't questioned it because he had no reason to— I'd never lied to him before. It didn't sit right with me now, but I hadn't been able to bring myself to repeat the words that had been running through my head nonstop since she'd said them.

You're the one who's hurting me, Carson.

"I have a football thing," I told Roman. "Go without me."

Again, he didn't question me, and I felt like the biggest ass for lying to him once more. But there was no way in hell I could tell him the truth—that Becca didn't want to see me. How the hell had it gotten to that? I'd never had a fight like this with either Roman or her. The Zizzos were more like family to me than my own.

She'll cool off. She'd gotten irritated with me about my protectiveness before, but she'd never been able to hold a grudge. I would admit that I was overbearing sometimes, but I couldn't stop myself. Even if Roman hadn't asked me to look out for her when he left for boot camp, I still would. I was hardwired to look out for that girl. Making sure she was safe and seeing her smile made me happy. Unfortunately, those two things weren't meshing lately.

You're the one who's hurting me, Carson.

But I wasn't. I couldn't be. I cared about her way too much to ever hurt her.

She'd been stone sober. Otherwise I could have blamed her irrationality on alcohol. Maybe she had just been tired and overwhelmed. Senior engineering classes were tough, and on top of that, she was going forward with the asinine plan of being on the homecoming court. I still couldn't figure that one out.

After Roman had left to meet her, my place was way too quiet. Good thing I knew exactly where to find the antithesis of that. And if I went to Jake's, then what I'd told Roman wasn't entirely a lie since Jake was my football buddy. *Integrity partially intact.*

I was out the door before I remembered that Becca had taken my Jeep. But there it was, parked in my spot. I stared at it in confusion then looked at where she'd parked her car last night. It was gone.

Of course she'd returned my Jeep already because she was responsible and considerate, though not enough to knock on the door to return the key. *Guess she really is pissed.*

No matter. I had a spare key.

When I got to Jake's house, Rachel answered the door, looking like she'd been run over. I could have seen that one coming. She held a hand over her eyes to block out the sun that was shining through the open door. "Come in."

"Thanks."

Cringing, she put a hand on the wall to brace herself. "Why are you yelling?"

I raised my eyebrows. "I'm not," I whispered. If I were in a better mood, I would totally take advantage of the situation and give her hell, especially after some of the things she'd said last night, but I wasn't feeling it.

"That's better." She resumed the trek to the living room and carefully stretched out on the couch. Closing her eyes, she flung an arm over her face. "Jake's in the shower."

"Is he as hung over as you?"

"No. He was reasonable last night, so he's all bright-eyed and bushy-tailed. I kind of hate him right now."

"That's not true." She and Jake were still in the phase where they made googly eyes at each other all the time. While I was happy for them, it could be nauseating to watch.

"You're right." She moved her arm and peeled open an eyelid. "It's me I hate. I'm sorry for last night. Those Bahama Mamas turned me into a Bitchy Mama."

Her apology made me glad I hadn't given her a hard time a moment ago. "You weren't bitchy." Rachel was a sweetheart. I doubted she had full-on bitch mode in her programming.

She closed her eyes again. "Maybe not bitchy but definitely obnoxious."

"A little," I allowed. But I'd dealt with much worse.

"I need to apologize to Becca too."

"You're not the only one," I muttered. I'd come to Jake's house to be distracted from thinking about her, but I couldn't even be pissed at Rachel for bringing her up because I'd been a fool to think it would be that easy to take my mind off Ziz.

You're the one who's hurting me, Carson.

Every time those words echoed in my mind, salt poured into the wound.

"Was she pissed about that thing with Stossel?" Rachel asked. "I noticed she left right after that." With as drunk as Rachel had been, I was surprised she'd noticed, but girls paid attention to that sort of thing, apparently even when they were drunk.

"She wasn't thrilled," I said tightly.

You're the one who's hurting me, Carson.

I scrubbed my hands over my head, wishing I could scrub those words from my mind. It was like she'd known the perfect thing to say to gut me. She couldn't have come up with more effective words if she'd tried. But she wasn't like that. She would never try to hurt me on purpose.

Rachel opened her mouth, closed it, and then repeated the sequence several times. She looked like a fish gasping for air.

I blew out a breath. "Just say it." I really didn't want to talk about it, but I could admit that a woman's insight might be helpful in clarifying everything. The faster I could get back to normal with Ziz, the better.

"Are you sure you're not dating?" Rachel cringed. "I mean, Becca told me you aren't, but—"

"But what?" I challenged, hating myself a little for how confrontational I sounded. But it was a dumbass question. I would know if I was dating someone, and since Ziz had told Rachel we weren't, that should have been the end of it. Besides that, Ziz was practically my sister. We'd grown up together. She was family.

"You acted like a jealous boyfriend."

I scoffed. "I did *not* act like a jealous boyfriend. I was just looking out for her. That's all." Anyway, I wasn't the jealous type. Case in point—I'd dated plenty of girls, and I had never gotten jealous over any of them. I tried to ignore the small part of my brain that was waving a red flag like a damn matador. I'd never dated anyone worth getting jealous over. Ziz was definitely worth it... but we weren't dating. Jealousy hadn't been the reason for my actions.

"Stossel didn't do anything wrong, though," Rachel pointed out. "They were in the middle of a bar, laughing and joking around." When she put it like that, I felt like a Neanderthal. She was missing the bigger picture, though.

"That's fine, but she shouldn't date a football player." *Or any other player.* I knew better than anyone that almost all guys were players. Becca didn't need some jackass breaking her heart.

Rachel sat up. "Why not? I'm dating a football player. My best friend is dating a football player."

Shit. This was entrapment. I should have known better than to get into a relationship discussion with a woman. Luckily, Jake walked in, so I could appeal to his better judgment. "Would you let your sister date a teammate?"

His gaze went back and forth between his girlfriend and me. "Considering my sisters are twelve and eight, that's a hard no."

"Don't be dense," Rachel said. "What if they were in college?"

Again, Jake's gaze slid between us. "Why do I get the feeling I'm being set up to fail?"

"Ugh... I'm too hungover for this," Rachel said. "Carson, I'm going to ignore the many contradictions with your argument that football players are undateable, especially since you are one. Instead, I'll just say this: It's a shame you won't 'let'"—she put air quotes around *let*— "Becca date a football player, because the two of you would be adorable together."

Puppies were adorable, and kittens, too, if a person was into them, but the idea of me dating Ziz wasn't adorable. It was ludicrous. We were too close for that. Even if that weren't true, it was still crazy. I would never be good enough for her.

Too bad, because I was probably the only one who knew how she deserved to be treated. My chest tightened at the thought of some other guy dating Becca and doing it completely wrong.

I forced a laugh. "Whatever you say, Rachel."

Shaking her head, she stood. "I'm going to soak in the bath. If I'm not out in thirty minutes, that means I've drowned myself to put myself out of my misery. Effing Bahama Mamas."

***

Carson

OUR SECOND GAME of the season, and we fucking lost. The University of Miami was a conference rival and always a tough match-up. This time, they were too tough. They'd beaten us by three, and it fucking sucked. But we weren't the same team we were last year. For starters, we had no running game. All of our running backs were rookies, and so were half of both our offensive and defensive lines. The offensive line in particular had struggled to get it together. They'd barely protected Wyatt, forcing him to scramble. We were probably lucky we hadn't lost by more. Hell, we were probably lucky our players hadn't gotten injured. The Miami linemen were beasts.

Still, after winning the national championship last year, a loss so early in the season was tough to take. At least I'd played well. So had Wyatt and Jake, but we were about the only ones. We weren't destined for a national championship this season, but with any luck, the three of us were destined for the draft. *Eyes on the prize.*

I skipped most of my classes for the first part of the week. That probably was not my best decision, but the travel to Miami had kicked my ass, not to mention the game itself.

I logged into my course websites and groaned when I saw that the sociology professor had assigned another written assignment. I should have dropped that class when I'd had the chance, but now it was too late. It was my own damn fault. I knew I was no good at this shit, but I hadn't wanted to look bad in front of Zi—*shit*—Becca. She was still pissed at me. She hadn't said as much, but she'd kept her distance for almost two weeks, which spoke volumes. Her absence weighed on me, but I was letting her have space.

Most of what Rachel had said the other day was bullshit. The main piece of bullshit was the part about Becca and me dating. When the right guy came along for her, he would be the luckiest bastard alive. But that guy wasn't me, and until he came along, I would continue scaring away the losers.

I had considered some things Rachel had said, though. I'd known that Becca didn't particularly like being called Zizzo, but I'd ignored it. Now, I was trying to stop. Also, I'd decided I needed to be a little more subtle when I was looking out for her. I would have to figure out how to protect her without letting her know I was doing it. I had no idea how the hell I was going to manage that. Not looking out for her wasn't an option.

I couldn't tell her either of those things, though, and not because she wasn't talking to me. Instead, I would have to show her by acting on them. Not that any of it mattered if she kept avoiding me, which was some horseshit.

For the first time, I was actually a little grateful to have a difficult assignment, because as pissed as Becca was, she wouldn't leave me hanging. I sent her a text.

Carson: *Got another written assignment for soc ed.*

I stared at the phone, waiting for a response. The seconds ticked by. In the past, she'd responded right away. She was probably just busy, yet I couldn't help but wonder if she was punishing me. Becca didn't normally play games like that.

Becca: *Send it when you're done, and I'll proof it.*

Damn. I was hoping she would say that she would be right over like she used to. It was past time for things to get back to normal.

Fuck it. Eating crow wasn't normally my MO, but I was willing to take one for the team.

Carson: *Can you come over later? I'll make you dinner.*

When she didn't respond right away, I sweetened the deal. I could get by in the kitchen, but I wasn't the best cook.

Carson: *Or I'll take you out to dinner. Your choice.*

Since I'd gotten behind with schoolwork this week, I didn't really have time to hang out, but Becca was more important than my grades. Besides, all I needed to do was maintain the minimum GPA to keep my eligibility. I wasn't a genius, but I wasn't a complete moron either.

My phone rang, and I saw that it was Stacey. Definitely not a welcome call, but she was easier to deal with than my mother.

"Hello?" I answered.

"Carson?"

"Yeah?"

"Hold, please."

Shit. I knew what that meant—my mother would be on the line in a few seconds. I shouldn't have answered.

A click sounded as my mother came on the line. "Carson, I have your RSVP for Chelsea's engagement party here."

Hi, Mom, how are you? Yeah, I'm fine too. Thanks for asking.

I didn't think I'd ever said anything remotely close to that on a call with my mom. If niceties didn't get her anything, then she didn't bother. Her political rivals called her a hard-ass bitch. Her supporters cried foul, saying that if she were a man, she would be applauded for being direct. The truth was most likely somewhere in the middle. All I knew was that she was never more maternal than when the cameras were rolling.

"Okay." I'd sent back the RSVP a few days ago, well ahead of the deadline. I'd patted myself on the back for that because usually I was a last-minute kind of guy. For this, I probably should have been, just to delay this conversation.

"You need to be there."

"I can't. I have a game that weekend." I didn't bother mentioning that it was family-appreciation weekend because I wasn't feeling very appreciative of my family. Maybe if I played for a school in my home state of Maryland, she would be more interested in my games because then she would be able to use her appearances to further her political career.

"You need to come." Her voice sounded strained, which was new. She always sounded cool, calm, and collected. Though I had personal issues with my mother, she was actually one of the better politicians. She acted in the best interests of her constituents. I just wished that behavior extended to me, her son. *Hey, Mom, remember I'm registered to vote in Maryland too.*

"I need to play in my game."

"Surely they can do without you for one game."

What the fuck? College football was basically the minors. I didn't get why she didn't understand that. I'd seen guys play with broken bones and while sick with the flu. There was no way I could miss a game for a stupid social engagement.

"It's not little league," I told her. "Games aren't optional."

"Neither is a family event."

Huh. So I guess the VVU family-appreciation game isn't a family event. I wasn't even going to get into that because, frankly, if they didn't want to come, then I didn't want them there.

"Sorry. You'll have to do without me."

My mother let out a lengthy breath. "Fine." She sounded resigned, like she'd expected as much. *Then why did she bother calling? To give me a guilt trip?* It wouldn't work, especially since I was pretty sure my mom simply wanted me there as a prop. *Here's my lovely, perfect family—don't forget to vote for me for governor!* "Your sister will be disappointed."

I snorted. "I'm sure there will be so many guests, she won't even notice I'm not there."

She didn't bother denying it. "All the same."

"If that's all you wanted, I need to go."

"Make sure you behave." The words themselves sounded like something a mother would say, but the intent behind them wasn't motherly. She wasn't concerned for my safety or well-being. Instead, she wanted to make sure I didn't do anything that would embarrass her and hurt her campaign.

I wouldn't but not for her benefit. I didn't want to do anything that would be a strike against me in the draft. I supposed I was running a campaign of my own. These days, the pro teams didn't want to take a risk on a player with questionable character.

"I always do." I hung up without saying a proper goodbye. I pushed the phone away and ran my hands over my head. Normally, I didn't let my family get to me. Every family had problems. Mine were first-world problems.

My phone buzzed, and I was tempted to ignore it, but then I remembered I'd invited Becca for dinner. I hoped she chose going out somewhere. I was no longer in the mood to cook.

Becca: *Sorry. I've got a thing.*

Fuck.

CHAPTER 9

Becca

I SAT IN my car outside the student center, watching the clock. I had seven more minutes before I had to pull up my big-girl panties and enter the building. The previous week, I'd left the homecoming court interview with a smile on my face. *Nailed it.* I'd spent the evening before it prepping by reviewing general interview questions I'd found online. That had turned out to be overkill since the questions they'd asked were beyond basic. After the interview, I'd been reasonably certain that I would get on the court and wasn't surprised when the congratulatory email showed up in my inbox. But I also knew with certainty that I wouldn't win. *Not the point,* I told myself sternly. *Winning isn't everything.*

Yeah, right. My competitive nature was rearing its ugly head. I came by it honestly, especially after growing up surrounded by Roman and Carson. Although I still wasn't ready to make nice with Carson, I'd loyally watched the game against Miami this past weekend and chewed my nails down to the quicks. *Good thing the game had been after the interview.*

I felt bad for Carson, and I'd had to stop myself from reaching out to see how he was taking the loss. Since the incident at Bleakers, I hadn't talked to him, even though he'd texted me. I wasn't ready, not necessarily because I didn't want to hear what he had to say but because I didn't know what *I* wanted to say. All I knew was that I didn't want to fall back into the status quo. Something had to change, but I wasn't quite sure what or how.

Earlier this evening, he'd texted me, wanting to have dinner. Actually, he'd offered to make me dinner, which I knew was his way of trying to smooth things over. I couldn't decide whether it was good or bad that I had a homecoming meeting, which made dinner not an option. At least I didn't have to feel bad for declining the invite.

Two minutes. Ugh. My stomach clenched, reminding me exactly why I hadn't wanted to be on the homecoming court. But I had committed, so I swiped an extra coat of lip gloss on my lips and headed into the building. I found my way to a room full of sorority girls and fraternity guys. That wasn't entirely correct—two candidates for homecoming king were sponsored by non-Greek organizations, but I was the only non-Greek girl. As expected, I felt immediately uncomfortable, like I didn't belong. Roman would have fit in better. If he had gone to college, he would have made the perfect frat boy.

I wandered over to a table along the wall and snagged a bottle of water. The homecoming committee had also provided a cookie platter, so I grabbed a chocolate chip cookie to have something to do other than scroll through my phone. But the second I took a bite, a guy walked over to me.

He held out his hand. "I'm Blake."

Cheese on a cracker. I awkwardly tried to switch my bottled water into the hand holding the cookie.

He laughed and dipped his chin to his chest. "Sorry. I caught you at a bad moment. It's my gift."

I quickly finished chewing and swallowed. "No, it's okay. I'm Becca." Despite the awkward introduction, I was glad not to be standing alone anymore.

He gestured toward the name tag I'd dutifully stuck on my shirt. "WIE? What's that?"

"Women in Engineering," I told him.

"Oh, cool, so you're an engineering major?" He grinned. "I was too for a semester. It didn't take long for me to realize I couldn't hack it."

That happened a lot. First semester, freshman year, engineering majors took what we referred to as "weed-out" classes. At least a quarter of those enrolled didn't make it through.

"What major did you switch to?"

"Business management." He grinned. "If I can't be an engineer, then maybe I can manage them."

"Oh." I didn't know how to respond to that. I peered at his name tag. "Sigma Chi." My tone came out more accusatory than I'd intended.

"Yeah. I'm the vice president." He rubbed the back of his neck in a sheepish gesture, making me feel like a jerk. It had sounded like I was judging him for being Greek, which I guessed I sort of was. I was being a total jerk.

"That sounds like a big responsibility." *Oh... my... God.* I could not believe how lame I was being. But it was rare that I actually got to talk to a guy longer than a minute without Carson breaking it up. *Especially one as cute as this one.*

Blake had clean-cut good looks—neatly trimmed dark hair, clean-shaven cheeks with strong lines, and blue eyes that crinkled at the edges when he smiled. That, combined with his polo shirt and boat shoes, made him look like he belonged in the pages of a Ralph Lauren ad.

"It's a pain in the ass," he said. "We almost lost our charter last year because of... Well, let's just say some of my brothers are total dipshits. You probably don't have to deal with that in WIE."

"Um, no." *Again, Becca, could you try to be a little more interesting?* Luckily, the committee member asked everyone to take a seat so the meeting could start. *Thank God.* I needed to be saved from myself. I was an introvert, but I could normally handle small talk for a few minutes. I was out of my element surrounded by all these sorority girls, which really wasn't fair. I had no reason to think they were anything but nice people.

The presentation covered the basics of being on homecoming court. I was relieved to learn that unlike in high school, the girls weren't required to wear formal dresses. The guys would wear suits, and the girls were expected to "dress smartly," whatever the hell that meant. I would have to look up pictures online of past years' courts because I'd never paid attention to the court in general, much less their clothing.

Campaigning wasn't required either, which was another relief. Part of the reason I had resisted being on the court was that I didn't want to have to sell myself. I wasn't good at that. I was better behind the scenes, like in a lab. *Hence the reason I'm majoring in biomedical engineering.*

The court representatives had two major responsibilities—well, three if I counted the court presentation at the homecoming game. We had to film an interview that highlighted our platforms. These would be posted online for the student body to view. The other unexpected responsibility was attending the homecoming alumni event the night before the game, which didn't seem like a big deal. Overall, I was getting off easy. Being on the court really wasn't all that complicated.

Although judging from the serious and contemplative expressions on some of the other girls' faces, they took it a lot more seriously than I did. I wasn't willing to put in the effort it would require to beat them. While I was competitive, I also knew when to cut my losses. They had a whole sorority full of girls to back them. I had Hanima, Courtney, Nicole, and whatever WIE members we could actually get to participate. *Sigh.*

The presenter finished speaking and invited us to stay as long as we wanted to get to know one another. *Um... no, thank you.* I'd barely managed small talk with Blake without coming across as a dimwit. I looked at him out of the corner of my eye. He *was* handsome, and with his preppy exterior, he was the exact opposite of my normal type, which was mainly Carson. Maybe getting to know him better wouldn't be such a bad thing.

"What's your platform?" I asked him.

"Breast cancer. My aunt is fighting it now."

"That's awesome." I cringed. *I should give up on the small talk.* "I mean, it's not awesome that your aunt is sick, but that's an awesome platform."

He smiled easily. "I knew what you meant."

"Your platform makes mine feel silly."

He looked at me expectantly. "What is it?"

"Oh, sorry. Promoting girls' education in science and technology."

He shook his head. "That's not silly. It's important too."

"It is," I allowed. And while I wholeheartedly believed in it, it still felt insignificant compared to finding a cure for a life-threatening illness that affected millions. My family was fortunate because we didn't have a history with breast cancer, but a girl I'd known in high school had a scare when she was just seventeen.

"Think about it this way," Blake said. "Girls think differently than guys, right? So we need girls in science. We need all the different perspectives we can get. A woman might be the one to cure cancer."

The nerves that had wound themselves tightly in my stomach uncoiled. "Thanks."

"For what?"

"For getting it. I feel the same way." Our eyes met, and I looked away, feeling exposed.

The other candidates started filtering out. *Guess I'm not the only one who doesn't want to mingle.*

Blake held his hand out for my empty water bottle then walked over to the recycling bin to toss both our bottles in. He turned back toward me. "We should exchange numbers. You know, in case either of us has a homecoming emergency."

I arched a brow, suddenly feeling very much in my element. I definitely knew how to handle cheesy pickup lines. They were my favorite kind. "What constitutes a homecoming emergency?"

He grinned. "Anything at all. Basically, whatever gets you to text me."

My heart fluttered. That was the first time in a long time it had done so for someone other than Carson. But for some inexplicable reason, that made me sad.

***

SO FAR IN the twenty-four hours since the homecoming meeting, I hadn't had a "homecoming emergency." What that really meant was I hadn't come up with a reason to text Blake. Or maybe I just hadn't yet decided if I wanted to. But he hadn't texted me either. I wasn't sure what the protocol was.

As an engineering student, I didn't have much time for a social life. What little time I did have, I spent with Nicole or Carson. Early in my freshman year, I'd dated a few guys who had also been engineering students, and it had become immediately clear to me that while I loved being friends with other engineers, I didn't want to date one. So I didn't have many opportunities to meet guys I would actually want to date, especially because I turned into a homing device for Carson whenever I was downtown and chatting with a guy. If I were in a spy movie, I would check myself for a tracking device.

Now I'd met a good-looking, smart non-engineer who was interested in me, and I was stalling. It made no sense because this was the exact reason I was angry with Carson—because he had prevented opportunities such as this one.

"Text him," I muttered to myself. "Stop being a pansy."

Lucy stuck her head in my room. "Did you say something?"

"Sorry. I was just talking to myself."

She eyed me warily. "Why are you staring at your phone like it did something to you? Was Carson an ass again?"

"What? No." I'd told her that Carson and I had a fight, but I hadn't gone into detail. I'd rehashed it enough in my own head, so I didn't want to discuss it. Plus, I wasn't confident that Lucy would understand. When I'd occasionally griped about Carson's behavior, she'd been less than sympathetic. *Champagne problem*, she'd called it.

"Okay. Do you want to run some lines with me?"

"You know I don't." I *hated* helping her memorize her lines. She'd talked me into it once. *Never again.* And this play was Shakespeare. That made it a double-hard pass.

She sighed and looked at me forlornly. Lucy was a master at the guilt trip, but over the years, I'd built up my immunity.

"I'll make you a deal," I said. "I'll help you if you'll quiz me for my cellular mechanotransduction test."

"Cellular mechano-what?"

I laughed. "Mechanotransduction. *Duh.*" *Yeah...* it was a mouthful.

She looked at me blankly for a moment then shook her head. "I'm glad there are smart people like you who can do that stuff because I sure as hell can't. You have fun with that." She wandered out of the room, leaving me to stare at my phone again. I wasn't normally such a coward. But I also didn't normally exchange numbers with hot frat guys.

"Just text him," I muttered. "For coffee. Just coffee."

The whole reason I was giving Carson the cold shoulder was because he'd overstepped his bounds where my dating life was concerned. But I was hesitating, and I wondered if it was because even though my head was ready to get over Carson, my heart wasn't having any of it.

It's just coffee... Eff it.

Becca: *Hey, Blake, it's Becca! Want to grab coffee sometime?*

I dropped my phone on my bed like it was on fire and continued to stare at it for a moment before shaking myself out of my stupor. The ball was in his court now.

***

Carson

PRACTICE WAS GRUELING for the rest of the week. Apparently, Coach Coyle did not take well to losing, especially when we could have won, at least in his opinion. His Texas twang had given me the impression that he was laid back, but I discovered exactly how wrong that was. I felt like I was in one of the clichéd high school sports movies, yet I was one of the players who hadn't screwed up. *Christ.* I never thought I would say this, but I felt bad for the offensive line.

Wyatt didn't. He merely shrugged. "They need to get their shit together." I could understand his point of view because he was the one who suffered from their ineffectiveness. The last thing he needed was to get injured because of other players' ineptitude.

Beside me, Jake hurriedly grabbed his stuff from his locker and shoved it into his bag. "I gotta run. It's open house tonight for Ashley's school."

Damn. I had hoped he would want to chill and unwind. Jake had been MIA for almost the past year, first because his parents had died and now because he had the responsibility of his siblings. Any free time he had, he preferred to spend with Rachel. I got it—it just sucked for me. I supposed I could see if Jimmy or Demarcus wanted to chill, but I didn't know them as well. I wanted to hang out with someone I could completely relax around. There were only two people that fit that description at VVU, and one of them was still avoiding me.

Fuck it. I was over that shit. She might be able to blow off my texts, but no way would she slam her door in my face... I hoped. I couldn't believe it had come to that.

I parked outside her apartment building and headed up to the second floor. I knocked, and her roommate opened the door. She leaned against it with a smile on her face that bordered on a smirk. "Hi, Carson." She and Becca had almost nothing in common, but they somehow got along perfectly.

"Is Becca here?"

Lucy stepped aside so I could enter. "In her room."

Her door was ajar, and she was sitting on her bed with papers spread out around her and a highlighter in her hand. I knocked, feeling like a tool. I'd never felt like I had to knock on her open door before. *Christ.*

She looked up, and her eyes immediately became guarded.

You're the one who's hurting me, Carson.

The words I'd worked so hard to forget flashed in my mind, and I was immediately filled with regret. But for what, I wasn't sure. There were too many things to narrow it down to only one, and I would never consciously admit to most of those.

"What are you doing here?" she asked.

Ouch. But I refused to be deterred so easily. I walked in and shut the door behind me then sat in her desk chair. "I'm sorry." *Simple and to the point.*

She cocked her head. "Are you, though? Or are you just sorry that I'm mad?"

Damn. She had me pegged, and she wasn't letting me off easy. "Both."

"Really?"

Shit. I couldn't lie to her. For one thing, she would know. But also, she deserved better than that. "Not exactly. I'm sorry I did something to upset you, but I'm not sorry I kept you from dating some loser."

Looking up, she shook her head in disbelief. "I was *talking* to a guy in a bar, not dating him. But even if I were, that's none of your business. And that 'loser' is your teammate. Have some respect."

Now I felt like a total ass. I didn't have anything against Stossel personally, and once I'd explained the situation to him the next time I saw him at practice, he understood. We were cool. It was in no one's best interest to have infighting on the team. *Which is why everyone knows to keep their damn eyes—and hands—off Becca.*

"You can do better than him is my point." I mentally patted myself on the back for my diplomacy. *Guess politician blood runs in the family after all.* "I'm always going to look out for you."

She held my gaze for a moment, like she was gathering her thoughts. "I appreciate that, but you take it too far."

"Maybe." That was all I was willing to admit. She would never understand how deep my protective streak ran when it came to her. Hell, I didn't understand it myself.

She studied me. "Are you okay?"

I ran a hand over my head. I must look as bad as I felt. "It's been a rough week."

"Tough loss on Saturday."

I was pleased she'd still watched the game. All this time, I'd been telling myself that Becca wasn't going to finally be done with my dumb ass once and for all, but I guessed I'd been worried she might be.

"I miss you." *Holy hell.* Where had that come from? It was true, but I hadn't consciously thought it, much less planned to say it. Becca knew how much she meant to me, just like Roman did. We didn't talk about feelings and shit.

"I miss you too," she said softly, and the words were music to my ears.

"Does that mean you forgive me?" I flashed the smile I'd used a million times to soften up Becca's mother after I'd done or said some dumbass thing. It had worked ninety percent of the time, much to Roman's dismay. She'd never let him get away with shit.

"That means I'm working on it." Becca looked like she wanted to say more, but I didn't push. I was just happy to be back on speaking terms. Besides, I'd met my daily quota for heart-to-hearts. Hell, I'd met my monthly quota.

"Have you eaten yet?" I asked, grateful to be moving on to something more normal.

She shook her head. "But I need to study for this test, so I can't go anywhere."

I wasn't in the mood to go out anyway, so I took out my phone. "I'll order something. Is that cool?"

"I really do need to study. That wasn't an excuse."

I had half a mind to ask if the *thing* she'd had the other night had been an excuse, but I didn't want to reopen that can of worms. If it had been an excuse, maybe I'd deserved it. *Maybe.*

"You won't even know I'm here."

She frowned at me like she was trying to figure out if she could believe me, which was justified. I had a history of being a pest when she had work to do and I didn't. As she studied, those cute wrinkles on her forehead formed, and I grinned at her.

"What?" she asked without looking up.

"Nothing." I stretched out next to her on the bed and dozed until the Chinese food arrived. Even though I was starving, I waited ten extra minutes—a freaking eternity—for her to get to a stopping point before digging in. *Because I'm thoughtful as fuck.*

She rooted around in the bag. "Is there duck sauce?"

"Here." I tossed a packet into her lap. "But seriously, you should try the mustard."

She wrinkled her nose, something that always made her look extra cute. *Damn.* She was full of cute expressions this evening.

"Mustard is gross."

"But this is special Chinese mustard."

"That doesn't make it better."

As we ate, I rolled my shoulders, trying to work out the tension that had been there all week and finally feeling some relief. Spending time with Becca was good for me. Damn, I'd missed her. I hadn't realized how much until now.

She cast a suspicious glance my way. "Why are you looking at me like that?"

"Like what?"

"I don't know. Just like... weird." *Well, that clears it up.*

I laughed. "I'm just happy to be hanging out with you again."

"Happy enough to help me with my shower?" She batted her eyelashes in an exaggerated fashion.

The blood drained from my face. "Is it full of hair?"

"Huh?"

"The drain, because I'll gag if there's a giant hairball in there." I'd shared a bathroom with my sister growing up, and our drain would always be full of her hair. I'd literally had nightmares about it.

"No. I already pulled all the hair out."

I shuddered as visions of long hair clumped together with soap ran through my mind. Suddenly the Chinese food wasn't sitting so well in my stomach.

Becca rolled her eyes.

"It's a legit phobia," I protested. I didn't give her shit about her clown phobia. *Oh, wait.* There was that one time, but I'd been fifteen. I hadn't known she would literally pee her pants if I climbed into her bedroom window on Halloween, dressed like a clown. Yeah... we didn't talk about that incident.

She ran her fingers through her long locks. "It's just hair."

"No, it's not. It's..." I swallowed. "Can we stop talking about it, please?" I wasn't normally a puker, but my stomach might make an exception if we kept going, especially after eating greasy Chinese food.

"Sure, whatever. Anyway, the drain is fine. It's the showerhead that's the problem. I bought a new one. The old one is stuck on there, though."

I flexed my arms. "So you need my muscles." I did my best Arnold Schwarzenegger impression, which was pretty damn pathetic. *Looks like it's time for a* Terminator *marathon.* I wondered if Becca would watch them all with me. There were no clowns in it, so I might be able to talk her into it, especially if I invoked her *movies are genderless* argument.

"Actually, yes," she said wearily, like it pained her to admit it. Becca had a can-do attitude and didn't admit defeat easily.

After we stowed the leftovers in the fridge, we went into her bathroom, and she handed me a gigantic wrench. It was the length of her entire arm.

"Well, that's the problem," I commented. "You don't have a big enough wrench."

She shot me a wry look. "Very funny. Lucy borrowed it from the drama tech room. It was the only one she could find." It was comically large, making me wonder if it was used as a prop in a play rather than as an actual tool. "If it's too big for you to handle—"

"Don't worry. I'm used to large... equipment." I wriggled my eyebrows and grinned.

She rolled her eyes. "I'd expect nothing less on account of how big of a tool you are."

"Touché." I stepped into the tub, keeping a tight hold on the wrench. If I dropped it on my foot, I would likely end up with a broken toe. I could just imagine having to explain that injury to Coach Coyle. *No, thank you.* I screwed the wrench onto the showerhead and gave it a light tug. The sucker was on there good and tight. The apartment building was at least twenty years old, and it wouldn't surprise me if the showerhead was the original.

"Can you get it?" Becca asked impatiently. She had a tendency to micromanage, but I was used to it.

"Give me a second. I don't want to break something and cause a bigger problem than a crappy showerhead."

She sank down onto the toilet seat so I could work. It took a fair amount of torque to get the thing loose. There was no way Becca would have been able to do it herself. I handed her the old piece of junk and quickly installed the new one.

"There." I stepped out of the tub and reached for the shower spigot to test it out. "Good as—*shit*."

Becca had chosen the exact second I turned on the spigot to step into the shower to check out my handiwork. She gasped as she took a direct hit from the cold spray. "Turn it off!" she shrieked.

"Shit!" I fumbled with the spigot, my hands suddenly having trouble grasping it. When I finally got it off, she turned to me, her eyes wide and wet strands of hair clinging to her face. My gaze traveled south, and I swallowed. Becca's shirt wasn't white, but it might as well have been. The thin, pale-blue material was see-through when wet, and she looked like she'd taken first place in a wet T-shirt contest. The material clung to her, outlining the gorgeous curve of her breasts. Her nipples were fully erect, and the sight of them made me fully erect.

"Cold," Becca managed to say through chattering teeth.

"Shit," I said, which was obviously my word of choice for the last minute. I yanked a towel off the rack and wrapped it around her, rubbing her arms and pulling her against my chest.

Bad idea. Because even through the towel, I could feel her hard nipples against me. I had to angle my lower half away from her so she wouldn't be able to feel that I was hard. Christ.

She shivered. "If I didn't know better, I'd say you were getting back at me for being mad at you."

"Passive-aggressive isn't my style," I said absentmindedly. It was a miracle I was able to form any coherent thought with her wet body pressed up against me. But my words were true—I was more likely to get up in someone's face and tell him to fuck off like I'd done with Stossel.

"Well, I guess we know the new showerhead works."

I let go of her just enough so that I could look at her face. She grinned, and her eyes twinkled. *Thank God.* It had been an accident, but I still felt bad about it. And now that I knew she wasn't upset, I could admit it was funny. Maybe not as funny as the clown incident, but again, we didn't talk about that.

I lifted her out of the tub. It had seemed like the gentlemanly thing to do, but I sure as hell didn't feel like a gentleman. Not when I wanted to peel the layers of wet clothing off her body and dry her skin inch by blessed inch.

Becca clung to me, still shivering. Using my thumb, I smoothed a wet tendril of hair away from her face. Her gaze met mine. Her beautiful brown eyes were open wide, but I couldn't read them—I had no idea what she was thinking.

But I knew what I was thinking, and it wasn't right. I was thinking that I wished to God she were someone else, not Roman's sister, but just a perfect girl I'd met. Because I wanted nothing more than to put my mouth on hers, to strip off her wet clothing and warm her body with mine.

I wanted her, more than I'd ever wanted anyone. I'd never admitted it, even to myself, but I couldn't deny it any longer.

Abruptly, I released her before I did something she would hate me for. "I've got to go." I left the small room, afraid to meet her gaze, afraid she would be able to read me like a book. But mostly, I was afraid of her reaction if she figured out the truth—that I loved her and not like a sister.

CHAPTER 10

Becca

LUCY FLEW AROUND her room like a lunatic, tossing clothing into her suitcase. "*Hamilton!*" she squealed for the eighth time.

"But you've already seen it twice."

Her body immediately went rigid, and she slowly spun to face me. "Excuse me?" She looked affronted by my comment, like I hadn't simply stated a fact.

"You've seen it twice, right?" I was pretty sure she had because I remembered hearing her squeal "*Hamilton*" in that exact cadence before.

She lifted her nose in the air. "When one gets offered a free *Hamilton* ticket, one takes it."

"I stand corrected," I said. Except I didn't get it. I would like to see *Hamilton* as much as the next person—well, I guess not as much as Lucy—but I wasn't about to drive nine hours and miss several days of classes to do it.

"Peter's boyfriend's flu is my gain," Lucy said. Peter was her cousin who lived in New York. He was a budding actor, which meant he shared an apartment with three other people and waited tables to pay the rent. It sounded miserable, but then again, I'd never had the desire to be famous, not even when I was a kid.

Lucy had only gotten the call from Peter thirty minutes ago as she was getting ready for her *Othello* rehearsal. She planned to go to that then start her trip immediately after, which meant she would be driving overnight. When I'd voiced my concern about her falling asleep at the wheel, she'd waved me off, saying nighttime was the best time to travel, especially to the city, because there would be less traffic.

"Text me when you get there," I told her, setting myself up for a snarky *okay, Mom* retort. She was too giddy to realize she'd missed the opportunity.

"I will." Her smile glowed. "If I get there early enough, I might try to snag some cheap tickets for a matinee show."

"Lucy, you've got to sleep at some point." Man, I wanted to *okay, Mom* myself. Jeez. I wasn't usually such a mother hen.

She dismissed my concern with a shake of her head. "I'll sleep when I'm back home. I like taking advantage of every minute I'm in the city." She slammed her suitcase closed and zipped it. Then she grabbed it with one hand and threw her other arm around me for a split-second hug before racing out the door.

Stretching, I looked around the empty apartment, not quite sure what to do with myself. I was one hundred percent caught up on my schoolwork. Actually, one hundred and ten percent because I had already started the reading for next week. I needed to proof an assignment for Carson, but he hadn't sent it yet. I hoped he would soon because I was exhausted.

I had done my recorded interview for homecoming court earlier that day. Lucy had applied my makeup and styled my hair to make sure I would look amazing on camera. And I had looked amazing, just not like myself. The thick layers of makeup she'd applied felt like a mask I was hiding behind, and since the interview was sandwiched between two of my classes, I'd spent the whole day feeling like a stranger to myself. I was more than ready to scrub the makeup off my face and wash the product out of my hair.

In the bathroom, I turned on the shower, and my gaze got stuck on the showerhead. What an awkward situation that had turned into. When Carson had wrapped the towel around me and pulled me against him, I'd practically moaned when my wet boobs had pressed up against his warm chest. Heck, with the way he'd run away afterward, maybe a moan had slipped out.

I stripped out of the dress I'd worn for the interview and tried pulling a comb through my hair. It got stuck halfway down. *Sigh. This is not going to be fun.* I carefully disentangled the comb and took it into the shower with me.

The water was starting to run cold by the time I was ready to get out of the shower. I wrapped a towel around my head, slipped into my thick terry cloth bathrobe, then shoved my feet into obnoxiously large slippers that made it look like I was wearing stuffed animals on my feet. Perhaps by the age of twenty, I should have given up my love of huge character slippers, but nope. I asked for a new pair every Christmas, and my mom always delivered.

In my bedroom, I flopped onto my bed then reached for my phone and noise-canceling headphones. Wanting to drown the world out for a little while, I selected a meditative music playlist on Spotify and closed my eyes.

***

THE SILENCE IN my headphones woke me. Groggily, I pulled my earphones off my head and inspected them. *Damn.* The stupid things barely held a charge anymore. I should have taken the time to find the cord instead of using the Bluetooth feature. *Oh, well.* I'd been dozing for nearly an hour, and if I slept any longer, I was in danger of being up all night.

Pulling the towel off my head, I padded into my bathroom to comb out my hair. As soon as I caught sight of how tangled it was, I was angry at myself for being too lazy to deal with it before I'd lain down. I tugged at the knots with a comb, cringing when huge tufts of hair stuck in the teeth. Next time Lucy wanted to put so much gunk in my hair, I was putting my foot down. I cleaned the hair out of the comb and smiled at it. If I was feeling mischievous, I would save it and play a prank on Carson later. I'd had no idea wet hair grossed him out so much. Granted, pulling wet clumps of hair out of the drain wasn't my favorite thing to do, but it wasn't *that* big of a deal.

Thinking of Carson made me remember we'd put the leftover Chinese food in my fridge. *Score!* I wandered out into the kitchen to retrieve it. As I was dumping what was left of the General Tso's chicken onto a plate, I heard Lucy rustling around in her room. *Huh.* Rehearsal should have ended by now, which meant she was supposed to be on her way to New York.

"Did you forget something, Lucy?" I called. It must have been important if she'd come back for it. She'd been so eager to get on the road that she had even considered sneaking out of rehearsal early.

I stuck my plate in the microwave, hit the reheat button, then walked toward Lucy's room. Spying her phone-charger cord on the couch, I backtracked to grab it. "Your charger is out here!" Ever since the cord she normally kept in her car went missing, she'd been taking this one with her everywhere, at least when she remembered it. But she would definitely need it for a solo eight-hour road trip at night.

I got to her door just as it flung open, hitting me with a smack. I yelped, putting a hand to my forehead, where there was sure to be a mark. "What the hell?" I knew Lucy was excited for New York, but *cheese on a cracker*. She didn't have to maim me.

Instead of Lucy's chagrined apology, I heard a grunt. I stepped back, and my eyes widened at the sight of a man I didn't recognize standing in the doorway of Lucy's room. His dark eyes locked onto mine, and I backpedaled, but there was a wall at my back. "You're not Lucy," I whispered, which was the most idiotic thing I could have said, because *no shit*.

The man snapped out of his stupor and slammed into me, flinging his elbow into my temple. My head knocked back into the wall, then everything went dark.

***

Carson

"FLECK! WHAT THE hell are you doing?"

I stopped in my tracks at the assistant coach's shout and surveyed my teammates. *Damn it.* I had run the wrong route. I had *never* made such a rookie mistake, even when I was a rookie. The playbook was the one book I didn't mind studying.

I jogged back to the line of scrimmage. "My bad, Coach." *Fuck.* After the hard loss to Miami, the last thing I needed was for Coach Coyle to think I was incompetent.

Wyatt stood with his hands on his hips. "You're supposed to run the burst four route."

"I know," I muttered.

He shook his head and handed the ball to the center.

Jake clapped a hand on my shoulder. "Don't worry about it. It's the first mistake you've made in a long time."

It was a stupid mistake, though, because that route was beyond basic. The truth was I'd been off all practice. My personal life had never affected my game before. True, it was only practice, but I practiced like I played—*hard*. And I didn't mess up easy stuff. I couldn't seem to get my shit together because my mind was too crowded with visions of Becca in a wet T-shirt.

Ignorance is bliss. Too bad I couldn't go back to being ignorant of how she'd looked in that wet shirt. *Jesus.* It wasn't like I'd never seen her in a bathing suit before, but something about that T-shirt was getting to me.

Plus, there was the whole revelation that my feelings for her were far from platonic. I'd always cared about her—*deeply*—but I hadn't realized until now that the reason I was so fiercely protective of her wasn't because she was like my little sister. The shock of seeing her soaking wet like that had broken illusions I hadn't even realized I was clinging to, but now I couldn't go back.

I wanted her. Not just her body but her heart, soul, and everything in between.

Fifteen minutes later—and fifteen minutes past when practice was supposed to end—Coach Coyle called it. I started stripping off my equipment on the way to the locker room, eager to shower off the stench of my poor performance. It was a disgrace. I'd always said I was only good at one thing, so it really sucked when I couldn't even manage to do that well.

Normally, I stuck around to shoot the shit with Jake, but I wasn't in the mood. He would tell me to shake it off, and I would have to stop myself from telling him to go to hell. When I was in a foul mood, I didn't want to hear any Pollyanna bullshit. I was doing us both a favor by going off to sulk on my own.

I swung through a drive-through on the way home. Maybe that was part of my problem. My diet had been horrible lately, and I wasn't taking care of myself as well as I normally did during the season. But just like the blindfold had been removed from my eyes last night at Becca's, I couldn't delude myself about this either. I'd been utterly distracted at practice, too busy thinking about Becca and wondering if she'd figured out why I left her place like a bat out of hell.

That wasn't the only Becca thought I was having, though. I couldn't stop thinking about how her curves fit against my chest or how her nipples felt. *God... her nipples. Payback is a bitch.* I'd started the semester with an incident of Becca being preoccupied with my nipples, and now I couldn't stop thinking about hers. Though she had the better end of the deal since I'd never seen her topless.

Christ. Part of me thanked God that Roman wasn't with us at VVU, but the other part wished he were. If he knew what I was thinking, he would kick my ass, and I would let him because I deserved it. I was supposed to protect Becca from dirtbags like me. I didn't deserve her and had nothing to offer her, but the thought of seeing her with someone else made me want to punch something... or *someone.* Namely, the faceless guy I was imagining.

When my phone rang and Becca's name popped up, I swallowed hard, my mouth suddenly dry despite the fact that I'd just downed half of the super-size soda from my food order. *Play it cool.*

"Hey, Bec, what's up?" As the words came out of my mouth, I wondered why she was calling. Normally, we texted. *Shit.* I hadn't sent her the paper she'd agreed to read for me. She hated when I waited until the last minute, and to be fair, it was a shitty thing to do when she was doing me a favor.

"Carson, are you busy?" Her voice was shaky, immediately setting me on edge. Even if I were busy, the tone of her voice would make me drop everything.

"What do you need?"

"Can you come over? As quickly as you can?"

"What's wrong?" My heart thudded in my chest. Becca had never sounded like this before. Something was not right.

"I... Just come. Please."

I hung an illegal U-turn. "I'm on my way." I tried not to let my imagination run wild, but when I got closer to her apartment, I saw flashing lights in front of her building. *Oh, fuck.*

I floored it, wishing I still had the Camaro so I could take the turns without slowing down. Still, my tires squealed as I skidded to a stop next to the source of the flashing lights—an ambulance. Two cop cars were parked beside it, but their lights were off. Two officers leaned against the hood of one cruiser, chatting. Their nonchalance should have calmed me, but it didn't. It took a lot to rattle a cop, but that didn't mean the situation wasn't serious.

Becca called. That means she's okay. If something had happened to her, she wouldn't have been able to call. *Shit. It must be her roommate.* Relief filled me, making me feel like an ass. It wasn't as if I wanted something bad to happen to Lucy, but I wanted even more for Becca to be safe. Becca came first. *Always.*

Not caring that I was double-parked, I flung open the Jeep door. God, I hoped Lucy wasn't hurt too badly. If it were really serious, the ambulance would have whisked her away to the hospital by now, so the fact that it was still here was a good sign.

I rushed toward the scene. The sight of Becca sitting in the back of the ambulance sent ice speeding through my veins. I jumped into the vehicle, not caring if I was allowed to do that, and pushed past the EMT. I gripped Becca by the shoulders, probably much too roughly given the circumstance, and pulled her against me, cradling her head in my hand. I couldn't breathe. But thank God she was.

Her breaths were shuddered, but the rise and fall of her chest against mine was a sweet feeling. "I'm okay," she whispered. "I'm okay."

But I couldn't force myself to let go of her just yet, much less speak coherent words. She was hurt. It was my job to protect her, and I hadn't.

"Miss Zizzo, would you like us to give you a minute?" the cop sitting next to the EMT asked.

"Yes, please."

It was only after we were alone in the back of the ambulance that I released her, but only so I could look her over myself. A nasty bruise was forming above her right eyebrow, and a small cut on her temple had been closed with a butterfly bandage.

I instinctively reached up to touch it before drawing my hand back. "You're not okay."

"It looks worse than it is," she said meekly.

"What happened?" My voice was much calmer than I felt.

"I feel so stupid." Her words made me think she'd fallen and hurt herself or done something else that was equally stupid. "For eff's sake, I'm a cop's daughter."

That sentiment chilled me. Tony Zizzo had been a cop for nearly thirty years, and I'd been at their house when he'd come home from being on duty with a tortured look in his eyes. He'd seen some shit in the line of duty. He'd made his entire family—even Roman—take self-defense classes and learn basic medical training, like CPR. *Just a precaution*, he'd always said. *You'll probably never need it.* It sickened me that he'd been wrong.

"What happened?" I repeated.

"I was in my room, listening to music with my headphones on, and I fell asleep. When I woke up, I went into the kitchen. I thought I heard Lucy in her room, but it wasn't her. Someone had broken in while I was listening to music or sleeping. I don't know how long he'd been there. He knocked me out and ran off. It could have been a lot worse."

She wrapped her arms around her middle, and for the first time I noticed she was only wearing a bathrobe. *Holy fuck.* She was already almost naked. He wouldn't even have had to remove her clothes if he'd intended to rape her. If she hadn't already had that thought, I wasn't going to enlighten her. *But holy fuck.* It could have been a lot worse, but it could have been a lot better too. *I* could have been there.

"Did you see him?"

"Yes, but it's a blur. I looked him right in the eyes, and he got this *oh shit* look because he knew he'd been caught. That's when he slammed his elbow into my temple."

I'll kill him. If the cops did their job and found that guy, they were going to have to protect him from me.

"How did he get in?"

"The deadbolt wasn't locked. See? Stupid. But it's Bleaksburg, you know? I never thought..."

I knew what she meant. I had buddies who regularly left their apartments unlocked because they didn't feel like having to take out their keys. "Lucy left earlier with a suitcase, so it might have looked like the apartment was empty since I had the lights off. The officer said there were two break-ins at apartments last week, so he might have been looking for empty ones."

"What the hell? Shouldn't they have put out an alert or something?"

"They probably will now. The other apartments were actually empty." She let out a shaky breath. "It could have been so much worse, Carson. What if my bedroom was closer to the front door? He could have walked right into my room, and I wouldn't have known because of those stupid headphones. Or what if Lucy had been home? Oh God. He was *in her room.*" Her calm expression was replaced by a panicked one, like what had happened was finally registering.

"You're okay," I said firmly. "That's what matters." I put my thumb under her chin and tilted her face up so she was forced to meet my gaze, holding it until she settled again.

"Excuse me," the police officer from earlier said. "I'd like to finish up now so we can all get on our way."

"Sure," Becca said then turned to me. "Can you call my dad? I don't think I can deal with him right now." She winced. "That sounds bad, but you know what I mean."

I knew exactly what she meant. Tony Zizzo was going to lose his shit when he learned that his baby girl had been attacked. The Zizzo men's protective nature was embedded in their DNA.

I gently pressed my lips to Becca's forehead. "Got it covered." Then I climbed out of the ambulance to make room for the officer and EMT.

CHAPTER 11

Becca

I WATCHED FROM inside the ambulance as Carson talked to my dad, catching brief snippets of the conversation.

"She's a little banged up, but she'll be fine. You raised one tough girl." He paused so my dad could talk, and I smiled. Carson knew exactly what to say to my father to calm him down. However, the best that could be expected was to take him from an eleven down to a ten. No doubt he would be on the phone to the Bleaksburg Police Department first thing in the morning to inquire about the incident. "No, sir. I don't think you need to come."

Shit. I was worried about that. I loved my dad, but he could be overwhelming at times like this.

"Miss Zizzo?"

I turned my attention back to the officer. "Sorry."

"I have the description of the perpetrator you provided earlier, but there's not much to go on. Is there anything else at all you remember?"

I shook my head. "I'm sorry. I was too stunned to look for any distinguishing marks or characteristics." The officer blinked at my words. "My father is a cop."

The officer smiled kindly, and I snuck a glance at his name tag for at least the third time. *Officer Perez.* He'd told me his name earlier, but I couldn't seem to remember it. *Stupid concussion.* I hadn't shared that gem of a diagnosis with Carson yet because he'd been freaked out enough.

I was angry with myself. Though Bleaksburg was a safe town, my complacency was unacceptable. My father had taught me better than that. This might have been prevented if I'd done the simple task of locking the deadbolt. It had probably only taken that guy seconds to pick the lock on the door handle.

I declined yet again to be taken to the hospital, and Carson assured the EMT he would keep an eye on me. Once the woman realized that Carson was a football player, she felt a lot better about his ability to monitor my concussion. After the ambulance left, Officer Perez escorted Carson and me to my apartment so I could pack a bag.

"You didn't tell my dad about my concussion, did you?" I asked on the way to Carson's place.

He frowned. "No, because when I talked to him, I didn't know you had one."

Shit. My brain really was fuzzy. I'd just been thinking that I hadn't told Carson about it. "Well, that means you didn't lie to him." I closed my eyes and rested my head against the headrest. The shock from the incident was wearing off, so I was feeling the effects of the concussion more. My head was pounding. *Ugh.* I did not have time for this shit. I'd just been patting myself on the back for being ahead in my classes, but now, I would likely fall behind. I inhaled deeply and wrinkled my nose at the scent of fried food. Carson's vehicles normally smelled like new cars because, well, they were usually new. He switched out his cars more often than a lot of people switched out their toothbrushes. "What's that smell?"

"Sorry, is it bothering you? I had just hit the drive-through when I got your call."

I tried to remember his practice schedule. It wasn't consistent like it had been in previous years because of the new coach. He'd probably come straight from practice.

I looked in the back seat and saw a big bag of abandoned food. "You must be starving. I didn't even think about you just getting out of practice. I'm sorry. I shouldn't have called."

"You don't have to apologize. You can always call me, whenever and for whatever reason. I would have been pissed if you hadn't called me." He pulled into his parking spot and cut the engine. "Wait for me to get out of the car."

"What?"

Not answering, he got out of the car and came around to my side. I opened the door, and he took hold of my arm. "Concussions can make you dizzy and unsteady on your feet. I don't want you crashing to the ground and getting a lump on the other side of your head to match the first one."

I grimaced. "I look horrible, don't I?" Looking in the mirror hadn't exactly been a priority. Maybe if it had, I would have paid more attention to the fact that I was still wearing nothing but a bathrobe. I had it pulled tightly closed around my neck, but still. One stiff breeze, and I would be pulling a Marilyn Monroe.

"Your injuries look painful," Carson admitted.

I laughed then regretted it because it made my head feel like BBs were ricocheting around inside my skull. "Clever way to dodge the question." *And he calls himself stupid.*

We'd made it to his front door. He faced me and ran his fingers along the outside of my injuries so softly, I had to question if I was imagining him touching me so tenderly. If getting beaten up was what it took for him to touch me like that, I would have done it back in high school.

"You're always beautiful."

It was on the tip of my tongue to quip that he was required to say that because of the best friend's little sister code, but I stopped myself because I didn't want to know if that was true. I'd had a bad enough night, so I let myself take his words at face value. "Thank you."

"Now let's get you in bed."

Yes, please. Although I highly doubted he meant it the way my compromised brain interpreted the phrase. *Wishful thinking.* The last time I'd slept over at Carson's, I'd ended up playing with his nipples. I hoped I could keep myself in check this time. *Though I could blame my behavior on the concussion.*

"Okay." I had been tired to begin with, and now that the adrenaline had worn off, I was exhausted. I let him lead me to the stairs. Although I gripped the railing, he still held on to my other arm and put his hand on my lower back. A tiny, minuscule part of me wanted to milk the whole concussion thing and ask him to carry me up the stairs. Not because I wasn't capable of walking up them myself but because... well, just because.

Ugh. A concussion was no excuse for my thoughts. I was supposed to be figuring out how to move on from Carson, not falling deeper into my *never gonna happen* fantasies.

"Before I forget to tell you," he said, "I invited your parents to come for the family-appreciation football game."

"What about your parents?"

His expression hardened, and I cursed my thoughtlessness. *Stupid concussion strikes again.* Carson's parents weren't bad people—they were just uninterested parents. "They can't make it."

That made me sad for him, but I knew he wouldn't appreciate me feeling sorry for him. In general, he didn't like talking about his family because, as he'd once said, "there's nothing to say."

"That was really thoughtful of you to invite mine."

He shrugged. "I practically lived at their house for the second half of my childhood. They had a fair hand in raising me."

Hanging out with him the previous night had made me realize that I'd missed him more than I'd let myself admit. He'd been the first person I'd called after I'd dialed 911. The reaction had been knee-jerk. I'd been stupid to think I could cut him out of my life. Even if he weren't so intertwined with my family, I wouldn't want to.

It was time to woman up and put my childish crush to rest... but maybe after I let him coddle me a bit. I would need those memories to last a lifetime.

***

CARSON WAS DRIVING me crazy. And I meant honest-to-God, wrap-me-up-in-a-straitjacket crazy. I took back everything I'd ever said or thought about him being irresponsible. He was taking his promise to the EMT to monitor my concussion way too seriously. I hadn't gotten more than an hour of continuous sleep last night on account of him waking me up every hour on the hour. He'd refused to listen to me when I'd said I was fine. Now the end result was both of us being exhausted and snippy. Though if I told him he was being snippy, he would likely just become snippier.

He jingled his keys. "I'm going to the grocery store. Tell me what you want."

"You have class," I told him. "Or practice. Or something." I couldn't keep up with his schedule, but I knew he didn't have an entire weekday free.

"I already emailed Coach Coyle and told him I was going to be out today."

"What?" My voice had a screeching quality to it. "You can't skip practice. You have a game this weekend." I knew better than to bother protesting his skipping classes. His attendance had never been stellar anyway.

He tossed his keys in the air and caught them without looking then continued to repeat the process. "I have a Becca with a concussion."

"You don't have to babysit me." I wasn't ready to return to my apartment just yet, but I'd had enough of his coddling. I couldn't believe I had wished for it last night. I should have known better.

He narrowed his eyes at me. "That's right. I don't. I could call your dad and let him know your injuries are much more serious than originally reported. In fact, you've taken a turn for the worse. I bet he'd break some traffic laws getting here with your mom in tow." Carson would do it too. He didn't make idle threats.

I crossed my arms. "Now you're just playing dirty."

"I don't play dirty. I play to win. Now tell me what you want to eat."

I gave him a short list of things he could buy just so he would leave me alone. I realized that made me sound ungrateful, which I wasn't. I appreciated everything Carson had done and was continuing to do for me. But if I'd wanted to be mother-henned, I would have called my mother.

While he was out, I used the time to text my friends and tell them what had happened. Even though I started every conversation with "I'm fine," no one seemed to believe me. Lucy had actually offered to miss *Hamilton* and drive straight home. However, I could practically feel her relief from hundreds of miles away when I assured her that wasn't necessary. Nicole was going to come by that afternoon to make sure I wasn't underplaying my injuries. I was about to tell her not to bother, but I held off. If Carson had afternoon practice, I could talk him into going if Nicole would hang out with me while he was gone. It was bad enough that my life was being adversely affected by the asshole who'd broken into my apartment. I didn't want all my friends to suffer as well.

When Carson got back, he made pancakes and sausage links, surprising the hell out of me because he wasn't a fan of cooking. After we ate, we settled on the couch.

Taking a deep breath, he placed the remote in my hand and looked at me meaningfully, like he'd bequeathed me a crown jewel instead of a hunk of metal and plastic. "With great power comes great responsibility," he said. "Please don't make me suffer."

"But I haven't seen the latest season of *Say Yes to the Dress*."

He gulped. "I... uh... I didn't know you watched that."

I pointed the remote at the TV and hit the power button, trying my best to keep a straight face. "I don't. That's why I haven't seen it."

He sighed with relief. "That's not nice, Ziz."

"But it was funny. See? My cognitive function isn't impaired. You're overreacting about the concussion. The EMT said it was mild." But if this sucker was mild, I would hate to feel a full-blown concussion. I didn't get hurt or sick often, so I wasn't the best patient.

"Concussions are nothing to mess around with, mild or otherwise." Carson was as serious as I'd ever heard him. Though as a football player, he probably knew more about concussions than I did. Still, this was a *do as I say and not as I do* moment.

I arched my uninjured brow, which was luckily the one I could raise by its lonesome. "Aren't you the same one who tried to talk the coach into letting you play after a direct helmet-to-helmet hit?"

"That's different. If I lose a few brain cells, then so what? I'm slightly dumber than I am now. No big loss. But your brain is too precious to risk."

I looked past the compliment and zeroed in on the insult he'd paid himself. "You're not dumb."

"Debatable."

I hated when he got down on himself, especially because he used a matter-of-fact tone, like he was reciting facts from an encyclopedia instead of spewing lies about himself. Carson had never been the most academically inclined, but that didn't make him stupid. Still, it had to be hard to live in the shadows of a sister who was about to graduate with honors from Harvard Law.

Neither of my parents had gone to college, so academically speaking, I was the most successful person in my family. My parents didn't care about that, though. They were simply proud that both my brother and I were productive members of society. Well, he was, at least, and I was well on my way.

My head was throbbing—not that I would admit that to Carson—so I didn't try to reason with him. It had never worked before, and I doubted I would be successful when my thinking was fuzzy.

I opened Netflix and started scrolling through the options. "What do you want to watch? *Gilmore Girls*?"

He hesitated. "Sure."

I laughed. "I'm just messing with you again. I know you don't want to watch that." Heck, I wasn't sure if I wanted to watch it. I'd never seen it since I wasn't a big TV watcher.

"But I would if you wanted to."

I turned my attention back to the television. "I know." It was times like these, when Carson was being more than sweet to me, that my resolve to get over him wavered. Because damn it, aside from turning into the Hulk whenever another guy talked to me, he was good to me, better than he should be for just a friend. And if we were together, then the Hulk thing wouldn't be an issue. But I'd known Carson for half my life, and he'd never once shown any indication that I was more than a little sister to him. My college years were coming to a close, and other than a few random dates, I'd spent the entire time pining after Carson.

I would always love him, but maybe it was time I found someone who loved me back.

CHAPTER 12

Carson

I PROGRAMMED MY number into Nicole's phone.

"You know that's overkill, right?" Becca held up her own phone. "Your number is right here. In the unlikely event of an emergency, we can call with this."

Ignoring Becca, I handed the phone back to her friend. "Call me if she seems disoriented, blacks out, or displays any sign the concussion is worse. And don't let her talk you out of it." I shot Becca what I hoped was a stern look. She been downplaying her concussion, but I could tell it was bothering her more than she was admitting.

Nicole looked up from the paper I'd printed out about concussion symptoms. "It says irritability is a symptom. In that case, I think she's getting worse."

Becca shot Nicole a dirty look. "Are you trying to give him a reason to skip practice?"

I'd already skipped the morning practice, so I really couldn't afford to skip another if I expected to play this weekend. I would, though, if I needed to. I was more serious about football than I'd ever been with anything else in my life because it was the only thing I'd ever excelled at. But it paled in comparison to Becca.

I let my bag slip off my shoulder and fall to the floor. "That's it. I'm staying. She's definitely taken a turn for the worse."

Becca got up off the couch, stomped around me, and flung open the front door. "You're going," she said through clenched teeth. Then she tried to push me out the door. It was cute, really, the way she was putting all her weight into it. Too bad she hadn't moved me an inch. For as smart as she was, she still hadn't learned she couldn't push me around, literally or figuratively.

Laughing, I picked up my bag. "I'm going." If I actually thought she was getting worse, I would skip practice, but she wasn't. Plus, Nicole was there to keep an eye on her. I hated that Becca was hurt, but I sure as hell wasn't hating the license it gave me to pamper her like I wanted. Soon, she would be better, and I would have to put the pseudo-big-brother line back in place.

Practice was grueling, but it went well. I didn't have any missed routes. *Thank God.* We had another tough game this weekend, but luckily it was a home game. Home-field advantage was definitely a thing, especially in college football, and that went double for us because of VVU fans. A good player needed to be able to perform in any conditions, but I felt like I played better at home because I fed off the energy of the fans.

After practice, I filled in Wyatt and Jake on what had happened to Becca. "Make sure you tell your girls to lock up."

"Fuck that," Wyatt said. "Katie can stay with me until that asshole is caught."

"Same for Rachel," Jake said. "Do the police have any leads?"

I shrugged. "I'm not sure. Becca's dad is a cop back in Maryland, so he's all over it. It was all I could do to stop him from driving down here last night." I was actually flattered that he'd trusted me enough to stay put. *Take care of our girl, Carson.* As if I wasn't already planning to do that. I wondered what he would think if he knew just how much I wanted to take care of her.

Christ. The man had a gun. As much as he liked me, I was sure he wouldn't approve of me for his daughter.

"I wouldn't blame him if he did," Jake commented. "I'd do the same if something like that happened to Ash or Em." Even though Jake had had custody of his siblings for months, I still wasn't used to him playing the fatherly role. He would be the first to tell me it wasn't like that, that he was still solidly their brother and not their parent, but I didn't see it that way.

"It wasn't targeted or anything," I said. "I don't know if that's better or worse. The cop thinks the guy was looking for signs of empty apartments, and Becca's roommate had left a few hours earlier with a suitcase."

Jake rubbed his chin. "I should probably tell the kids about this so they'll take extra precautions, but they've already been hitting me up for a dog."

"Dogs are good protection," Wyatt said.

"I know, and they know that too. Trust me. They've already hit me up with a bulleted list of why we need one." Jake sighed. "I swear I'm the one in charge of those girls and not the other way around."

Laughing, I clapped him on the back. "Keep telling yourself that."

I headed home, and as soon as I opened the door to my house, the smell of pizza hit me. *Hell yeah.* I'd bought chicken and other healthy shit at the store earlier, but that required cooking and frankly didn't taste as good. I really needed to get my diet back in check. I didn't plan to go all crazy with macrocounting ape shit like Wyatt had, but maybe not eat so much junk.

Tomorrow. I would start eating better tomorrow.

I spread my mouth into the smile that had once been called panty-dropping by a girl I'd dated. "Hello, ladies. Miss me?"

Nicole's eyes widened a bit, making me realize she wasn't used to guys flirting with her. I didn't know her well, but she'd seemed like a good girl the night we'd all hung out. I'd thought something might be happening between her and Jimmy, but nope.

"Oh, were you gone?" Becca grinned. "I hadn't even noticed my warden was missing." Her accusatory gaze slid over to Nicole.

She put her hands up. "What can I say? He scares me a lot more than you do." *Yup. I definitely like her.*

Becca crossed her arms. "I just wanted to go for a walk, not run a marathon."

"You're skinny but not light enough for me to carry your butt if you pass out." Nicole looked at me for support, and I nodded in approval. Becca might be going stir-crazy, but it wouldn't kill her to take it easy.

"Don't worry, though. I can carry you," I said with heroic flair. "Give me a minute to eat, and then we can walk."

"There you go. Your knight in shining armor has arrived." Nicole stood and gathered her stuff. "Will you be back to class tomorrow?"

"No," I answered for her.

Becca's face twisted. "What? You're not the boss of me." That was totally a tween thing to say and a sure sign that Becca was hitting rock bottom. Too bad I wasn't going to cave.

"Forty-eight hours. That's how long you need to lie low." I would prefer that she take an entire week off, but I would feel good if I managed to get her to rest for two days.

Becca wasn't really good at relaxing. Even as a kid, she was always doing something.

"You aren't doing yourself any favors if you don't allow your body to heal," Nicole said gently in contrast to my tough love. *Good cop, bad cop.* Becca should be familiar with the tactic.

She sighed. "I know. This sucks."

Nicole flashed a tight, commiserating smile. "Text me if you need me."

I quickly scarfed down two slices of pizza and grabbed a third one to eat while we walked. Becca was waiting for me by the front door, impatiently tapping her foot. *No, my girl does not relax well.*

There wasn't a good place to walk in my townhouse community, so we settled for trekking around the sidewalks that ran in front of the homes. It worked well enough to burn off Becca's nervous energy. Once we got home, though, it was back to resting.

Grumbling, she settled on the couch. "I've watched more TV in the past twenty-four hours than I have in the past twenty-four days."

"Then let's do something else. Want to play a game?"

"Like Monopoly?"

"Sure."

"Do you even have any board games?"

"Not exactly." I grabbed my PlayStation remote. "But this is almost as good." It only took a few minutes to find the game and download it.

"I want to be the car," Becca said immediately.

"Damn," I muttered. I hadn't played in years, but I was always the car. I settled for the dog instead. It probably didn't matter either way. I always got my ass whipped in Monopoly. The game took too long, and I usually got bored with it before the end. My family hadn't done a lot of things together when I was a kid, but playing Monopoly had been one of them. It was right in my father's wheelhouse, and my mother enjoyed the cutthroat aspect of it. My sister excelled at just about everything, and Monopoly was no different. I, on the other hand, sucked at it. Part of it was that I'd been too young, and my parents were unyielding when it came to helping me. They weren't the sort of parents who let their kids win.

"Shit," Becca said suddenly. "I never proofed that assignment for you. Wasn't it due today?"

"I already submitted it." Even though I hadn't gone to class, I was still able to turn it in through the online portal. I was fairly certain it was good enough to get a passing grade. *Probably.*

"Sorry," she said.

I shrugged. "It's no big deal." I wished I didn't need her help, but writing did not come easily for me. "It's your turn."

She rolled the electronic dice, and her pawn moved to Oriental Avenue. "How do I buy it?"

"Here." I pointed to the button on her control. Next it was my turn, and sure enough, I landed on her property. *Story of my life.* I should have suggested another game. It figured that she would like this one because she actually fit in with my family better than I did. My parents had always been impressed with her intelligence and drive. I didn't hold that against her because, hell, it impressed me too.

Becca laughed. "Pay up."

By the time our pawns made it around the board for the fourth time, Becca had curled up next to me and laid her head on my shoulder. "I don't know why I'm tired. I barely did anything today."

It could be that neither of us had gotten much sleep last night on account of me waking her up every hour, but

I wasn't going to remind her of that. She was pissed about it enough already.

"It's the concussion," I said. "You should go to bed."

"It's not even nine o'clock."

"So?"

"I just need to rest my eyes for a minute. Then we can finish the game." As she closed her eyes, I stared down at her. Did she really just use the "rest my eyes" line that octogenarians used?

It only took her a minute to doze off, and her head started to slide off my shoulder. I carefully wrapped my arm around her and tucked her against my chest. She snuggled against me.

Hell. I'll just let her rest her eyes for a few minutes like she wanted. But then a few minutes turned into twenty, which turned into an hour. All the while, I watched her like a creeper. I couldn't help it. Even with her injury, she was still the most goddamn beautiful creature I'd ever seen. I wanted to keep her like this—safe and in my arms.

Her eyelids fluttered, and I sighed. While I would be happy to hold her like this the entire night, she would get better rest in a bed.

"Bec," I whispered.

She blinked sleepily then turned her face toward mine. "What?"

"Let's get you to bed."

"No," she moaned. "I'm comfy right here." Then she sighed. "Okay." She pulled herself to a sitting position, and I stood, offering my hand. She took it, but when she straightened, she swayed and gripped my shoulder.

I wrapped my arm around her waist to steady her. "You okay?"

"Sorry. I got dizzy. I just need a minute."

"I've got you." I wondered if she would protest if I scooped her up and carried her to the bedroom. God, I really wanted to, and not for the innocent reason of letting her rest.

I'm such an asshole. She was injured, and I was having the most inappropriate thoughts, ones that were wrong on too many levels to count. But when she looked up at me with her big, vulnerable eyes, she undid me.

What if my thoughts aren't so wrong? She was already wrapped around me. All I needed to do was lower my mouth to hers, and that question would be answered in an instant. It was so tempting, especially when her mouth was so damn pink and plump. She licked her lips, and I nearly groaned. It was like she could hear what I was thinking and daring me. Then she closed her eyes, and my face shifted toward hers, just a fraction of an inch.

When I'd fixed her shower and she'd been wet with her hard nipples taunting me, I'd almost lost it. But now when she was so vulnerable, I was having a harder time reining myself in.

She opened her eyes. "Carson." Her voice was barely a whisper.

"Yes?"

"I think I'm okay now."

"Good."

Because I sure as hell wasn't.

CHAPTER 13

Becca

"WHAT DO YOU mean you're going out?" Carson asked.

I gingerly patted my forehead with the makeup sponge, doing my best to cover the bruise. If Lucy were there, she would be able to mask it perfectly. She'd actually decided to stay in New York for a few more days since she was about as eager as I was to get back to our apartment. Though she hadn't been there, it had been her room that had been rifled through, first by the burglar then by the police. Plus, she would use just about any excuse to spend time in the city. No doubt she was racking up credit card debt with all the Broadway tickets she was buying.

"I'm going out," I said again, being purposefully vague. Last night, I'd been so close to giving in and kissing Carson. I had gotten dizzy when I'd stood up, but I hadn't needed nearly as long as I'd taken to recover. Instead, I had been fighting for control, trying to talk myself out of doing something that might end up becoming my biggest regret. Because if I kissed him and he rebuked me, I would never recover from it. Though I'd been exhausted, I'd lain awake, thinking about what had almost happened. Hell, it would have happened if Carson weren't so much taller than me. If his face had been level with mine, I wouldn't have been able to stop myself.

So that morning, I'd texted Blake to set up a coffee date. We'd been texting back and forth since my original text but hadn't managed to meet up yet. After last night, though, I was so desperate to distract myself from Carson that I was willing to go on a date with a huge bruise on my face. If Blake was put off by it, then I could write him off. *Consider it a test.*

"You still shouldn't drive."

"Blake is picking me up."

Carson cracked his knuckles, and the sound echoed off the tile in the small bathroom. "Who's Blake?"

Here we go.

"He's on homecoming court with me." I spun and braced myself by gripping the sink behind me. "You promised you would be cool about this sort of thing."

He wouldn't meet my gaze. "I am. I just didn't think you'd be going out this soon."

I turned back toward the mirror to apply the final touches. "No time like the present."

I glanced at him in the mirror. He still wasn't looking at me, and I could tell by the way he was grinding his teeth that despite what he claimed, he was not okay with this. I didn't expect him to change overnight, but if he could keep his behavior in check, that would be good enough. *For now.*

"When's he coming?" Carson asked gruffly.

I checked the time on my phone. "Shit. Any minute."

"I'll wait downstairs." He turned on his heel and left. I heard his footsteps thundering down the stairs. *Shit, shit, double shit.* I did not want poor Blake to be greeted by Carson, especially because I couldn't trust the big football player not to go into Hulk mode.

I rushed into the guest bedroom and stuck my feet into my shoes. I was going casual—jeans, a purple long-sleeve shirt, and Toms. We were just going for coffee, so dressing up wasn't really required, but I'd packed my bag in such a rush and hadn't expected to be going on a date, so my options were slim. *Oh well.* Again, if Blake was put off by how casual I was, then that was a reason to write him off.

Am I looking for a reason to write him off? Because I seemed to be coming up with a lot of them. Blake was a nice guy, and I was definitely attracted to him, so I didn't understand why I was already dreaming up scenarios in which I cast him aside. Although, if I were honest, the reason was downstairs, probably watching out the front window for my poor, unsuspecting date.

Damn Carson. If I wanted to move on, I was going to have to cut him out of my life. I was beginning to see that there was no way around it. If it really did come down to that, though, the problem would naturally take care of itself. The odds of us winding up in the same place after graduation were slim.

I grabbed my purse and went downstairs just in time to hear the knock on the door.

Carson opened the front door, saying nothing. I couldn't see his expression from my angle, but I doubted it was friendly. *My own personal guard dog.*

"Uh, hi." Blake swallowed and twisted his neck to look at the house number. "Do I have the right house? I'm looking for Becca."

I pushed Carson aside. "Hi, Blake. Remember I said I was staying with a friend?" I jerked my thumb at Carson. "This is my friend, Carson."

"Oh, okay." Looking Carson up and down, Blake frowned. "Wait. Carson? Are you Carson Fleck?"

Carson shoved his hands in his pockets. "Yeah." Better than him cracking his knuckles. It was such a caveman habit.

"I'm a big fan," Blake said excitedly. "We got robbed in the Miami game. Another two minutes, and we would have won."

"Maybe," Carson said begrudgingly. His glare softened a bit, though. Plus, I didn't know Blake well, but I could already tell he was the type of person who was difficult not to like. Carson was actually like that, too, at least when he wasn't pulling his Hulk routine.

"Are you ready to go?" I asked. I hadn't realized Blake was such a football fan, but considering the way he was staring at Carson with stars in his eyes, I was in danger of him wanting to take Carson out for coffee instead of me. *Now wouldn't that just be some shit.*

Blake looked at me. "Sure. Of course." It sounded like he would rather stay and shoot the breeze with Carson for a while longer.

I grabbed his hand and pulled him out of the house. He nearly stumbled as he looked backward at Carson. Total man crush. Carson didn't close the door behind us like a normal person would. Scowling, he crossed his arms and watched us walk all the way down the parking lot to the guest spaces.

"You didn't tell me you were friends with Carson Fleck," Blake said. "Do you know Wyatt Archer too?"

"Yeah," I admitted. "But not like I know Carson. He's my brother's best friend from home, so I've known him forever."

"What about FM4? Do you know him?" Blake was in total fanboy mode.

"I've met him, but I wouldn't call us friends."

"That's so cool. I played football on my high school JV team, but I didn't have the size to make it on varsity." He sounded wistful.

"Football is definitely a sport where size matters." Carson definitely had that advantage, but even if he didn't, he had natural ability. He also had a dogged determination once he set his mind to something. *Like me not dating.*

"That's what everyone told me, but I was too stubborn to listen. I should have played soccer." Blake slid his eyes over to me. "How are you feeling?"

Instinctively, my fingers went to the wound on my forehead. I'd done my best to cover the bruising, but there had been no hiding the butterfly bandage I was still sporting. "I'll admit I've been better."

Blake chuckled. "I'm glad you weren't seriously hurt. Though your forehead looks painful. That was another reason football and I didn't mix—I don't deal well with pain. I'm a wimp."

That reminded me of another reason Carson was a solid player—pain didn't bother him.

Blake took me to Beans and Buns, a locally owned coffee shop that was famous for their sticky buns. It was downtown on Main Street right in the middle of all the bars. It was fairly busy for a weeknight, but we were able to snag a prime table right up front. I held the table while Blake put in our order.

The sight of students around me poring over textbooks and laptops caused a sinking feeling in my stomach. I'd missed two days of classes, and I would probably miss another one as well. The last time I'd missed class was when a stomach bug had swept through my dorm freshman year.

It only took a few minutes for Blake to get two coffees and a plate of sticky buns. I eyed the mountain of sugary goodness. "Did you invite some other people and not tell me?"

Taking the seat across from me, he handed me a fork. "I forgot to ask which kind you wanted. So I got regular, chocolate, nutty, cinnamon, and caramel."

"All of the above."

He grinned. "I was hoping you'd say that. We can share them all if you're cool with that. I can never decide which one to get, so this is a dream come true."

Smiling, I waved my fork at him before digging into the cinnamon one. "I knew I liked you."

***

Carson

I WAITED TO close the door until Blake had driven off. Then I slammed it so hard, it shook the front wall of the house. Even though I was pissed, I realized that was an asshole move since I shared walls with my neighbors. *My bad.*

When I'd pledged to be better about Becca dating, I hadn't realized how damn hard it would be. I hadn't expected it to be easy, but seeing her walk off with another guy gutted me from the inside. To top it all off, the guy was starstruck by me. I hadn't seen that one coming. Hopefully I wouldn't have to kick his ass. Maiming a fan probably wouldn't make me attractive to the pros when it was time for the draft. *Christ.*

I turned on the TV and flipped through the channels, landing on ESPN by default, but I couldn't sit still. I paced as various images of Becca and Blake ran through my mind—*his hand on her lower back as they walked, her smiling and laughing at something he'd said, their faces close together, and—*

Fuck. Don't go there, Fleck. I eased my grip on the remote control before I crushed it.

Exhaling, I tried to talk some sense into myself. They'd only been gone a few minutes, so it was doubtful they'd even gotten to the coffee shop yet, if that was indeed where they were going. For all I knew, they weren't actually going for coffee. They could be—

You already decided not to go there. Besides, Becca wouldn't lie to me.

God, this sucked. It was like I was being punished. The fact that her date had picked her up at my own goddamn house was salt in the fucking wound. She shouldn't be on a date right now, anyway, not while she was still recovering from her concussion. She had a good head on her shoulders, but her thinking was impaired. Surely that was the only reason she would go out with a preppy frat boy. He wasn't her type, but hell if I knew what was. I'd been good at what I considered my job—keeping her safe from asshole guys, which meant *all* guys, in my opinion. I knew the thoughts running through college guys' heads better than anyone.

I couldn't do it. I'd promised Becca I would be cool, but what she didn't know wouldn't hurt her. I grabbed my keys and stormed out of the house. The most popular coffee shop in town was on Main Street, and I was betting on him taking her there. And damn it, she liked that place. *Score one for him. Fuck!* Why couldn't he have taken her to a stupid Starbucks?

I tried to convince myself Beans and Buns was better because I could easily drive past the coffee shop without it arousing suspicion. A person couldn't get anywhere in town without driving down Main Street.

As I neared downtown, part of me hoped to get caught at the red light so I would have longer to look in the coffee shop window. But the other part of me knew that my Jeep stood out, and if Becca was facing the window, she would see me. While I could justify driving down Main Street, I couldn't justify craning my neck to peer in the window.

Damn it. The only sensible thing to do was park and go check it out on foot. Not only would I get a clearer view, but it would be easier to keep from being seen. Since it was a weeknight, I was able to find a place to park quickly. I strode down the opposite side of the street and casually leaned against a light pole across from the coffee shop. I spotted Becca right away at a table right inside the door. Luckily, her back was facing me.

Okay, so now what?

They were there, drinking coffee, and—*fuck. Are they eating off the same plate?* At first, I had the unflattering thought that he was too cheap to buy her her own damn sticky bun, but then she shifted, giving me a better view of the table. *Nope.* He definitely wasn't cheap—the plate was more like a platter, and it was overflowing. It was the sort of thing I would have done, which made me hate the guy more. *Is he trying to impress her by buying the whole damn menu? Asshole.* I didn't care if he liked me. I didn't like him, not one bit. But the real question was if Becca did. *God, what if she likes this guy?*

He turned his head toward the window, and I jumped back behind the light pole, knocking into someone.

"Sorry," I said immediately, stooping to pick up the person's bag that had fallen without even looking to see who I'd bumped into.

The person giggled. "That's okay."

I looked up and into the eyes of a girl who looked like she was in high school, maybe a freshman in college at the oldest.

"Sorry," I said again, handing her the bag. She smiled at me, and another giggle slipped out, reminding me of Jake's sister Ashley. *Shit.* With one last look at the coffee shop, I hightailed it out of there. On the walk back to my Jeep, the absurdity of what I'd done hit me. I was a bona fide creeper. Not only that, but if Becca learned that I'd spied on her, she would never forgive me. In the end, it hadn't even been worth it because I didn't feel any better about the situation.

When I got home, I made myself a whiskey and Sprite, heavy on the whiskey. I normally stuck to beer, but that wouldn't cut it that night, not after I'd spied on Becca on a date. It wasn't my pathetic actions that bothered me, though—it was the fact that Becca had been on a date at all.

One drink led to a second then a third as I watched the clock. *How long does it take to drink one damn cup of coffee?* She should have been home by now.

I didn't need to know Blake to know that he wasn't good enough for her because *no one* was good enough for her. Becca was special. I'd known that since the day I met her. Roman had brought me to his house for the first time, and Becca had been pissed at him because he'd downloaded some things he shouldn't have on their shared laptop. It had been so full of viruses, Becca couldn't fix it herself, and Roman had refused to cough up the money to have it professionally cleaned, even though it was his fault. When we later tried to go on his Xbox, we found that she'd hacked all of his accounts and locked him out. She'd hit him where it hurt and refused to budge. I can clearly remember her calmly crossing her arms and evenly meeting her brother's gaze while he yelled until he was blue in the face. I might have fallen in love with her just a little in that moment.

And maybe it was the whiskey talking, but if she was going to end up with someone who wasn't good enough, then why couldn't that someone be me?

CHAPTER 14

Becca

BLAKE WAS A ridiculously sweet guy, and the more I stared at him, the more good-looking he became. Unfortunately, he was already in love with someone else. *Womp, womp.*

Technically, I was, too, but the whole point of me going out with Blake was to forget about Carson. But Blake? Not so much. He had just broken up with his high school sweetheart who attended George Mason. After almost four years, the long distance had finally proven too much.

"I'm sorry," he said as we walked to his car. "I didn't mean to talk your ear off about Sadie."

"It's okay." I was a little disappointed, but I wasn't going to tell him that. He already felt bad enough.

Blake flashed a wry grin. "I suppose now is not the best time to ask for a second date."

I stared at him for a moment before it clicked. He didn't even realize he was still hopelessly head over heels for his ex. "You're not over her." *Lucky girl.* Blake really was a nice guy. For his sake, I hoped they could work things out.

"Yeah, I am." At my stern glance, he sighed. "I'm working on it. But I definitely could be with the right girl."

I shook my head. "That's not the way it works. That's called a rebound. You need to get over her first."

Blake's situation was eerily similar to my own but with one key difference. He was definitely rebounding, but I'd never actually been with Carson, so technically, I wasn't rebounding. Basically, though, we were two hopeless fools. Part of me wasn't surprised in the least about this new development. For whatever reason, I seemed to attract guys who were friend material. Case in point? Evan, Blake, and Carson.

Blake apologized the whole way home, sounding completely miserable. *Poor guy.*

"Seriously, it's fine," I told him. "I was going stir-crazy in the house and needed to get out. Mission accomplished. The sticky buns were a nice bonus." I patted my belly, which I'd filled to the max. On my lap, I held a to-go box with a bun for Carson. Just one, though, because I actually knew what kind was his favorite—cinnamon. Lucky for him, I was so full that I wouldn't poach his treat. *Maybe.*

When we pulled onto Carson's street, I told Blake he could drop me off in front of the townhouse instead of bothering to find parking. Even if the date hadn't been a bust, it wasn't as if I would invite him into Carson's house. That would have been weird on so many levels. Aside from that, I didn't think Carson had it in him to be civil to my date for an extended period. He'd barely managed the two minutes when Blake had come to the door.

As I walked toward the townhouse, I tried to talk myself into believing what I'd told Blake—that everything was fine, that it didn't matter that the first date I'd been on in over a year was a wash. Blake was a nice guy, and his intentions had been good, so I wasn't upset with him. I wasn't *upset* at all exactly. I was just... I didn't know what I was. Disappointed, maybe? No, that wasn't it. I was simply tired. Everything about my life exhausted me at the moment, most of all this damn concussion. I was so over it. I might not have been ready to go back to my apartment yet, especially since Lucy was still out of town, but I was going to class tomorrow no matter how much Carson protested. Friday was the perfect day to go back because if it wiped me out, I could rest all weekend.

I tried the doorknob before bothering to fish my key out of my purse and found the door unlocked. Carson was sitting on the couch, a glass in his hand. His eyes immediately went to my face, searching. I had no idea what he was looking for, though. His expression reminded me of a puppy who'd been kicked, and it made me glad I'd gotten him a treat. The loss to Miami was weighing on him. He didn't talk about the pro draft much, but he had to be worried about it, especially since the team wasn't playing nearly as well as it had in previous years. Then he'd skipped practice. Though I'd told him not to, I felt guilty about it. If I'd only made sure the deadbolt on my apartment door was locked, all of this might have been avoided.

I held up the to-go box containing the sticky bun. "I got something for you."

Unfortunately, the sight of the Beans and Buns box didn't change his expression. "Where is he?"

Okay, so he's not moping about football. Totally got that one wrong. I put the box on the table next to the couch and crossed my arms over my chest. "On his way home." It was on the tip of my tongue to put Carson out of his misery and tell him that Blake and I would just be friends, but it wasn't any of his business. I didn't understand why he cared so much.

"Good."

I could not even do this with him. "I need to take my contacts out." I'd been sleeping in them longer than I was supposed to because I hadn't felt like dealing with them. Now, though, they were simultaneously dry and dirty. The first major thing I planned to spend my money on once I graduated and got a job would be corrective eye surgery. I'd been shoving contacts in my eyes for the last decade, and I was over it.

I guessed I was over a lot of things this evening—the concussion, my poor eyesight, and Carson's attitude. I sighed. I couldn't do anything about two of those three, but I contemplated going to my room and closing the door to avoid Carson. I definitely didn't want to talk to him about my failed date, but I didn't want to quietly reflect on it either. It really wasn't a big deal except for the fact that I'd had to psych myself up to even text Blake in the first place. *Wasted energy.*

I returned to the living room, and Carson hadn't moved. He was still sitting on the couch, staring at nothing. The TV wasn't even on. Maybe I hadn't misjudged the situation. This had to go beyond his frustration that I had pulled the plug on his protective detail. The guy needed a hobby other than football and scaring away my potential suitors.

I sat next to him and put my hand on his knee. "Is everything okay?"

His jaw worked as he stared straight ahead. "He's not good enough for you."

I retracted my hand and leaned away from him. And to think I'd felt sorry for him. "I can't do this with you. You promised—"

"Because no one is good enough for you," Carson continued like I hadn't spoken. "You're smart and pretty and funny and kind. You're perfect."

I scoffed. "No one is perfect, Carson. Least of all me." *God, is he drunk?* He knew me better than anyone, which meant he knew all my faults.

He finally looked at me, and there was a tenderness in his eyes. "See? You're humble too. And you're so sexy, especially when you're wearing those damn librarian glasses."

"Librarian glasses?" I focused on the part of his statement that I could comprehend. Because had he really just called me sexy? He must have somehow confused the word *sexy* with *nerdy*.

"I'd think you were torturing me, but you're too nice to ever do something like that."

Torturing him?

"I... I don't know what you're talking about." My mind was spinning, and I was having trouble sucking in enough air to stay conscious. Because he couldn't be saying what it sounded like he was saying. I peered at the drink still clutched in his hand and sniffed, faintly smelling whiskey. "Are you drunk?" That had to be it. I supposed it was good payback after what I'd done the last time I was drunk. Maybe I should've been grateful he wasn't trying to pinch my nipples.

Carson looked down at his glass then put it on the table and shook his head. "No, I'm not. For the first time, I'm thinking clearly."

Before I could react, he cupped my chin in his hands and pressed his lips to mine. Time stopped as I marveled at how his lips were both strong and soft at the same time. Yet they were also tentative as they worked over mine, like he was unsure of himself.

Carson is never *unsure of himself. What in the hell?*

My heart pounded, threatening to punch its way out of my chest. *I can't believe this is happening.* The feel of his hand on my knee broke my paralysis, and my mouth moved against his.

That was all the permission he needed. He pulled me onto his lap, which put our faces at an equal height. I gripped his shoulders, needing to steady myself. My lips parted, and when his tongue delved into my mouth to sweep against mine, I moaned. Carson was such a good kisser. I knew he would be.

He wrapped one arm around me, and his other hand skated up my rib cage, his splayed fingers brushing the underside of my breast. Though my skin was separated from his by my shirt, heat shot to my core. My body trembled, the fire inside me having gone from nonexistent to an inferno in mere seconds.

Stilling, Carson abruptly stopped kissing me. "Oh, shit." Pure terror filled his eyes.

No, no, no... I wanted to pull his face back to mine, to rewind to a few seconds ago, to replay the kiss again and again. But the inferno running through my blood turned to ice, because now we were at the part where he apologized and told me he really was drunk. I squeezed my eyes shut, not able to bear seeing that look in his eyes, the one that signified he regretted kissing me. With a sob, I tried to jerk away, but his arm was still wrapped tightly around me, holding me on his lap.

"I'm sorry. Oh, God, Becca, I'm sorry." He sounded pained.

Here we go. I turned my face away so at least he wouldn't see my tears. I felt so stupid, beyond humiliated. I'd been trying unsuccessfully to put distance between us, but now I would be forced to. I wouldn't be able to face him after this. The trouble was that I'd wondered for years what it would be like to kiss Carson. Too bad the reality was way better than I'd ever imagined. So while my curiosity was satisfied, my desire for him had only grown.

Carson put his fingers under my chin and tried to turn my face toward his. "Becca, please look at me. I'm so sorry."

"Don't apologize." My voice was so hoarse, I barely recognized it.

"The last thing I ever want to do is hurt you."

No, I silently corrected. *Apparently, the last thing you ever want to do is kiss me.* When was I going to get it through my thick skull that my feelings were one-sided? Carson had hurt me, but I couldn't blame him for that. I'd never told anyone, especially not him, how I felt. If he'd known how one little kiss would gut me, he would have been more careful to prevent whatever had come over him. *What the hell had come over him?*

"Why?" I asked. "Why did you kiss me? Why would you do that to me?"

"Becca, I'm sorry." His voice was thick. "The whole time you were out tonight, I couldn't stop wishing you were with me."

"Why?" I asked again.

"I've always wanted it to be me. I was just too stupid to realize—"

"You're not stupid," I said automatically.

"About you I am. I just wish it could be me."

I finally met his gaze. "What are you talking about? You wish what could be you?"

"I wish I could be with you."

I stared at him, waiting for the bottom to drop out. But his expression was more serious than I'd ever seen it. Closing my eyes, I exhaled slowly. In my mind, I replayed hundreds of conversations and interactions, especially the ones from the past month. I'd always thought there was a spark between us, but when nothing had ever come of it, I'd written it off as being all my imagination. But what if it wasn't? What if we'd both just been so incredibly and terribly stupid?

I opened my eyes and studied this man I had loved since he was a boy. Misery and utter confusion colored his face.

Be brave, Becca.
"What if you could be with me?"

CHAPTER 15

Carson

SHE DIDN'T HAVE to tell me twice. I covered her mouth with mine, moving so quickly, she gasped in surprise. It only took her a moment to recover, though, and she gave as good as she was getting. Her tongue battled mine, like she was unleashing years of pent-up aggression. I knew I was. I'd been so stupid for so long, not seeing what was right in front of me.

But I couldn't think about that anymore. Hell, I couldn't think at all, not while Becca was in my lap and writhing against me. Instinct took over.

Wrapping her arms around my neck, she arched her back, which pressed her perfect breasts against my chest. My hand snaked up under her shirt, wanting to feel her skin. *Fuck that.* I yanked her shirt up, startling her, but once she realized what I was doing, she took it off the rest of the way. I pulled my own shirt over my head.

Her bare skin against mine felt like a dream. Both of us were breathless as our eyes met. Then she cupped my face in her hands and assaulted my mouth with hers. *My girl is hungry.* If my lips weren't otherwise occupied, I would have grinned. Becca was feisty—she always had been. But God, I'd had no idea how fucking awesome that was.

My hands traveled every inch of her exposed skin. But that wasn't enough—I wanted to taste her. I pulled away from her mouth and trailed my lips along her jawline. She tilted her head, causing her hair to cascade over my face. The flowery smell of it was intoxicating. The last thing I'd expected was the damn scent of her shampoo to make me even harder, but there it was. My cock strained painfully against my pants.

When my tongue found the tender spot behind her ear, she shuddered and let out a little moan. Her hips rotated in my lap, causing her sweet ass to rub against me. Heat spread to every cell of my body. I gripped her ass to pull her closer.

Suddenly, her fingers dug into my shoulders, and she stilled. Her breath was shaky.

I paused. "Are you okay?"

"Yeah. I got dizzy. Give me a second."

I pulled back and brushed her hair away from her face. Her eyes were closed, and she was taking deep breaths. "I've got you."

She opened her eyes. "I'm good now."

Instead of returning my attention to her throat, I shifted so that I could stretch out on the couch. I positioned her on top of me so that her head was nestled between my shoulder and neck. "Comfy?"

"But..." She seemed perplexed, something that didn't happen often since she was so damn smart. "I was comfy before."

I chuckled, and I could almost feel her cheeks redden against my chest. "You're still dealing with the effects of the concussion. We'll have plenty of time for other things." *Because now that you're in my arms, I'm never letting you go.* "I'm just happy to be close to you."

No one was more surprised than me that that was true. I'd always been a love-'em-and-leave-'em guy. Cuddling wasn't in my repertoire. But everything was different with Becca.

She was quiet for a moment, and because I knew her so well, I could tell she was trying to figure out how to say something. "I wasn't lying when I said I was comfy before. Because now you're kind of poking me."

I frowned. *What the hell?* I wasn't wearing a belt or anything. Maybe it was the remote. Then I laughed as I realized what she meant. I reached down and adjusted myself so my erection wasn't pressing into her belly. "Better?"

"Yes. I would have fixed it myself, but..." She trailed off, and I had to squeeze my eyes shut as images of Becca "fixing" me filled my mind. My cock pulsed, and I managed to stifle a groan.

"Yeah," I said wryly. "There's only one way you'll be able to fix that, and I don't think you're ready."

She lifted her head up and propped herself up on her arms. "I am ready, Carson. I've been ready for years." Her wide brown eyes combined with her trembling lower lip made her look so vulnerable. This was a confession she'd been holding in for a long time, and I'd had no idea. *Years?* I couldn't believe she'd kept her feelings from me for so long. I tried to imagine how my life would have been different if I'd known sooner.

I tucked her hair behind her ear. "Why didn't you ever say anything?"

"Because I didn't want to screw things up between us. You never gave me any indication you'd be open to the idea."

I wouldn't have been because Becca was Roman's little sister, which meant she had always been off limits. I'd believed that for so long that it was just a fact of life, something I never questioned. Anything I'd felt for her was suppressed so quickly by my subconscious that I'd never recognized it. But I had loved Becca for as long as I could remember. It had taken her getting attacked and me seeing her walk out my door with another guy for me to realize I was *in* love with her.

Even though moments ago, I'd thought about what would have happened if I'd been aware of her feelings earlier, I was now suddenly glad I hadn't known. I still didn't trust myself not to fuck this up, but I knew my younger self definitely would have made a mess of things.

"I don't deserve you," I said.

"Stop." Her expression was pained. "I hate when you devalue yourself like that."

"It's true, though." I'd never pretended to be anything I wasn't, and I wasn't about to start now.

Sighing, Becca laid her head down on my chest again. "I think you have an overinflated opinion of me."

I laughed. "You are probably the only girl alive who would try to talk a guy into thinking less of her."

"Maybe you've been hanging out with the wrong girls."

I kissed the top of her head. "Obviously." Because no girl had ever felt so right in my arms. I never thought I would be content simply holding someone like this. *Don't get me wrong*—I definitely wanted to do more than just hold Becca. But for now, this was perfect.

Just like her.

***

Becca

I WOKE WITH a smile on my face and snuggled closer to Carson. *Is this really my life?* I'd never been more tempted to pinch myself. Any minute now, I expected him to realize he'd made a mistake, that—

Nope... Don't go there. I didn't know what the future held for us, but I wouldn't let my fear rob me of this moment.

Staring at Carson's sleeping face, I forced myself not to touch him. *God, he's handsome.* When awake, he had a roguish look about him—mischievous with just a hint of danger. Sleeping, though, he looked peaceful and somehow softer. *Not that soft, though.*

My gaze traveled lower to his chest, which was only partially covered by the sheet. Nothing about his body was soft. He was all muscles and cut lines. My eyes landed on his tattoo. He'd gotten it the day he turned eighteen, and I was pretty sure he'd only done it to piss off his parents. *Mission accomplished.* It was a tribal design that was shaped into a wave, but a closer look revealed the wave actually had arrows running through it. When he'd first gotten it, I asked him what it meant, but he'd simply laughed and said it looked cool. That was Carson in a nutshell, but I believed the tattoo symbolized something, even if he didn't realize it.

He twitched, and I watched him for a moment, hopeful he was waking up. But when his body remained still, I sighed. He might not have a concussion, but he still needed sleep. He pushed his body to the limits on a daily basis. I couldn't begin to imagine how exhausting that was. So while I wanted nothing more than to wake him up and continue what we'd started last night, I left him alone.

I peered at the alarm clock, but because I didn't have my contacts in, I couldn't see it. I felt around the nightstand, finally laying hands on my glasses. Slipping them on, I looked at the clock. *Shit!* I hadn't set an alarm because I hadn't anticipated sleeping so late. Then again, I also hadn't anticipated staying up until way past midnight, cuddling with Carson and talking about everything and nothing. Long conversations with him were nothing new, but somehow every word had taken on new significance. It was so weird to experience something so new with a person but also to be completely at ease with him.

Because seriously, did last night actually happen? I felt like I was in a dream.

I'd already missed my first class, but if I hurried, I could still make the last two. I moved to get out of bed, but a glance at Carson stopped me. Not able to resist, I trailed my fingers along his arm then leaned down to press my lips on his hand. I repeated the gesture with the other one. As I pulled back to admire him in all his shirtless glory, I realized I was being totally stupid to let him sleep. If I was missing stuff, so was he.

I gently shook his shoulder. "Carson, you should wake up." He didn't wake. "Carson," I said a little louder. Suddenly his hands shot out and grabbed me. He flipped our positions before I even registered what had happened, caging me against the bed with his arms.

A lazy grin formed on his face. "Good morning."

"Is that a smile or a smirk?" I teased.

"A smile. It's always a smile where you're concerned."

I shook my head. "That's not even true." I could list the times I'd irritated him over the years, but I wasn't going to go there.

"You're right, but I have a feeling that will change from now on."

"Why's that?"

"Because I'll never have to watch another guy hit on you again."

Oh, really? I wasn't a guy magnet, but I cleaned up well enough when I wanted to. I stuck my chin out. "I'm hot enough, so—"

His smile widened. "Yeah, you are."

I ignored him. "Guys are still going to hit on me."

"And now you can't argue when I hit them."

My eyes widened. "Don't hit anyone. Promise me you won't." *Shit.* I hadn't anticipated that if we were together, he would feel even more entitled to turn into the Hulk. The teasing look on his face made me sigh with relief. To be fair, he'd never actually laid a hand on anyone. Well, at least not where I was concerned.

He didn't make any promises, instead pressing his lips to mine in a chaste, pre-toothbrushing kiss. Then he rolled to his side and pulled me against him, nuzzling his face in my hair.

Sighing, I closed my eyes and let myself enjoy the moment. But as freaking wonderful as it was, we both had shit to do today.

"Carson, I've got class. And you've got... I don't know what you have, but something."

"I know." But he didn't move.

I wriggled, trying to maneuver out of his arms. I never thought I would be doing that.

He groaned. "You might want to stop doing that." He paused. "On second thought, never mind. Keep doing it."

Gasping, I stilled, suddenly realizing the reaction in him I had unwittingly invoked. *Good morning to you too.* I rotated my hips again, this time slowly and with purpose.

Carson groaned again. "You are killing me."

It was a weird feeling to know I had that kind of power over him. Who knew? I sure as hell hadn't. But I was going to have to exert my power another time.

"Seriously, we need to get moving. Do you have practice?"

He sighed. "Yeah. In fifteen minutes."

I jumped up. "What the hell, Carson? You need to go! You can't miss practice the day before a game!"

He moved to a sitting position. "I know. But I'd much rather stay here with you." He stood and walked over to me then tilted my chin up so my eyes met his. "You know that, right?" His expression was strangely serious, just like it had been last night.

I could ask him to skip practice for me, and he would likely do it. But I would never ask that of him. Once he came to his senses, he would surely resent me for it. Besides that, I wouldn't want him to give up his passion for me.

But if I'd had any doubt in his sincerity, this moment would have erased it. "I do now."

***

CARSON MANAGED TO make it to practice on time because all he'd had to do was brush his teeth and walk out the door. Hopefully the fact that he hadn't had breakfast wouldn't affect his performance too much. At least he'd been in a fantastic mood. That had to help, right?

I'd personally never slept so well in my life. My body fit against his perfectly, and when he'd thrown his arm over me, I'd never felt more safe and secure. I never would have pegged Carson to be a cuddler. That was probably the least surprising thing from the past twenty-four hours, though.

I couldn't figure out what had opened Carson's eyes— my getting injured, being picked up for a date from his house, or a combination of the two. Had I known what it would take, I would have given myself a concussion ages ago. A tiny voice inside me whispered that everything had fallen into place too easily. It was like I was waiting for the catch. *Please don't let there be a catch.*

I made it to my last two classes, and though I had trouble paying attention, I was glad I'd gone. Fortunately— or unfortunately, depending on how I looked at it—the game this weekend was in Boston, so I would have plenty of time to get caught up. The first order of business was going to my apartment to retrieve some things. I wasn't ready to go back, but I didn't want to put it off any longer for precisely that reason.

I parked outside my building and watched my neighbors go about their business like normal. A tiny bubble of fear took root in my chest, so I exhaled and tried to talk some sense into myself. *It's broad daylight. There's no reason for the guy to come back. There are plenty of people around.*

Still, I would feel much better when the cops caught the guy. So far, the police hadn't had any luck, and my father was sure as heck getting daily updates. At least the perp hadn't struck again. Maybe running into me had scared him enough that he wouldn't break into anyone else's place. *Not likely.*

Clutching my bag of dirty laundry, I climbed the stairs to my apartment. I unlocked the door and pushed it open, not realizing until I saw the empty living room that I'd been holding my breath. Exhaling, I entered and closed the door behind me then slid the deadbolt home. *Not going to make that mistake twice.*

After I dumped a load of laundry into the machine, I headed to Lucy's room to survey the damage. Her drawers were open, and some of their contents were spilled onto the floor. The only thing she'd had of value was a couple hundred dollars in emergency cash, which she kept in her nightstand. The best I could tell, that was the only thing that had been taken. It could have been so much worse.

Not wanting her to come home to such a mess, I gathered up all of her clothes and sorted them into loads. I was going to wash every piece because that was what I would have wanted if the burglar had had his hands on my things. It felt good to be putting things right.

With the laundry all sorted, I made myself some dinner: soup from a can, the dinner of champions and poor college students everywhere. My phone rang, and I smiled at the caller ID. "Hi, Carson." Unfortunately, I hadn't gotten to see him before the team left for Boston. He'd told me before that he didn't like away games. The farther they had to travel, the more of a pain in the ass it was.

"Hey. What are you doing?" In the background, I heard his teammates and what sounded like road noise. He was probably on the bus on the way to the airport.

"I'm in my apartment, doing laundry and getting caught up."

"What?" He sounded alarmed. "What the hell? Why are you there?"

"I can't stay away forever." I appreciated his concern, but he knew that as well as I did. Despite the recent development in our relationship, it wasn't like I could just move in with him. Besides not wanting to abandon Lucy, that would be moving way too fast. Things were good right now, and I didn't want to risk doing anything to screw it up. As happy as I was, I felt a little like I was tiptoeing on cracked ice, waiting for the bottom to fall out beneath me.

It was so strange, though, to suddenly be in a relationship with someone I knew almost as well as I knew myself. There would be no cute getting-to-know-one-another phase. We would probably skip straight to the old married couple phase, in which we annoyed the hell out of each another. I was oddly looking forward to it.

"Is Lucy back yet?" Carson asked.

"No, not until Sunday. So don't worry—I'm still planning to stay overnight at your place."

"Good." He sighed. "I wish this game weren't away."

Me too. But I wouldn't tell him that. Life had to go on, and I wasn't going to give more power to the situation by letting it dictate my actions. With the exception of not staying alone in my apartment, I planned to take reasonable precautions and go about my life as normal.

Except my life was no longer normal because everything with Carson had changed. It hadn't even been twenty-four hours, but nothing would ever be the same. *In a good way. Please, God, let it stay good.* Butterflies filled my stomach as I remembered how it had felt waking up next to him. I hoped I would never take that for granted.

"You'll be back Sunday," I told him. "Focus on the game. Don't worry about me."

"I always worry about you. I always did, and I always will."

"I know." I wondered if his overprotectiveness toward me had always been more than just him acting like a surrogate big brother. It had probably started that way, but it must have morphed at some point without him realizing it. Or without me realizing it, for that matter. I'd had no idea his feelings for me had been percolating beneath the surface.

A thread of doubt wormed its way through my thoughts. I didn't doubt that Carson cared for me, but I wished his realization that he wanted to be with me wasn't a result of jealousy over me going out with Blake. When there was no longer a reason to be jealous, would he still want me? I shook my head, trying to clear the dangerous thought. I didn't understand why I was doing that to myself. I'd gotten what I had longed for for years, but for some reason, I couldn't fully relax and enjoy it.

"Shit, we're at the airport," he said. "I gotta go."

"Okay." I hesitated. "I miss you." There was so much more I could say, but though my feelings had been strong for years, I didn't want to move too fast. Carson might need some time to catch up.

"I miss you too. Always."

Perfect.

CHAPTER 16

Carson

WE WON, BUT it wasn't a satisfying victory. Boston's quarterback got injured in the first quarter, and his replacement was so green, he fumbled the ball without any of our players near him. At the end of the day, a win was a win, but I would have preferred to beat them when they were at full strength. *But whatever.* I played well, which was more important than ever with the draft coming in just a few short months. With every game, the pressure to put in a flawless performance grew. I didn't like it—it was sucking all the joy out of the game for me. In general, I tried not to take things too seriously and just have fun, but my future was looming, and that was hard to ignore. My record was solid, but memories were short. The next few games could determine my place in the draft.

Jake, Wyatt, and one of our linemen were also feeling the pressure. The four of us were the only players with a real shot of getting picked up by the pros. Strangely, all four of us were seniors. A lot of players entered the draft their junior year, like Freddie had. I didn't know why the lineman had waited, but Wyatt had wanted to finish his degree, and Jake had gotten sidelined by his parents' death. I had waited because, while I'd always been a solid player, I hadn't gotten enough playing time my first two years. I needed more time on the field to show the scouts what I was capable of. Or perhaps I'd just been chickenshit.

Anyway, it didn't matter. I was here, so there was no point wondering.

It was past midnight by the time the bus finally pulled into campus on Saturday night. Games that required air travel were rough, especially since the closest airport was an hour away.

I was in my Jeep, peeling out of the parking lot, before a lot of the guys had managed to shuffle off the bus. I was always eager to get home after an away game but never more so than now. When I got to my townhouse, I frowned at the empty parking spot. Where the hell was Becca's car? I quickly spotted it in guest parking. I'd told her to take my spot, but of course she hadn't.

As I walked toward the door, I saw the blinds move as Becca peeked out. Then the front door flung open, and she barreled down the walkway. I dropped my bag as she launched herself at me. I caught her easily, and she wrapped her legs around my waist and her arms around my neck.

I chuckled. "Did you miss me?" I'd hoped she had. It had been the worst time to be away from her because she was still reeling from the break-in. More than that, though—now that I'd gotten my head out of my ass and realized how I felt about her—I wanted nothing more than to be with her. I'd always wanted to be around her, but it was different now because I finally didn't have to hold anything back. I'd been such a fucking moron.

Instead of answering with words, Becca pressed her mouth to mine. *Hell yeah, she missed me.* I gripped her ass and walked through my front door, kicking it closed behind me.

"Wait." She pulled back. "Your bag is out there."

"Forget the bag."

"But—"

"Forget the bag."

"Even if someone doesn't take it, it'll get covered in dew."

I sighed. She wasn't going to forget the bag, and I knew her well enough to realize it would be quicker to retrieve the damn thing than to talk her into understanding that I honestly didn't give a shit.

I deposited her on the couch and strode back out front to get the stupid bag. When I came back inside, she wasn't where I'd left her. Instead, she was waiting at the door.

Going up on her toes, she wrapped her arms around my neck. "You were awesome. That might have been your best game yet."

I grinned. "You think so?" It wasn't, but I sure as hell wasn't going to discourage her gushing praise. I could totally get used to that. *Yeah, I'm shallow.*

"I do. I wish it had been a home game so I could have seen it in person."

"Me too." But not for the same reason as her. If it had been a home game, then Becca would have been wrapped around me hours ago. "How are you feeling?"

"Much better overall but still tired a lot."

Damn. "You shouldn't have waited up. It's late. Let's get you to bed."

The side of her mouth stretched into a half smile, and a wicked gleam filled her eyes. "Yes, please. Except I'm not tired right now. I took a nap earlier." She unwrapped her arms from my neck, trailing them down my chest as she stepped away.

I swallowed, feeling like my sixteen-year-old self, who was about to go to third base for the first time. My knees were weak, and my palms were sweaty. *Christ.* Becca had an effect on me like no one else. I would say she didn't know what she was doing, but she knew. And somehow that made it even hotter.

She walked toward the stairs, suggestively swinging her hips. Paralyzed, I watched her walk up the first few steps. Just as she was about to disappear from sight, she turned and raised an eyebrow. "Are you coming?"

That snapped me out of my stupor. "Uh, yeah." I was normally a pretty smooth guy, but this petite blonde I'd known half my life undid me, turning me into a fumbling idiot.

I took the stairs two at a time, scooping her up on my way. She yelped in surprise. *Who knew a yelp could be so goddamn sexy?*

I carried her to the bedroom. Somewhere in the back of my mind, I had the errant thought that we should slow down, that she still wasn't back to one hundred percent. Then her fingertips dug into my back, and I couldn't hold a coherent thought if I tried.

Aw, hell. I laid her on the bed, and she yanked her shirt over her head. Going on her knees at the edge of the bed, she pulled me toward her using the waistband of my pants. Then she tugged my shirt off. She ran her hands down my chest, pausing ever so slightly at my nipples.

Grinning, I pressed my lips behind her ear. "Feel free to do anything you want to my nipples."

She stilled. "Oh... my... God. I was hoping you'd forgotten about that."

I laughed. "No way in hell. I needed to take a cold shower that night."

She pulled away so she could look at me. "Really?"

"I didn't, but I probably should have. I hate to admit it, but it was a turn-on. I've been attracted to you way longer than I should have been. Hell, I shouldn't be—"

She put her finger to my lips. "Stop. I don't want to hear any reasons why you think you shouldn't be with me because they're all lies."

Debatable. But I wasn't going to actually engage in a debate with her. For starters, that would require deep thought, and my blood was nowhere near my brain at the moment. Also, I didn't want to think about it. Deep down, I knew I would never be good enough for her, not to mention she was Roman's little sister. But I wanted her so goddamn much. I loved her so goddamn much.

I pulled her body flush with mine and kissed her deeply. Then I flicked open the button on her jeans and unzipped them so I could slide my hands in to cup her ass. It was tight, round, and firm. Perfect. Was anything about this girl not perfect?

"Wait." She pulled away. "We should talk about something."

That. That's not perfect. Why did she want to talk when all I wanted to do was worship her body? If she said anything else about that goddamn bag, I was going to lose my ever-loving shit.

Closing my eyes and leaning my forehead against hers, I tried to summon up self-control. "What is it?"

"I want to be with you, Carson, in every way, but... I don't know how to say this. Um..." She swallowed thickly, and alarm bells went off in my head. *Shit.* My damn dick was leading the charge, and she wasn't ready. *I'm such an asshole.*

"There's no rush." I tried to keep my tone light. I didn't want her to think this was a deal-breaker for me. She knew my history, that I tended to sleep with girls quickly, but that was in the past. Everything was different with her. I would be celibate if it meant I got to love her. *Please, God, don't make me be celibate.*

"No, you don't understand. I feel like I've already waited for you for forever, so it's not that we're rushing. It's that, well... I'm a virgin."

I didn't know what I'd expected her to say, but it wasn't that. I looked down at her, but she'd tucked her face against my chest, like she was hiding. "Becca?"

She didn't move. "What?"

"Can you look at me?"

After a few deep breaths, she lifted her head and met my gaze.

"I didn't know," I said. "We can wait." God, I'd had no fucking idea. But then again, it made sense. She'd never had a serious boyfriend, and she wasn't the type to have casual sex. It should have been obvious to me that she was inexperienced, but fuck, she was just so sensual, it had never occurred to me that she was new to this.

She swallowed. "I don't want to wait. I feel like I've been waiting for you my whole life."

My heart swelled, and so many emotions flooded me, I couldn't discern them. What had I ever done to deserve this girl? This woman? *Nothing.* Because I didn't deserve her. But that didn't mean I was willing to give her up either.

I might not be worthy of her, but I sure as hell would make her feel loved.

***

Becca

I WAS AFRAID to look at Carson, afraid of what I would see in his eyes. I didn't want him to treat me like a delicate flower just because I didn't have sexual experience.

But when I mustered the courage to meet his gaze, I found the same need in his eyes as before.

"I always wanted you to be my first," I said softly. I already felt so vulnerable and exposed admitting I was still a virgin, but I felt like I might as well put it all out there. Yet part of me was afraid. I'd wanted this, wanted him, for so long that I was petrified I would screw it up.

"I don't know what to say," he said. "I didn't know any of this."

"You weren't supposed to," I replied. "I wouldn't have told you now except I'd be so embarrassed if things got weird, and—"

"It could never be weird with you, Becca." He kissed me. "But we can stop whenever you want."

"I already told you—I've been waiting for years. I'm not going to want to stop." I tried for a wry smile, but I was so damn nervous, it probably came across as a grimace.

He took my lead and smirked. "I just hope I'm worth the wait."

I ran my hands over his shoulders and his chest, my fingers tracing the grooves of his muscles. *Oh yeah.* Even if I weren't already in love with him, it was worth the wait to have my first time be with someone who could be a body double for Thor. But mainly it was worth it because I was in love with him, and I'd never wanted anyone but him. That didn't mean I wasn't going to give him hell, though. Old habits died hard.

I looked him up and down with what I hoped was a scrutinizing expression. "I hope so too."

He grinned, and any awkwardness that had been in the air over my big announcement dissipated. "Oh, it's on."

He slipped his arm behind my knees and stretched me out on the bed. Joining me, he propped himself up on his elbows and hovered over me. His hand palmed my ribcage, covering nearly all of it and making me feel tiny. I wasn't normally into feeling like a damsel in distress, but I liked how protected I felt because of his size and strength. It wasn't just that, though. It was the possessive way he put his hands on me. I'd joked that he was a caveman when he cracked his knuckles, but maybe I liked some of his caveman tendencies.

He sucked my lower lip into his mouth, and my brain short-circuited, ending my analysis of the situation as every pore on my body tingled. I lost myself in the feeling of Carson's warm mouth and the sensation of our skin being pressed together. His attention moved to my throat, and he trailed kisses from my next down to my chest, kissing my breasts through my bra. I arched my back so he could fit his arm under me to unhook it, but he'd already moved on to my belly. He took his time, exploring with both his hands and mouth. Pushing the flaps of my unzipped jeans aside, he ran his tongue along the band of my panties. Sucking in a breath, I turned my head to the side as heat shot to my core and vibrations started at the vee of my legs. Only my shirt was off, but he'd already pushed me so close to the edge.

Because this was Carson. He was very good at what he was doing, but no one could ever make me feel as much as he did.

I put my hands on his shoulders to ground myself physically, mentally, and emotionally. Then I gripped his arms and pulled him up toward my face, wanting to kiss him more. He understood what I wanted and brought his mouth to mine. I arched off the bed and wrapped my arms around his neck. My bare foot entwined itself around his calf.

I slipped one arm between us to undo the button of his jeans, but my fingers suddenly wouldn't work, and the damn thing wouldn't come undone.

Without missing a beat, Carson did it for me then stripped himself of his jeans. He smiled at me. "You need to get caught up."

Lifting my hips, I wriggled out of my jeans as he watched. His eyes grew heavy. He bit his lip like he did when he was reading, and it was so sexy knowing he was fixated on me. He ran his hands down my body, starting at my shoulders. I sucked in a breath as he got to my belly. When his fingers skimmed over my panties, I closed my eyes and threw my head back.

"You're gorgeous," he said reverently.

I propped myself up on one elbow and reached behind to unhook my bra. Sliding it off my shoulders, I watched as Carson's eyes darkened and his breath hitched.

He leaned down to draw one nipple into his mouth while he caressed the other breast with his hand. His kisses trailed lower again, but instead of stopping at the top of my panties, he slid one finger under them to tug them down my thighs. Heat rushed to my core as his mouth moved against my inner thigh.

Carson moved back up my body, and I eagerly leaned forward to kiss him. His fingers slipped between my folds, and suddenly I forgot how to kiss as my entire body quaked.

"Is this okay?" he whispered.

"Yeah." The only reason I managed to form a word was because I was desperate for him to keep touching me. He stroked and teased, building the pressure within me until it felt like I couldn't take anymore. Then he plunged a finger inside me, and I cried out as my muscles gripped him tightly. His thumb pressed on my clit as his finger worked. I moaned, my breath coming in short pants.

"Hold on to me," he said, his breath warm in my ear. I did as he said. Moments later, my entire body seized as I rode the wave of pleasure.

"That was so fucking hot," Carson said. He put his mouth all over my body, not giving me time to recover. The pressure began to immediately build again.

I ran my hands over his body, tracing each line of his abs then following the trail of hair that disappeared into his boxers. Taking a deep, courage-inducing breath, I dipped beneath the fabric and took him in my hand.

Tentatively, I stroked, and he let out a grunt of approval. I pushed his boxers down his thighs, and he shed them the rest of the way. Then he rolled away from me to fish in his nightstand. Hearing the tear of the condom wrapper, I swallowed and exhaled slowly.

When he turned back to me, he kissed me tenderly, running his fingers along my face. "If you're—"

I gripped his shoulders and met his gaze. "I've never been more ready. I want to share this with you." I wanted to share *everything* with him.

Emotion flooded his face. "I love you. I've always loved you."

Cupping his face, I smiled. "I know." I'd always felt the pull between us, but I'd almost given up on it. I thanked God I hadn't.

He positioned himself between my thighs, and I felt him against my opening. My instinct was to tense up, but I forced myself to relax.

As Carson kissed me tenderly, he pushed inside slowly, and my legs spread farther to accommodate him. I wrapped my arms around him, clinging to his shoulders. When he was all the way in, he met my gaze. A silent question lit his eyes. *Are you okay?*

I nodded. He withdrew, leaving me feeling suddenly empty. Then he filled me again, and I hissed at the sweet feeling of the friction. It only took me a moment to catch on to the rhythm, and then my hips moved to meet his.

Being with Carson was everything I'd hoped it would be—full of love and tenderness. Choking up, I reveled at the feeling of him moving inside me.

When his body shuddered with his release, I clung to him and rode the wave.

***

Carson

I WATCHED BECCA sleep. Stretched out beside me and tucked next to my chest, she seemed so tiny. And so sexy. God, I couldn't forget that. *So much sexy in a tight little package.*

She stirred. Opening her eyes, she stretched as a sleepy, contented smile formed on her face. *I did that.*

I kissed the tip of her nose. "Good morning."

"Morning."

"I was thinking we could go out for breakfast."

She raised her eyebrows with a coy smile. "Aren't you supposed to buy me a meal *before*?"

I grinned, glad that the playful part of our relationship was still intact. "You know I don't play by the rules. But I do have something serious to ask you."

Pushing her hair out of her eyes, she sat up, much more alert. "What?" Her voice was slightly alarmed, and I almost felt bad. *Almost.*

"Was I worth the wait?"

She burst out laughing. "Do you really want me to answer that?"

Shit. That was not the reaction I'd expected. Last night had been fucking amazing. Hell, I could have simply held her hand for several hours, and that would have been amazing, too, because I just wanted to be near her. But being inside her and feeling her body tighten around me had been fucking heaven.

"Maybe?"

She tapped her chin with her pointer finger. "I might need some more information in order to form an opinion."

I perked up. "That could be arranged."

Just as I was reaching for her, her phone rang. She frowned. "Why would someone call me at nine on a Sunday morning?" She grabbed her phone off the nightstand. After looking at it, she answered. "Hey, Dad."

Talk about a mood killer. I shifted to the other side of the bed. *Awkward.*

"No, you didn't wake me." She paused and listened. "They're sure they got the right guy? Thank God. I'll sleep easier now." She glanced over at me and grinned. "Yes, Carson's been taking great care of me."

My balls iced over. *Holy fuck.* I respected the hell out of Officer Zizzo, and I was pretty sure he liked me but as Roman's friend. Becca was his little girl, and the man carried a gun. That wasn't a combination I wanted to test. Sure, he was tasked with upholding the law, but all bets were off where Becca was concerned.

Becca ended the call and laughed. "Relax. Be glad you don't have to do the whole 'meet the parents' thing."

"This is worse," I muttered.

"Why?"

"Because they know me." I could turn on the charm when I wanted, making parents and grandparents adore me, but there would be no charming the Zizzos. They knew everything about me, from how shitty of a student I was to the fact that I'd dated more girls than I could remember. I was not the kind of guy they would choose for their daughter. Hell, I wouldn't choose me for Becca either.

And then there was Roman. *Fuck.* Talk about breaking the bro code. I couldn't even think about talking to him without breaking into a cold sweat.

"Exactly." Becca scooted closer, wrapped her arms around me, and rested her cheek on my chest. I inhaled the sweet scent of her hair. "They already love you, just like I do."

Despite my newly realized anxiety, I smiled. "You love me?"

"I wasn't exaggerating when I said I've waited for you for years. I can't remember a time when I didn't love you."

"Why?" The question just slipped out.

She sighed. "I wish you could see yourself like I do."

I was never one to look at the world, much less myself, through rose-colored glasses. I knew what I was—good-looking, a solid football player, and fun to be around—but I also knew what I wasn't, and that list was so much longer. But I was selfish enough to ignore the fact that I could never be half the man Becca deserved. I was going to love her as long as she would let me. With any luck, she would never come to her senses.

But I wasn't counting on it. Becca was a smart girl.

CHAPTER 17

Becca

"OPEN UP!" CAME a muffled voice from outside my apartment.

With quizzical glance at Nicole, I went to the front door and peered through the peephole. All I could see was a huge cardboard box, but since I recognized Hanima's voice, I opened the door.

She immediately shoved a box into my arms. "I'll go help Courtney with the rest of it." She trotted off down the steps.

I deposited the box on the kitchen counter. "What is all this stuff?"

Nicole shrugged as if she didn't know, but it was unconvincing. Before I could grill her further, Courtney stumbled in the front door I'd left open, carrying two huge shopping bags. She dropped them in the living room and collapsed on the couch. "Remind me to tell Hanima *no* the next time she asks me to help her carry a few things."

"What is all this stuff?" I asked again, hoping to get an answer this time.

Before Courtney could respond, Hanima strode in the door, kicking it closed behind her. "Your campaign."

"Excuse me?"

"Those sorority girls have posters all over campus."

"I've noticed." At the homecoming court meeting, the chairperson made it sound like campaigning was almost discouraged. Or perhaps I'd simply interpreted her comments to suit my own needs. "But I hadn't planned to campaign." It just felt weird putting myself front and center like that, essentially demanding that people pay attention to me. I was more comfortable behind the scenes.

"That doesn't mean you get to spoil our fun," Nicole chimed in. "You don't even have to participate if you don't want."

"I'm the one on the court," I pointed out. "Isn't that the exact definition of participating?"

Pursing her lips, Nicole shot me an annoyed look. "You know what I mean."

Hanima pulled a stack of thick photo paper out of a box, and I saw a flash of my own face. *Cheese on a cracker.* "What is that?"

Smiling smugly, Hanima held one of them out. In a three-inch circle was my picture and the slogan, "Becca Zizzo supports Women in STEM. Do you? Vote Becca!"

I gaped at it. "Where did you get that picture?" When I'd spoken at the education conference last year, I'd had to supply a headshot for the program, so I'd gotten a photography student to take it. I hadn't been wild about the end result, but I'd put it off for so long that I hadn't had any other options. Now it looked like the entire campus would see it. *Ugh.*

"Lucy helped us," Nicole said. "By the way, you really should update your password on your computer."

"Believe me, I will." I pinched the bridge of my nose. I didn't know why I was getting upset. If anything, I should have been grateful. It just bothered me that they'd gone behind my back to plan all this. Then again, if they would have asked me, I would have told them no. Nicole had said this was fun for them, and I had to admit, they looked like they were enjoying the whole charade. Heck, I would've been more likely to enjoy it if one of them were in the spotlight.

"The pictures will be used with these." Hanima fished in the box and came up with a plastic bag full of buttons. "There wasn't enough time to send them out, so we're going to have to put them together ourselves."

"Please tell me we don't have to cut out all those circles," Nicole said.

Hanima snorted. "Do you think I'm an amateur? I got a punch. All you have to do is line up the picture and press. Hang on. I'll show you." She dug around in the box and found a craft punch. It seemed she had thought of everything, which didn't surprise me.

The buttons weren't the only thing she'd gotten. In addition, she'd printed up flyers all about women in STEM and how the proceeds from my homecoming candidacy would support local Bleaksburg students.

As I read over what she'd written, my heart swelled. A person would have to be heartless not to want to support the cause. "This is so good."

She beamed. "I took a creative writing class last year. I guess I picked up a few things. And that's not all." She held up a bag of chocolate candy. "We're going to attach these."

"I can't believe you went through all this trouble," I said. "I hope it didn't cost a lot."

Hanima passed me a roll of tape. Apparently, I was on chocolate duty. "We took up a collection at the last study hall. The freshman girls are especially excited. Speaking of that, Dr. Hanover is also really excited you're on the court. She wants you to speak in her Tuesday morning class. I checked your schedule, and you're clear for that." Dr. Hanover taught one of the dreaded freshman engineering weed-out courses. Despite that, she was one of the most popular professors in the department.

"Okay," I said slowly, not entirely comfortable with the idea. "Are you sure she wants me to take up class time for this?"

"It actually fits in with her curriculum. Do you remember that unit about the role of engineering in society? I told her you'd give a dumbed-down version of the paper you presented at the conference."

I hadn't looked at that material in months, but since I only had to provide a broad overview, I could probably do it without reviewing if I had to.

"Then when you're done," Hanima continued, "you hand out the flyers and buttons."

Even though I had been wary when Hanima first walked in with the boxes, I was incredibly moved by the lengths these women had gone to to support me. Granted, they were the ones who had talked me into running, but still. Tears unexpectedly formed in my eyes, and I quickly wiped them away. I usually wasn't a crier at times like these.

"Stop," Courtney said. "Because if you cry, then Hanima will cry, and if she cries, then I'll cry, and when I say I'm an ugly crier, I'm not exaggerating."

"What about me?" Nicole seemed put out. "What if I cry?"

Courtney stared at her for a beat. "Are you going to cry?"

"Anything is possible, right?" She gestured toward me. "Becca is proof of that."

"Oh, come on," Hanima said. "She was a shoo-in for homecoming court."

"That's not what I'm talking about," Nicole said. "I totally saw her making out with a hot football player on campus the other day."

The gasps that sounded from my other two friends were so exaggerated, they were comical. I ducked my face before they could see me blush. Carson and I had been keeping things under wraps. We weren't necessarily hiding. Rather, we were getting used to *us* before we let others know. Plus, no assurances I could give had settled his unease over how my parents and Roman would react once they found out. He was being ridiculous, but telling him that would only make it worse.

Nicole nodded. "It's true. I saw Becca from afar, looked away, and when I looked back, she was wrapped around a piece of man muscle."

My cheeks heated. She made it sound so dirty. I most definitely had not been wrapped around Carson's man muscle. Though I had been doing my fair share of that. My cheeks got hotter at the thought.

"If I weren't already late, I would have gone to get a closer look," Nicole said unapologetically. "My dating life is so stale, I've been reduced to living vicariously. So spill."

"Yeah," Courtney demanded. "Who were you making out with?"

"I wasn't making out," I protested. Carson had kissed me after we'd had lunch on campus, and sure, maybe he'd taken the kiss to a level I probably wouldn't have in public, but it most definitely wasn't a make-out session.

Nicole snorted. "Was there tongue?"

Oh God. I'd never been one of those girls who discussed these kinds of details with friends. Then again, I'd never had details to discuss, nor had I had close friends to discuss them with.

"I wasn't making out," I said again. "It was simply a very enthusiastic goodbye kiss."

My friends burst into laughter.

I wasn't fooling them. But it wasn't like Carson and I had been groping each other. Except I might have grabbed his ass. *Oops.* With an ass like his, though, who could blame me?

"Who's the guy?" Nicole asked. "That's what I want to know. And how the hell did you manage to keep this from your bodyguard? Because if you keep making out in public like that, Carson is going to find out, and then someone's going to die."

I waited for her to crack a smile, but she was serious. She didn't know. If she had been close enough to call out to me, she would have. That meant she must have been far enough away that she hadn't seen Carson clearly.

"Carson's totally cool with it," I said.

"Really?" Nicole asked. "I thought he broke bad on his teammate who tried to talk to you at Bleakers."

"I wouldn't say he 'broke bad,'" I corrected. That seemed like so long ago. "There were words."

"Why are you dodging the question?" Courtney asked. "Give us details! Who is this mystery guy?"

I grinned, not able to keep the ruse any longer. "It's Carson."

The girls squealed. Nicole grabbed my arm and squeezed. "Are you kidding me? I was in such a hurry, I didn't get a good look, but I should have known. It was only a matter of time."

If she says so. I certainly hadn't been that confident, especially after years of secretly pining for him. The reality of it was a lot less romantic than historical romances made it sound.

Courtney sighed. "I need to find a man."

Nicole nodded. "Girl, same."

They looked at Hanima expectantly, waiting for her to chorus her agreement. "What?" she asked. "I don't have to worry about this stuff. Arranged marriage, remember?"

"Huh," Nicole mused. "You know, I never would have thought I'd be on board for that, but if I'm still single when I'm thirty, can your parents hook me up?"

Hanima rolled her eyes.

***

MISS HINCHEY, THE teacher in charge of the STEM program at Bleaksburg Middle School, nodded enthusiastically. "I'd love to have a partnership with VVU."

"Well, it wouldn't be with VVU exactly," I explained as I shifted in the uncomfortable student desk I'd dragged over next to the teacher's. "I can't speak for anyone else in the engineering department, but WIE wants to get involved, specifically with underrepresented populations in STEM."

"Even better. This is only my second year, but the number of students involved has already doubled." The young teacher pursed her lips and drummed her fingers on her desk. "How do I put this nicely? Oh, forget it. It's just us talking. Mr. Adams should have retired fifteen years ago, or at least given up the STEM program. The man still carried a flip phone."

I cringed. "Not exactly cutting edge." Even my technophobic grandmother had a smart phone. Though most of the selfies she sent me were of her forehead or partially blocked by a finger.

"Far from it. Don't get me wrong. He was a nice man, just... past his prime."

"I get it."

"So anyway, I'll need to get everything cleared with the principal, but I don't see any reason why she would object."

Miss Hinchey grinned, making her look like she could be one of the middle school students instead of the teacher. She couldn't be much older than me. "This is going to be awesome. I wish my school had had something like this. I might have ended up in a much different career."

"Oh?" I'd only just met her, but she seemed perfectly suited to her position. I would bet anything her students absolutely adored her.

"I love teaching, but I wasn't even exposed to the concept of STEM until I was in college." She shrugged. "Maybe if I had been, I would have gone into engineering or scientific research."

As I left the school, her words stuck with me, and I became even more determined to make this work. I wished I had taken the initiative sooner since I would be leaving VVU after this year. But if everything went according to plan, a system would be in place for WIE to volunteer with the middle school STEM program for years to come.

I couldn't take all the credit for it, though. I never would have pursued the idea if Hanima hadn't pushed me to be on homecoming court. I'd gotten so caught up in my own life that I'd forgotten how great it felt to give back.

When I started my car, and the dash flared to life, I cursed. I hadn't realized how late it was. I'd gotten along immediately with Miss Hinchey, and we'd chatted for quite a while, which wouldn't have been a problem except now I would have to haul ass to make it to the stadium. I rushed to my apartment so I could change out of the business clothes I'd worn for the meeting and into my VVU fan gear.

As I hurried past Lucy in the living room, she fell to her knees.

I whirled around to face her. "Oh my God, are you—"

"Upon my knees," she cried out. "What doth your speech import?"

Should have known. She'd been trying to make up for the rehearsals she'd missed while in New York.

Shaking my head, I continued to my room to get ready. I'd never been late to a game, and I sure as hell wasn't about to start now. It was my first home game as a WAG, and I intended to enjoy it.

***

Carson

I SLIPPED MY earbuds in my ears for my normal pregame ritual. This game against West Virginia was a rare Thursday night game. I loved night games, probably because the fans loved them. Plus, there was something awesome about playing under the lights. Maybe it was nostalgia for high school when every player was probably the best in their high school, destined for something greater. For most guys on the team, their time playing at VVU was the end of the line. Only a select few would become professional athletes.

And by God, one of them would be me.

I was the first to admit that I was a slacker about everything but football. Except recently, I'd come to realize that perhaps my slacker ways extended to athletics as well. I wasn't half as disciplined as Wyatt, and for the first time, I wondered what I could have been if I were. Maybe I relied too heavily on my size and natural talent. Those two things could only take me so far.

I forced myself to focus on the beat of the music. The last thing I needed was to psych myself out before a game. It wasn't like me to be insecure. If anything, I was usually overconfident. Maybe that was the problem—I'd used up all my confidence.

Fuck.

Jake yanked out my right earbud. "Dude, calm the fuck down."

"I'm calm."

"Bullshit. What's going on?"

I shrugged my jersey over my head. "Nothing. I'm cool." I tucked my earbud back into my ear.

Jake pulled it back out. "Seriously, man. Are you okay?"

Scowling, I had to stop myself before I told him to fuck off. I rolled my shoulders. "Just nerves."

He clapped a hand on my shoulder. "Believe me, I understand. But you got this. I got this, and you got this. You feel me?"

"Yeah." I moved to put my earbud back in then paused. "Thanks."

Jake nodded then went back to getting ready.

A few games ago when I was talking him off the ledge, I never would have guessed our positions would be reversed. I didn't know what had gotten into me. While the team as a whole hadn't been playing the best, my stats were solid. *But what if solid isn't good enough?*

Coach Coyle ambled in, like he was on the way to a pig pickin' instead of coaching a nationally televised game. After our first pregame pep talk, he had given up on them altogether. Instead, he would come into the locker room and simply ask, "Y'all ready?"

When he did that this time, I didn't join in the chorus of *hell yeahs* that the other guys called out. But it didn't matter because it was game time. I shoved my earbuds into my locker and lined up next to Wyatt so I could carry one of the flags on the run out of the tunnel. All business, he jerked his chin up at me. The guy was a fucking machine. I'd never seen him rattled, not even when the offensive line was falling apart around him. I didn't get it because he had so much on the line.

I tended to live my life like I had nothing left to lose, which was why not much bothered me. But for the first time, I felt like I did have a lot to lose, and it scared the hell out of me.

CHAPTER 18

Becca

I GRIPPED RACHEL'S arm and leaned in so that no one could hear me. "Did I do something to piss off Ashley? She's been glaring at me."

Rachel glanced at the tween then chuckled. "She has a crush on Carson."

"Oh." Well, dang. There wasn't much I could do about that. *Awkward.*

"Aw, don't worry." Rachel patted my arm. "This is actually good. Maybe now she'll realize she's twelve and not twenty. She's a bit of a handful."

I smirked. "You know, I might have been about twelve when I first developed a crush on Carson."

Rachel rotated her glass in her hand so that the ice swirled. "That crush seems to have stuck."

She has no idea. I glanced over at Carson, who was manning the grill with Jake. Since the game had been on Thursday this week, the guys had a rare weekend free. The weather was gorgeous, so Jake and Rachel had invited us over for a cookout. The more time I spent with them, the more I liked them. Carson had good taste in friends if I did say so myself.

"Yeah," I agreed. "That crush definitely stuck."

"I'm going to say to you exactly what I plan to say to Carson because I'm petty like that." Rachel cocked her head. "I told you so."

I laughed. "Yeah, I guess you did. Are you always right?"

She held her hand out and wiggled it. "Like ninety percent of the time."

"Only ninety? My percentage is around ninety-five."

"Try teaching elementary school. Just when you think you have the kids figured out, they go and do something crazy." She paused. "It's actually not as bad as I thought it would be. I still don't want to teach long term, but if I have to do it for a year or two while I get my counselor certification, it wouldn't be the worst thing ever. What about you? Have you thought about what you're doing after graduation?"

"I want to develop medical devices," I said. "It's all I ever wanted to do."

"It sounds like there's a story behind that."

"There is. It's kind of sad, though."

"I'm curious if you're willing to share."

"My uncle was a soldier who got injured in the Middle East," I explained. "He lost his leg and his arm, and he never got used to the prosthetics. He fell into depression and had PTSD on top of it. He ended up committing suicide when I was nine."

Rachel shot me a sympathetic look. "I'm sorry. That is sad."

"He was my dad's younger brother, and he never lived near us, so I didn't know him well. But he was so fun when he came to visit. He had a zest for life that was sucked out of him after he got injured. Maybe if he could have adjusted to the prosthetics, he wouldn't have been so depressed." I kicked at the grass with the toe of my sneaker. "It's kind of a silly thought."

Rachel shook her head. "It's not."

"My brother is a soldier now. It scares the hell out of me." Laughing hollowly, I rubbed my forehead. "Sorry. I don't mean to be such a downer."

"I asked. Roman, right? I think I met him at Bleakers that one night, though my memory is kind of hazy. I was pretty drunk."

I chuckled. "I remember."

"Hey, babe!" Jake called over. "Do you want cheese on your burger?"

Rachel shrugged. "Sure." She turned to me. "I'm going to head inside to get everything out."

"Do you need help?"

"No, I got it. You can hang out with the guys."

I wandered toward the grill, grateful Ashley went with Rachel. It was stupid to feel guilty, but I could sympathize with having a crush on Carson. *Been there, done that.*

Carson wrapped his arm around me from behind, holding me against him as he continued his conversation with Jake. "Coyle's not doing a bad job," he said. "He's just not Gurgin."

Using a spatula, Jake lifted a burger to check under it. "No one is."

"Where do you think we'd be if Gurgin hadn't retired?"

Jake unwrapped a piece of cheese. "I haven't thought about it."

"Come on. Yes, you have."

"No, man, I really haven't. Gurgin is gone, so there's no point getting caught up in the what-ifs. I try not to waste energy on things I can't change."

Carson grinned down at me. "We've got fucking Buddha over here."

Jake laughed. "Whatever. Carson said no cheese for you."

"That's right," I confirmed. One of the perks of being with Carson was that he already knew all my preferences. The few things left to be discovered involved us being naked. *Not that I'm complaining.*

After dinner, Jake dragged an ancient set of cornhole boards out of the shed. The paint was flaking off so badly, I couldn't determine what picture had originally been on the worn boards. They were a giant splinter waiting to happen.

"Awesome." Carson circled them, appraising them like he would a vintage car. "Where did you get those?"

"Some guys were moving out of the house down the street, and they put them out for garbage collection."

"Uh, yeah," Rachel interjected. "Because they're trash."

Jake huffed. "They're broken in and well loved."

Rachel cocked her head. "If they're so well loved, then why were they out in the trash?"

"Hell if I know," Jake said with a tone of disbelief in his voice. "Do you want to play or what?"

Rachel hopped up. "Of course. I just hope everyone is up to date on their tetanus shots. There are some rusty nails on the bottom."

My team got to go first since we were the guests. Carson's first throw went wildly to the left, while Jake's landed solidly on the board. When Carson's second throw was nowhere near the board, I groaned. "What was that?"

Rachel and Jake laughed as they gathered up the bags.

"Those were warm-up throws," Carson protested. I eyed him skeptically. *Lame-ass excuse.*

Luckily for us, Rachel's aim was about as good as Carson's. On his next round, though, he didn't do much better.

"I thought you were supposed to be an athlete," I teased. At the rate we were going, I was going to have to carry our team.

"My job is to catch, not throw."

I sighed so dramatically, Lucy would have been proud. "Don't embarrass me, Fleck."

Grinning, Carson sauntered over. "I forgot how competitive you are."

I arched a brow. "Now that you remembered, can you tighten up?"

He wrapped an arm around my waist and pulled me close. "I'll definitely tighten up," he whispered in my ear, sending tremors running through my blood. I would never tire of his innuendos now that we acted on them.

Since his back was to Rachel and Jake, I reached around and grabbed his ass. "Is that a promise?"

He let out a little growl. "You're so fucking hot. I wish we were at my place right now so I could—"

"Hey!" Jake called. "Are you going to play or what?"

With a reluctant sigh, Carson released me and gave Jake the middle finger. He retrieved the bean bags and pressed them into my hand. "You can complete that sentence however you'd like. Your wish is my command."

I took my place at the throwing line, trying to pretend that my entire body wasn't quivering. *Fat chance.* I totally missed my throw.

***

Carson

I THOUGHT BECCA would never be ready to leave Jake's house. I'd just about had her out the door when Jake's youngest sister, Emily, came outside to ask if we were ready for dessert. I was about to decline, but once Becca learned Emily had baked the pie herself, she insisted we stay. She was a much better person than I was.

Now she held on to the *oh shit* handle in the Jeep, and I took corners too sharply on the way back to my place.

"Uh, the speed limit is thirty-five."

I was doing fifty-three. "You said to hurry."

"Yes, but if you get pulled over, that'll take way longer."

She made a good point, but I'd never gotten pulled over. I liked to believe I'd been blessed by the traffic gods. Still, I slowed down to a respectable forty-five. It felt like we were crawling.

Watching Becca hurl those bean bags had been such a damn turn-on. When it was her turn, she would narrow her eyes in concentration at her target. Then she would stick her ass out as she positioned herself to toss the bag. It was so fucking hot.

I pulled into my parking space and had my seat belt off before I'd even turned off the Jeep. I strode to the passenger side, and as soon as Becca got out of the Jeep, I closed the door and pulled her up the walkway. Though I didn't have to put much effort into it—she was in just as much of a hurry as I was.

Once inside, I closed the door and pushed her up against it. My mouth assaulted hers, taking everything she had to offer and still demanding more. No matter how many times I tasted her, it would never be enough.

She wrapped her leg around my thigh, and I responded by gripping her ass and picking her up. I carried her to the couch and laid her down. I was about to climb on top of her when she put a hand on my chest. Standing, she gently pushed me so that I was on the couch.

"I got something for you." She undid the top button on her jeans. *Hell yeah, she does.*

She pulled down the zipper slowly, revealing black lace. Then she turned her attention to her top, undoing each button slowly, all the while holding my gaze.

It was sexy as hell, especially because she seemed to enjoy teasing me. And fuck, it was working. My cock was so hard.

She slipped the shirt off her shoulders, revealing a black lace bra that matched her bottoms. Beneath the delicate fabric, her nipples were taut. *Christ. She's trying to kill me.*

Rotating her hips, she shimmied out of her pants, stepping out of her shoes so she could kick the pants aside. She stood, nearly naked except for the scraps of black lace.

"Holy fuck, you should come with a warning label," I said.

She smiled, telling me that was the right thing to say. "What should it say?"

"At your own risk."

She frowned. "What's at your own risk?"

"Everything. You're a fantasy come to life." She was the total fucking package, and I couldn't believe how goddamned lucky I was.

She stepped toward me. "You have no idea." Leaning down, she undid my belt then pulled it out of the loops and tossed it over her shoulder. Kneeling in front of me, she undid the buttons of my shirt and pushed it over my shoulders. Then she undid my pants, and I lifted my hips so she could pull them down my thighs. Straddling me, she wrapped her arms around my neck and lowered her mouth to mine.

I ravaged her mouth, taking possession. I gripped her ass, pleasantly surprised when my palms came in contact with her bare skin. *Fuck!* I wish I'd asked her to turn around so I could have appreciated every angle. But there was one thing hotter than Becca in skimpy black lace, and that was Becca with nothing on at all.

I unhooked her bra and discarded it then cupped one breast while sucking the other one into my mouth. Gasping, she arched her back.

I couldn't wait to get inside her, to feel her muscles clamp around me. And then I'd—

"Shit!"

Becca's body jerked away from me. "What? What is it?"

Talk about ruining the mood. All Becca had to do was lay a single finger on me, and any smoothness I had went out the window. "I don't have any condoms down here."

Her body relaxed. "Is that all? You scared me."

"Sorry, babe."

She climbed off my lap, which was a damn shame. Then she shifted, and I caught sight of the black lace disappearing into her ass. I grinned. "Your ass looks so hot in those."

Putting a hand on her waist, she cocked her hip out. "Yeah?"

Before she knew what was coming, I rushed her and threw her over my shoulder. She let out a yell of surprise. When I got her upstairs, I planned to make her scream again, only this time for entirely different reasons.

CHAPTER 19

Carson

BECCA CUDDLED UP next to me. "Truth."

I looked at her out of the corner of my eye. "This should be called truth and truth, not truth or dare." I grinned as all sorts of wicked thoughts filled my mind. We'd only just started the game, but so far, we'd only had truths, and I was dying to give Becca a dare.

"That look right there is exactly why I won't choose dare," she said. *Ah, she knew me all too well.*

My grin widened. "I think we'd both enjoy a dare." At least we would enjoy *my* dares. Becca had a devious streak and could be creative, so I was leery of whatever dare she might pick for me.

"Probably, but I need a breather after the last few... um... dares."

I stifled a laugh. She was so cute because as mature and intelligent as she was, she still blushed every time she talked about our sex life. Which was freaking amazing, by the way. What Becca lacked in experience, she made up for in enthusiasm.

"Is that what we're calling it now?" I couldn't help teasing her. That was one thing about our relationship that hadn't changed.

She groaned. "Shut up. And hurry up with the truth question."

"Okay, I got one," I said. "Remember that girl on your field hockey team?"

"There were a lot of girls on my field hockey team," she said dryly.

"You know the one I mean."

"You're going to have to be more specific." Though she tried for nonchalant, I could tell she knew exactly who I referring to. There was only one girl who looked like she was the missing Kardashian sister, only ten times hotter.

"Cheyenne."

"What about her?"

"Did you really threaten to beat her up if she asked me out?"

Becca lifted her head, her eyes blazing. "Are you kidding me? Beat her up?"

I shrugged. "Maybe it didn't go down exactly like that." All I knew was that one day Cheyenne had suddenly stopped flirting with me when we'd been going back and forth for weeks.

Becca was silent for a moment, telling me I was closer to the truth than far from it. "I might have strongly suggested that it would be unwise for her to approach you. I don't remember the exact conversation."

I laughed. I would've loved to have been there to eavesdrop, but Becca's admission that the conversation had even taken place was the closest I was going to get. I had no doubts that she remembered exactly how it had gone down, but she would never tell me.

She buried her face in my chest. "Don't laugh at me. We were co-captains of the team, and she had a big mouth. She always kissed and told. I didn't want to hear about the two of you getting naked together."

"I didn't get naked nearly as much as you seem to think I did in high school."

She snorted. "I guess you've been making up for it in your college years."

"You could say that." I kissed the top of her head. "But you know none of that meant anything, right?"

"Yeah. It doesn't mean I have to like it, though."

I ran my fingers along her bare arms, pleased to see goose bumps form at my touch. "I didn't know it bothered you. You never said anything." There was a lot Becca hadn't said, and again, I wondered how things might have been different if she had spoken up.

"Because what right did I have?" She shifted to look at me. "I wasn't going to be a hypocrite and get on your case about dating."

I wouldn't have listened to her anyway, but I didn't tell her that. "Except with Cheyenne."

"Fat lot of good that did," she muttered. "You dated another girl on the team later that year."

"Did I?" I tried to remember. A lot of high school was a blur. Though it was only a few years ago, it seemed like another lifetime. Back then, I'd felt like I was biding my time, waiting for something better to start. College had been fucking awesome. It was sobering to think that time was coming to an end.

She sighed. "You're unbelievable."

I laughed. "I'll admit I was a man whore. But you changed me. Isn't that what every woman wants?"

"No." She shook her head against my chest. "*No.* I don't want to change you. You're perfect just the way you are."

"That's not true." *Case in point—weren't we just talking about my man whoring?* I'd never considered that behavior a problem, but now I wished I'd been more prudent for Becca's sake. I hated that my past bothered her. *Another of the endless strikes against me.*

"You're right, because no one is perfect. But you're perfect for me, and that's what counts." She tilted her face up, and I obliged her with a kiss. "Now it's my turn. Truth or dare."

"Dare."

"I knew you were going to pick that."

"What can I say? I like living on the edge." I braced myself for whatever heinous task Becca would come up with.

"Hmm... How about this one?" She propped herself up on her elbow. "I dare you to love me forever."

Her request took my breath away.

***

I COULD TELL by the way Becca was wrinkling her nose that my essay was garbage, which wasn't surprising considering I'd spent about twenty minutes on it.

"Well," she said slowly. "This isn't your best work." *That was putting it mildly.*

I snorted. "Will it get at least a C?" That was all I needed to keep my GPA up long enough to finish the season. Beyond that, I didn't give a shit.

She tapped on her teeth with her finger. "I honestly can't say."

There was no way in hell I was wasting any more time on that stupid assignment. "It'll have to be good enough."

Becca's lips pursed. "But you can do better." *She's the only one who thinks so.*

Athletes weren't expected to be good students. The ones who were were anomalies. I stretched out on the couch and put my hands behind my head. "What's the point?"

She blinked as if she didn't understand the question. "It's your name on the paper, so don't you want it to be good?"

I really didn't see why it mattered as long as I got a passing grade. The professor would read it once, and then it would wind up in the trash. "I'm fine with decent."

She pressed her fingertips to her closed eyelids. "I just don't understand why you wouldn't want to do your best."

"What if that is my best?"

"It's not."

I sat up. "It might be."

She shook her head. "But it's not."

"It is." I didn't know why I was turning this into a pissing match. I knew as well as she did that I'd put in the minimum effort. But again, I didn't see why it mattered.

Letting the paper fall to the table, she leaned back in her chair. "I don't know why you shortchange yourself."

"It's not like I'm planning to go to grad school." *Or even graduate with my undergrad.* But if she hadn't figured that out by now, I wasn't going to tell her. At best, I was destined for a decade of playing pro football. At worst, I would wind up pushing paper for Fleck Holdings. Either way, my path wasn't an intellectual one. I wasn't like her.

"So what?" she asked. "Don't you want to do well for the sake of doing well?"

If there was no return on investment, then it was a waste of energy. I would get absolutely nothing out of putting more time into the assignment. But I was fighting a losing battle because Becca would never understand that. School was easy for her. When we'd been in high school, she and I had never had a single class together because she'd taken all advanced courses. She could've gotten honor roll with her eyes closed, but I'd had to work hard to get grades high enough to satisfy VVU's GPA requirement for incoming athletes.

I stood and walked toward the kitchen. "I do what I need to do," I called over my shoulder. I grabbed a beer out of the fridge and popped the top.

Becca followed me into the kitchen. "I'm not trying to pick a fight with you," she said quietly.

"It kind of feels that way."

"Well, I'm not."

I ran my hands over my head. "Look, I'm never going to be as smart and accomplished as you." In a lot of ways that mattered, I simply wasn't in Becca's league, and I never would be.

She frowned. "First of all, I don't care about your accomplishments. I care about *you*. But second of all, you're plenty accomplished. How many guys do you think get a shot at playing pro football? Or even college football?"

I didn't answer, figuring they were rhetorical questions. I understood what she was saying, but being good at football wasn't in the same league as being a biomedical engineer. Hell, in just a few years, she could develop a mechanical heart or some shit. And what would I be doing? If I was lucky, I would be playing with a damn football. My potential paled in comparison to hers.

I was crazy in love with her, but I would never be enough for her, not even close. But I wasn't ready for her to realize that yet.

"Just forget about it," I muttered. "I'll redo the stupid paper."

"You never used to get bent out of shape when I called you on stuff like this. Why is it bothering you now?"

I rolled my shoulders. "It's not."

"Bullshit." She looked at me expectantly, waiting for an explanation for why I'd been such a pain in the ass about the assignment. I didn't have a good excuse, especially since she was the one doing me a favor by helping me.

I gathered her in my arms. "I'm sorry. I had a rough practice, and I guess it's still getting to me."

"Why didn't you tell me?"

Because it's a lie. Practice had been fine. But I couldn't explain the truth. She'd always pushed me to be better, and in the past, I'd given a half-assed attempt at meeting her expectations. If I succeeded, great. If I didn't, no big loss. But now I had a hell of a lot to lose.

I could lose her.

I loved this girl so much, it twisted at my insides. I'd spent years screwing around because I couldn't even admit to myself how I felt about her. Now fear gripped me every day that this would be the day she finally realized I wasn't enough for her.

***

BECCA'S PARENTS WERE driving up the morning of the homecoming game because the closest hotel they could get was almost two hours away. Roman had managed to rearrange his schedule so he could attend the game, too, but he would stay with me the entire weekend. Or that was the plan anyway. He might change his mind after I talked to him.

Becca pursed her lips. "Roman will be fine. Even if he's mad at first, he'll get over it. But he'll be hurt if we wait a long time to tell him."

I snorted. The idea that Roman would be hurt that I was dating his sister was laughable. He was going to be pissed. I'd been putting off thinking about it, much less picking up the phone to actually have the conversation with him. Now I would be forced to face him. At least it would be in person, so he would be able to punch me if he wanted. I wouldn't stop him.

"I'm almost ready," Becca said. "But you can still change your mind if you want. I wouldn't mind."

I grinned, grateful for the topic shift. "Hell no. There's no way I'm going to miss your first appearance as a court princess."

"Candidate," she corrected immediately. "Calling them princesses is a high school thing."

I got off her bed and went over to where she was finishing her makeup in front of the full-length mirror on her closet. Wrapping my arms around her from behind, I nuzzled her neck. "You'll always be my princess."

She smiled. "You know I love it when you talk cheesy to me." She was such a nerd. I loved that about her, though.

"You look amazing," I said. Her navy-blue dress was conservative, much more business than party, but she looked amazing no matter what she wore. Tonight, though, her dark-blond hair was styled into loose curls that flowed down her back, making me wish we could blow off the alumni event. I wanted to see her in those curls and nothing else.

She turned so she could wrap her arms around my neck. "So do you, Mr. Fleck."

My clothes were nothing special—dress pants with a light-blue button-down shirt—but I cleaned up nicely when I wanted to. I was glad I'd put in the effort since it seemed to make her happy.

The homecoming alumni party was being held in the alumni center. It had recently been renovated, but since I'd never been inside, I couldn't tell the difference. It was super nice, though. I guessed it would need to be to entice rich alumni to donate large sums to the university. As I walked up the stairs with Becca on my arm, I idly wondered how much I would have to donate to have a building named after me. Maybe it was narcissistic, but that would be fucking cool.

We went to the lounge being used by the homecoming committee so that Becca could pick up a sash. I helped her put it on, holding my breath as I stuck a pin in the fabric near her shoulder and only releasing it once the sash was in place and none of her blood had been shed. "What do you do now?"

She shrugged. "Mingle, I guess. They're doing the court presentation at nine. I think we can go after that."

The lounge door opened, and Blake stood there. I instinctively stepped closer to Becca. The last time I'd seen this guy, he'd been sharing a plate of sticky buns with her. I really needed to take her to Beans and Buns to replace that memory for both of us.

Seeing us, Blake smiled widely. "Hey, Becca. Hey, Carson. Ready to go into the battlefield?"

"Battlefield?" Becca questioned. She glanced up at me.

"You have no idea, do you?" Blake laughed. "It's an open bar for alumni. Some of them are going to be drunk off their asses. It's like they come back to campus and try to drink like they did when they were students here."

"How do you know that?"

He shrugged. "I went to an alumni event as an officer of my fraternity last spring. It was a total shit show." For the first time, Blake seemed to notice my arm around Becca. "Are you two together?" His question made me tighten my hold on her.

She blushed slightly. "Yes."

"Cool. Carson, are you ready for the game tomorrow? It should be a blowout, right?"

Despite myself, I couldn't help but like the guy. Though I shouldn't have been surprised. Becca didn't stay friends with assholes. Except me. "If we can't whip JMU, we've got problems." This year, our homecoming opponent was an in-state rival, but they weren't anywhere close to being in our league. The timing was fortunate, though. It always sucked to lose the homecoming game.

We made our way to the ballroom, which was already packed. I checked the time—the event had only officially started two minutes ago, but the line for the open bar was already ridiculous. *Guess Blake knows what he's talking about.*

Blake straightened his tie. "I guess it's time to charm a cougar into donating a ton of money to the school."

Becca frowned. "Really?"

"Why else do you think they parade us out here? They can't tell us that, but that's our purpose." He nodded toward a group of cheerleaders. "That's why they're here."

"That's so cynical," Becca said.

"Is it cynical if it's true? Tickets cost three hundred a pop for this event," Blake said. "Trust me. They're hoping this crowd will donate."

Becca looked up at me for confirmation.

"I agree with Blake," I said. "This event has politics written all over it."

"I guess you would know," Becca muttered. I'd been coerced into attending events like these in the past, both for my mother and for her associates. It was all so fake. I would take a cold beer, a grilled bratwurst, and a bonfire over bruschetta on tiny toast any day. But I kind of wished Blake had kept his fat mouth shut. There was no reason Becca's view of this whole shindig had to be jaded.

"Excuse me," an elderly man wearing a bow tie said. "Are you Carson Fleck, by any chance?"

I squared my shoulders and pasted on a smile. I knew how to do this song and dance. "Yes, sir. I am."

Blake gave us a little wave and wandered off, probably to do his part and find an older lady to schmooze.

"Well, hot damn." The older man twisted his head to scan the crowd. "Where are the other guys?"

"They're resting up for tomorrow's game." That seemed the prudent thing to say, even if it wasn't true for a lot of my teammates. It was definitely true for Wyatt and Jake, though.

"Don't you need rest?"

"Yes, sir, but I'm here to support this lovely lady. She's on the homecoming court."

The man spared a glance for Becca. "How nice. Say, would you mind signing something for me for my grandson? Archer is his favorite, but he'd probably like something from you."

"Sure," I said easily. The man produced a pen, and Becca grabbed a flyer from a side table.

After I signed it, the man tucked it into his pocket and patted me on the shoulder. "Have a good game tomorrow, son."

"Thank you, sir."

Once he was out of earshot, Becca shook her head. "He was kind of a prick, even if he was an old man."

I shrugged. Quarterbacks were always kids' favorite players. It didn't bother me. Though the guy had been kind of a dick about the whole thing.

Becca and I made the most of the situation. While we didn't get to enjoy the open bar, we did gorge on hors d'oeuvres, and sure enough, there was bruschetta on tiny toast. Shortly before nine, she made her way to the stage. The cheerleaders did a routine and then created an alley for the homecoming court to walk through as they were announced. The alumni attendees clapped politely for each person, but it was obvious they didn't give a shit. After the first few candidates, the buzz of conversation resumed. When Becca's name was called, I stuck my fingers in my mouth and whistled obnoxiously loudly. Even from the back of the room, I could see her blush. *Mission accomplished.*

My phone buzzed with a text from Roman, telling me he was already at my place. I immediately started sweating, and my collar suddenly felt like it was choking me. *Damn.* I hadn't expected him for another hour. Normally, I would have been happy he'd arrived early, but not when we needed to have the conversation where I told him I was shacking up with his sister.

I reminded myself it wasn't like that. Once he saw that I genuinely loved her, he would be cool with it. He had to be. *Fuck.* I was not looking forward to this.

Becca returned to my side, and I scooped her up in a tight hug. "I'm proud of you."

She laughed. "All I did was walk through a spirit tunnel."

I grinned. "But you did it so well. Ready to go? I just got a text from Roman."

She sighed. "I totally misunderstood. We're supposed to stay until ten."

"Okay." I breathed a little easier, grateful for the excuse to avoid Roman a little longer.

"No, you go. I can catch a ride home with Blake."

"I'll stay. Roman can wait. He's early anyway."

"Roman just drove almost six hours. It's kind of shitty to make him sit in his car for another hour if he doesn't have to."

God, I'm such a dick. I hadn't even considered that. Even though Becca had a valid point, I didn't like leaving her.

Becca put a hand on her hip. "Don't be an ass about this. You were just planning to drop me off at home anyway." Although she said she was sure Roman would be okay with the two of us being together, she wasn't ready to stay the night with me under the same roof as her brother. I couldn't say I was ready for that either. Would I ever be?

"Fine," I muttered. "But I want to talk to Blake first."

Blake assured me multiple times that he would make sure Becca got home safely. As she walked me to the exit, she promised to text me when she got home. I'd run out of excuses to stay. *I'm such a chickenshit.*

Putting my thumb under her chin, I tilted her face up. "Be sure you do." It felt so ass-backward to entrust Becca to another guy, especially one she'd dated. Okay, it was just one coffee date, but still.

As I walked away from her, she grabbed my hand and pulled me back for another kiss. "I love you," she said.

"I love you too."

She playfully pushed me toward the door. "Now go talk to Roman. It'll be fine."

Easy for her to say.

CHAPTER 20

Carson

ROMAN WAS WAITING on my front porch when I pulled in. "About time your ugly ass showed up," he called.

I took my time getting out of the car. "Sorry," I said when I finally emerged.

He shot me a strange look. *Shit.* The fact that I didn't lob an insult right back at him warned him that something was up.

I unlocked the front door, and we shuffled in. Roman dropped his bag on the floor and wandered into the kitchen. "I'm fucking starving. You got anything good?"

"The same as usual," I said. Roman was always hungry. "We can order a pizza if you want."

He came back into the living room with his arm elbow deep in a bag of Doritos. "No, I'm good. I hit up a Wendy's on the drive here. I just need snacks."

"Cool." I sat on the couch, stretched my arm across the back, and propped my right foot on my left knee. *God, this sucks.*

Roman remained standing, probably because he'd just spent several hours sitting in a car. "Man, I wish Becca would've gotten on the homecoming court in high school. We really could have punked her, but I guess we can't really do that here."

"No," I agreed. Roman and I definitely would have tried to pull something in high school, though for the life of me, I couldn't think of what we would do. Maybe it was a sign I was finally maturing.

"You're acting weird." He shoved a chip in his mouth. "Are you okay?"

"I'm fine." I started bouncing my foot then stopped and planted both feet on the floor before leaning my elbows on my knees. "Actually, I need to talk to you." *There's no going back now.*

"What's up?"

"So, uh, yeah." I rubbed the back of my neck. "Becca and I are sort of... together." *Christ.* I shouldn't have put off thinking about talking to him. Then maybe I would've known what to say.

Roman's eyes filled with confusion, and his gaze locked on mine for a few tense seconds. Then he laughed. "Nice try, but you can't punk me that easily."

I blew out a breath. I hadn't expected that he wouldn't believe me. I'd expected him to be pissed. Though there was still time for that reaction.

"I'm not punking you."

Roman stared at me, like he was trying to make sense of my words.

"We're together," I said, wanting to make it perfectly clear. Then I braced myself.

Roman crumpled the empty chip bag and threw it on the floor. "*What... the... fuck?*"

"I didn't plan it." I didn't bother to tell him that Becca had had feelings for me for years. She could decide if and when she told him that. At this point, the fewer details Roman knew, the better.

Roman's hands were balled into fists at his sides, and a vein in his neck bulged. "How long?"

"Not long. A few weeks."

"You're supposed to be looking out for her, not fucking... *shit.*" Roman unclenched his hands and ran them over his head. With one last furious look at me, he stalked to the door and exited the townhouse, slamming the door closed behind him.

Fuck. That went as badly as I'd suspected it would. I supposed I should be glad he hadn't hit me, but I might've felt better if he had. Roman and I had grown apart because of distance, but I still considered him my brother. I stood and started pacing, wondering how long I should give him to cool down before I went after him. Because I sure as hell wasn't leaving things like this.

Just as I was about to open my front door, it flung open, nearly hitting me. I stepped backward, and Roman slowly stalked toward me, his eyes narrowed. I tensed, preparing to take the punch I deserved.

Instead, Roman poked me in the chest. "You know my sister is worth more than both of our sorry asses combined."

"Yeah." The word came out shaky. He was putting into words what had been going through my head for weeks.

"And goddamn it, I know your track record. You don't stay with girls."

"This is different," I said quietly. "I love her, Roman. Honest to God, I love that girl."

I didn't know what else to say to convince him of that. But he knew me, and I trusted that would be enough for him to see the truth.

He stared at me, processing my words. Closing his eyes, he hung his head. When he looked at me a moment later, he seemed calmer, more resigned. "If you hurt her, your ass is mine. You feel me? There's no going back from that."

"I know."

Roman stepped away from me and put his hands on his hips. "Fuck, man. You should have warned me."

"Would it have made a difference?"

"No."

"I figured." Not that it mattered. I'd been so chickenshit about telling him that I'd put it off. Hell, if he hadn't come to visit, I wouldn't have told him.

"Just be good to her, man."

"I will." I wanted nothing more than to love her and treat her well. That was the easy part. It was being enough for her that was impossible.

Though I should have felt better now that I had Roman's grudging blessing, a ball formed in the pit of my stomach, rolling and twisting. Screwing up with Becca was inevitable because at my core, I was a fuck-up. And now the stakes were higher.

I would lose them both.

***

Becca

ROMAN SHOWED UP at my door with half a doughnut hanging out of his mouth and a big box of them in his hands. I hugged him and pulled him inside. Chewing his doughnut, he sauntered to the kitchen and put the box on the counter, but he didn't take off his sunglasses.

"What's with the glasses?" I asked. "You look like Tom Cruise in *Top Gun*."

"My eye looks pretty bad," he replied. "I didn't want to freak you out."

"Oh my God, what happened to your eye?" I had no idea what went into SEAL training, but every military-training movie sequence I'd ever seen ran through my mind.

"Your *boyfriend* happened."

I gasped, and my hand clutched at my throat like I was a little old lady grabbing her pearls. "Roman, what did you do?" *Damn it.* I'd been so assured that Roman would be cool about Carson and me that I'd dismissed Carson's concerns. *Shit.* The last thing Carson needed was to have a black eye or some other stupid injury the day of a game.

"Hey!" Roman protested, pulling off his sunglasses. "Why are you assuming it's my fault?"

I stared at him, taking in his perfectly normal, uninjured eye. "You can be such a dick sometimes."

He laughed. "Before you ask, the answer is no, Carson didn't put me up to this. But I couldn't resist."

I wasn't going to ask because as worried as Carson had been, I doubted he would want to tease me. "So you're okay with everything?"

"I am now."

Shit, what did that mean? Had he been *not* been okay with it at first?

I tossed my hair over my shoulder. It technically wasn't his business anyway. Sure, Carson was his best friend, but we didn't need Roman's permission. Although his blessing would be nice.

"I told Carson you would be okay with it."

Roman poked around in the box and picked out a chocolate-covered doughnut. "I am. It just took me by surprise, though it shouldn't have. Carson has always had a thing for you."

I did a double take. "What?"

Roman paused, mid-chew. He swallowed. "Yeah. Wasn't it obvious?"

"Not to me, it wasn't." *And not to Carson either.* Unless there was something he wasn't telling me. I didn't think so, though. Carson wasn't one to keep secrets.

Roman shoved the second half of the doughnut into his mouth and wiped his hands on his jeans. "Well, just play nice with each other, because if I have to kick his ass to defend your honor or some shit, it's gonna get awkward."

Rolling my eyes, I went back to my room to grab my shoes. *Whatever you say, Roman.*

***

ROMAN ALMOST MADE me late. By the time we made it to campus, I barely had time to point him in the direction of Evan's tailgate and rush to the coliseum to meet up with the rest of the homecoming court. Since the game wasn't being televised, the homecoming court presentation would be during halftime instead of before the game. That meant the court had reserved seats in the first and second rows near the end zone. Though the seats weren't centered, that was probably the closest I would ever get to the action. It was a shame, though, because I would rather sit with my parents and Roman.

When Carson came streaming out of the tunnel, carrying the Virginia flag, my chest swelled with pride. I was glad Roman and my parents were there to see this. I knew they watched the televised games religiously, but it wasn't the same as seeing Carson in person and hearing how the crowd reacted to him. Everyone loved him. Wyatt Archer might've been the best player on the team, but Carson was the most fun.

He scored in less than three minutes on a pass from Wyatt that resulted in a forty-seven-yard run. I knew from years of watching Carson's games that that play was one of the most basic in their playbook. Yet the defense had done little to slow them down, much less stop them.

Beside me, Blake stuck his fingers in his mouth and whistled. He put both hands up to high-five me. "That's what I'm talking about!"

The entire first half went pretty much like that, with the touchdowns alternating between Carson and Jake. By halftime, it seemed like the game would indeed be a blowout since we were up thirty-five to nothing. It was also clear the other team was frustrated as hell. In a way, I felt sorry for them. The only reason they played us was proximity. It really wasn't fair to them. But that still didn't stop me from enjoying seeing my man jump into the crowd behind the end zone on his last touchdown. The fans couldn't get enough of his antics. Neither could I, really. I loved seeing him confident and in his element.

The homecoming presentation at halftime was nothing to write home about. I'd been so nervous about walking on the field, but at least a quarter of the audience had gone to the bathroom, and out of the people left, probably only half of them paid attention.

Spoiler alert—I didn't win. But Blake did. I was so freaking excited for him, even if he did look ridiculous in the furry maroon crown they put on his head. While the rest of us got to return to the stands, he had to stay on the field to pose for pictures along with the homecoming queen. But as soon as he got off the field and away from the cameraman who was broadcasting him to the jumbotron, he took the crown off.

"I think you should wear it," I told him. "You look, um, regal." I tried valiantly to keep a straight face and failed.

"Nope," he said quickly. "I did the requisite five minutes. Besides, that thing is heavier than it looks. Do you want to try it on?"

"Nope. But congratulations. For real."

He rubbed the back of his neck, looking bashful and adorable. "Aww, thanks."

I wanted to ask him if he'd talked to his ex-girlfriend, whom he was hung up on, but I didn't want to risk bringing it up in case it was still a sore subject. If things didn't work out with her, he was going to make someone else very happy one day. Hopefully he and I would remain friends.

By the fourth quarter, the other team still hadn't scored, and we were up by forty-nine. Coach Coyle pulled Wyatt out so his backup could get some game-time experience. By that point, a lot of people had already started filtering—or stumbling—out of the stands. There was a collective gasp several rows up, and I looked up just in time to see a drunk girl land on her ass on the concrete stairs. I winced on her behalf. That was going to hurt tomorrow. But she was probably lucky she didn't get arrested, considering security had been right next to her. *Sheesh.* She looked like she was a freshman.

Though a lot of the other homecoming court members had already left, Blake and I stayed. He grinned at me. "Always stay until the bitter end. Am I right?"

I nodded. "Always. Just glad that this time the bitter end is for the opponent."

"It usually is."

"True," I agreed. "We'll conveniently forget about the game..." I trailed off as I watched our backup quarterback bobble the ball in his hands, nearly fumbling. By some miracle, he managed to recover and send the ball sailing down the field. The throw was high, arcing up, which gave the defenders plenty of time to get down the field. Carson jumped, easily claiming the ball. The defender who had also been trying to catch the ball hadn't stood a chance, even though he had committed pass interference. I nodded as the ref threw down a flag at the spot of the foul.

As Carson turned to run, a defender rushed him. Carson dipped his shoulder, no doubt planning to plow through the guy. That might have worked, except another defender rushed up behind him. *Goddamn it. Where the hell is our offensive line?* The defender slammed into Carson's back just as the first defender went in for the tackle. He led with his helmet and crashed into Carson's arm, probably in an attempt to force a fumble. Carson got sandwiched between them and went down.

"Oh no," I whispered.

"It's okay," Blake said. "He still has the ball."

I wasn't worried about a damn fumble. It looked like Carson was hugging the ball to his chest, but I knew better—he was cradling his arm. He didn't hop up like he normally did. Something wasn't right.

A teammate jogged toward him then waved his hand toward the sidelines. The trainers rushed onto the field.

Oh no, oh God, oh no.

When Blake put his arm around me, I realized I was shaking. "Hey," he said in a soothing tone. "Don't worry. Carson is one of the toughest guys on the team."

That was what I was worried about. Carson was tough and had a ridiculous pain tolerance, so if he stayed down, then something was very wrong.

***

Carson

THE SECOND I heard the crack, I knew it was bad. *Motherfucker!* The pain was excruciating, but that wasn't what bothered me. My main concern was that Coach wasn't going to let me go back in the game with my arm bent like that.

I had the errant thought that I should use the hand on my good arm to massage the crooked arm straight again. But before I knew it, the trainers were hovering over me with concerned looks on their faces.

"Just stay still, Carson," one of the older ones named Hank said. What the hell did he expect me to do? I couldn't move with the wall of bodies around me. Hell, weren't they supposed to leave some oxygen for me? *Fuck. Give me some goddamn air.*

Hank undid my helmet strap and pulled it off. Nope, not better. The brim of the helmet had blocked out the sun, but now it was blasting right into my eyes.

"It's definitely broken," someone said.

No shit. I could have told you that.

"I'll be fine. Tape it up."

The trainers all stared at me. "Tape isn't an option for this one."

Fuck. I'd known that, but it was worth a shot.

"Can you walk?"

"It's my arm, not my leg."

"All righty then," Hank said. "Let's get you off the field." He leaned down to help me up, but I waved him off. Using my unbroken arm, I pushed myself up off the ground. I wasn't careful enough, and my bad arm got jostled. I nearly stumbled as a wave of pain hit me. *Holy fuck.*

The crowd cheered once I was on my feet. Grinning, I waved to them with my good arm, and the roar got louder. The grin fell off my face when I saw the flatbed golf cart waiting for me on the side of the field. *Oh, hell no.* They might force me off the field, but I sure as hell was leaving it on my own legs.

As I walked toward the tunnel, my gaze found Becca's in the crowd. *Shit.* Tears were streaming down her face, and I could tell that she was shaking. Blake's arm was around her shoulders, which should have pissed me off, but I was just glad she wasn't alone. *Look at me—maturing and shit.*

In the locker room, shit got real as I was handed off to Dr. Flores. After a brief inspection of my arm, he wanted an X-ray.

"How long will this take to heal?" I asked. "A few weeks?" That sucked, but at least we had a bye week coming up. So at most, I was looking at missing two games.

Dr. Flores's mouth pressed into a tight line. "You see that bump on your arm there?" He pointed to the misshapen part of my forearm. "That's your bone."

Well, shit. I'd suspected as much, but hearing the doctor confirm it was sobering.

"Can you push it back into place or something?"

The doctor stared at me for a moment and shook his head. "This isn't like a dislocated shoulder. I won't be able to confirm until I've seen the X-ray, but I suspect this is a displaced fracture."

I frowned. "What does that mean?"

The doctor held his hands out flat with his fingers touching. "This is what a normal bone looks like. See? All together. And this"—he pulled apart his hands and held each one at an odd angle—"is a displaced fracture. With any luck, there's just one fracture. But your bone has shifted so that the pieces aren't touching."

I appreciated him dumbing it down for me, but he still hadn't told me what I wanted to know. "How long until I'm back on the field?"

"It's starting to swell. Surgery can't happen until the swelling goes away."

I gritted my teeth. "How long?"

Dr. Flores shook his head sadly, and I knew before he said the words. "You're not getting back on the field this season."

CHAPTER 21

Becca

I WAS A wreck, sobbing in the uncontrollable way that also caused snot to run out of my nose. It was an ugly, ugly cry. To his credit, Blake didn't leave my side until he'd deposited me in the care of Roman and my parents. Then he took off. I couldn't blame him. I was hysterical and nonsensical, but I couldn't rein it in, not until I saw Carson. In my gut, I knew he wasn't okay.

Despite the chill in the air, I insisted on waiting outside the players' entrance. My mom wrapped her arms around me, providing the comfort only a mother was capable of. "I'm sure he'll be fine, honey. Yes, he's hurt, but he'll recover."

Her words made sense and were exactly right, but they didn't make me feel any better.

My father's cop eyes narrowed as a loud group of kids strode past. They were totally wasted, and my dad probably wanted to give them hell, but he was obviously out of his jurisdiction. As a general rule, he didn't arrest kids for underage drinking, but he did like to scare them into thinking twice about their actions. He was one of the best cops around despite the fact that I was biased. My mom kept pressing him to get a position in one of the local high schools as a school resource officer. So far, he'd resisted, but he would end up there eventually. He was good with kids.

Jake exited the building, and I pounced, wrenching out of my mother's arms. "Did you see Carson? How is he?"

"Strangely calm," Jake said, not seeming unnerved by how I'd grabbed him. "I expected him to be pissed."

My shoulders slumped in relief. "Then it must not be that bad." Carson got pissed whenever he had to sit out, even for a few plays. So if he was calm, then I must have overestimated the severity of his injury.

Jake grimaced. "His arm is broken. He wouldn't tell me much else, but that much was obvious."

I closed my eyes as my chest tightened.

"Shit," Roman said. "That's at least six weeks out, right?"

Please say no. But I knew it was a fruitless hope. Bones took time to mend, and it wasn't worth the risk for Carson to play before it was better.

"I couldn't say," Jake said. "But yeah, probably."

The exit door flung open, and Carson came out with his arm in a sling. I flung myself at his other side, trying not to jostle his arm. I inhaled his scent, but the tightness in my chest didn't relent.

He chuckled. "Sorry to worry you."

I stepped back so I could get a good look at him. Though he smiled, it was strained. He was probably putting on a brave face for my parents' sake—and hell, for my sake. I wasn't proud of how I'd fallen apart. *Thank God he hadn't seen me up close.* I'd been upset that I couldn't be with him right after it happened, but now I realized that was probably better. If I was in this for the long haul—and I was—I would need to learn how to deal. Injuries in pro sports happened all the time.

"Is it too late for you to switch to golf?" I asked meekly. Everyone laughed, and some of the tension dissipated.

Jake jerked his head up. "I'll see you later. Call if you need anything."

It was only after he had walked away that I realized I hadn't introduced him to my parents.

"That was Jake," I said apologetically.

"Jake Truitt. Yes, I know," my dad said. I wasn't surprised he'd recognized him. He'd always followed college football, and because of Carson and me, he was a devoted VVU fan. He turned to Carson. "That was an amazing game, with the exception of the last quarter, of course."

"Yeah, that part sucked," Carson said wryly. "Are you all hungry?"

"Oh no, Carson. We don't expect you to cook for us now," my mom said. "You need to rest."

"I have five pounds of steak in my fridge," Carson said. "You'd be doing me a favor if you'd come over and grill it for me, because I obviously can't." Grinning, he gestured to his arm.

Shit. I'd been shortsighted, only thinking about how his injury would affect football, but it was going to upset all aspects of his life. Already, I could see the battles ahead of me. While Carson was fine with accepting my help on assignments, he wasn't keen on showing what he perceived to be weaknesses. Needing assistance because of his broken arm definitely fell into that category.

My father clapped him on the back. "You got it."

Roman stuck with Carson to drive his Jeep, while my parents and I started the hike to our cars. The whole way, my concern for Carson grew as I thought more about what he'd said, or more accurately, what he hadn't said. Like Jake had said, he was eerily calm about the whole thing. Something was off.

He needs time. This had only just happened, and on top of that, my family had descended on him. He hadn't had a moment to think. *Him thinking won't make it better—it will probably make it worse.*

At Carson's house, my mother and I prepared side dishes while the guys manned the grill on the patio.

"I am so proud of you, honey," she gushed. "It didn't seem appropriate to tell you earlier while we were waiting for Carson, but I am really, really proud."

"It's not that big of a deal," I muttered, keeping my head down as I washed celery. "I didn't win or anything." I wasn't comfortable with praise in general but especially that which I hadn't earned.

"No, but I know that putting yourself out there like that is hard for you, so I'm proud that you did it."

"Well, thanks."

"So..." Her gaze slid over to me as she peeled potatoes. "Roman told us that you and Carson are dating."

Ripping the individual stalks of celery apart, I groaned. "Really? He just couldn't keep his fat mouth shut, could he? I swear, he's a gossip." That was another thing I needed to talk to Carson about. Though Roman had said they were cool, I wanted to hear Carson's side of it since he'd been worried about it.

My mom shrugged. "It was only a matter of time."

I blinked, trying to hide my shock at her statement. "What do you mean?"

"I've known for years how you felt about him."

I'd begun to cut the celery, but my hands paused mid-chop. "What?" That had been my most closely guarded secret, and there my mother was, nonchalantly telling me she'd known.

"Honey, I'm your mother," she said in a tone that indicated being my mother was reason enough for her to figure out my secrets. "And Carson was at our house nearly every day for almost a decade. Of course I knew."

"Did Dad know?" I was horrified. My parents shared everything. It was what made their marriage so strong and something I'd once considered as one of my marriage goals. But I was rethinking that stance now that it meant humiliation for me.

"*Pfft*. Please. The man is clueless when it comes to romance. Did I ever tell you he got me a toaster for Valentine's Day the first year we were married?" She chuckled at the memory.

"Really?"

"Yes. In his defense, he explained that I'd been complaining about the toaster burning my bagels every morning, so he thought he was doing a nice thing. I guess he was, but Valentine's Day?" She shook her head. "His other excuse was that one of the things he loved about me was how practical I am."

I snorted. "That sounds like a cop-out." I wondered how I would react if Carson gave me a similar gift. Probably not as coolly as my mother. Though she might have lost her shit at the time.

"He honestly thought he was doing a good thing." She made a clucking sound with her tongue. "Clueless, I tell you."

We continued food prep in silence for a few minutes. "You know," I said, "I was going to tell you about me and Carson. It's only recent, and he wanted to talk to Roman first."

"I understand, and I'm not upset. I'm just glad he finally got his head out of his ass."

I gaped at my mother. "*Mom.*"

Shrugging, she popped a cherry tomato into her mouth. "In some ways, Carson is as dense as your father. But like your father, he's a good man."

He definitely was, and my heart swelled to hear my mother say that.

I smiled as I looked out the sliding glass door at Carson. He sat next to my father and brother with a dazed look on his face, and my smile vanished.

Broken. He looks broken. And I wasn't referring to his arm.

***

Carson

I WATCHED THE clock from three a.m. to four a.m. Even with Becca sleeping beside me, I couldn't relax. The pain meds were wearing off, but the pain didn't bother me. What bothered me was that my broken arm wasn't an injury I could hide. I'd played through pain, but Coach Coyle wouldn't let me play with a cast on my arm.

And fuck. Of all the fucking games to get injured in, it had to be during one with a pansy-ass team who couldn't score a single point against us. It was insulting. Though I supposed I should have been glad the game hadn't been televised. At least that shit wasn't memorialized for the pro coaches to view. But they would hear about it regardless. Still, that wasn't the main problem. Last year, I'd been a solid player, but I'd been in FM4's shadow. Everyone had except for Archer. This was supposed to be my year to prove myself, even if we weren't destined for a national championship. Now that chance was lost, and I'd only gotten a fraction of the season in, all because some dipshit hit me with his goddamn helmet.

Spending the evening with Becca's parents should have been a highlight of the weekend. I loved them more than I loved my own damn parents. But all I could think when I looked at Becca's dad was that I'd just lost the one thing that made me worthy. I didn't have shit to offer her—I wasn't smart or particularly good at anything except football. Lucky for me, Americans treated athletes like royalty and massively overpaid them. I might not be the sharpest tool in the shed, but even I recognized that was ass-backward. People like Becca's dad, who risked his life keeping his community safe, and Roman, who was prepared to go to war to defend our freedom, and Becca, who would no doubt invent some kind of life-saving medical device, deserved much more than they would get.

My injury had clarified things for me in a hurry. I'd always said if I didn't make it to the pros, I would take whatever scraps my father was willing to pass my way in Fleck Holdings. But I'd never believed it would come to that. Now I had to accept that it was a real possibility. The thought was more than distasteful—it was unfathomable. Not only did I not want to work for my father, but he would be sure to remind me every day that I hadn't earned my place in his company, that it was a handout. The kicker was that he would be right. He'd started with nothing but debt from a few community college classes, and he had built Fleck Holdings into one of the most successful companies on the East Coast. Yet I couldn't manage to get my shit together enough to complete my college degree, which I wasn't even paying for. For the first time, I was starting to regret that I hadn't taken my studies seriously. Even if I changed my mind and decided to stay for the spring semester, I still wouldn't graduate on time. I'd done the bare minimum and had taken the easiest courses, which meant I would need at least another year to complete the required classes. The thought made me sick to my stomach, especially considering I'd chosen my major because it was the easiest one available.

I shifted, trying to get comfortable with my useless arm. I ran my left hand over Becca's hair and smoothed it away from her delicate features. I'd always loved her, but just like with everything else in my life, I'd been a total moron and hadn't recognized my feelings for her. Or maybe I'd been too chickenshit to admit to them. Either way, it didn't matter. Loving her made me a better person, and all I wanted was to do right by her. I just wasn't sure what that was anymore.

***

Becca

"HOW LONG HAVE you been awake?" I asked.

Carson looked rough, like he'd only gotten a few hours of sleep at most. "A while." He started to get out of bed, but I put my hand on his chest.

"Stay here," I said. "Try to rest some more. I'll make breakfast."

Instead of lying back down, he stood and walked toward the bathroom. "Don't bother. I'm not hungry," he said over his shoulder. Then he closed the bathroom door behind him.

Shit. Carson was *always* hungry. Not to compare him to a dog, but it was kind of like that—him not eating was a sign that something was seriously wrong. I'd already known that, but confirmation like this felt like a punch to the throat.

"I'm hungry, so I'm going to cook anyway," I said loudly so he could hear me through the closed door. "I'll make enough for two in case you change your mind."

I waited for him to reply, but after a few seconds of silence, I sighed and went downstairs. I wasn't much of a breakfast eater and normally had something light. But Carson usually ate a big breakfast, so I pulled the eggs out of the fridge. Hopefully the smell of scrambled eggs with cheese would awaken his appetite. And hopefully I was being overdramatic with my worry. It was the first time in my life I'd ever wished to have muddy thoughts about something.

The eggs were nearly done by the time he came downstairs, but he wasn't wearing the sling he'd come home in the night before. I had no idea whether he needed to be wearing it or not.

"Do you need help with the sling?" I asked. I knew he had to wait for the swelling to go down for the doctors to treat the break, but his unprotected arm made me nervous. I didn't want him to hurt it worse, if that were even possible. Though I was a biomedical engineering major, I knew surprisingly little about broken bones.

"No." His response was terse and in a tone he'd never taken with me before.

"Does it hurt?" I asked gently, even though I could tell he didn't want to talk about it. I couldn't stop myself, though.

"It doesn't bother me." Again, his words were clipped.

That meant it probably did hurt, but injuries to Carson were what mosquito bites were to most people—simply annoying.

I scooped the eggs onto two plates and set them down on the table. I was pleased when Carson sat in front of the bigger helping and picked up a fork. *See? Totally overreacting.* Still, my internal cheery voice couldn't persuade me.

"Did the doctor give you any instructions for today?" He had a consult scheduled for tomorrow. With my parents and Roman visiting, though, we hadn't gotten a chance to discuss anything. I was still as in the dark as I had been last night.

"Rest."

Damn it. His terse answers were killing me, but I didn't know how to make his mood better. False assurances that everything would be all right wouldn't help him. In fact, they would most likely annoy him.

We ate in silence, then I started cleaning up the dishes and pan I'd cooked in. As I stood at the sink, Carson came up behind me and wrapped his good arm around me.

He pressed his face into my hair. "I love you." His voice was laced with pain, and it broke my heart a little.

"I love you too. We'll get through this." I put down the plate I'd been rinsing so I could turn to embrace him, but before I could, he was gone.

***

I CHECKED MY phone for the millionth time. Normally, I tucked it in my bag during class, but Carson's consult with the doctor should have ended by now, and I was anxiously waiting to hear his prognosis.

Around me, my classmates chuckled, making me realize I hadn't heard a word the professor had said in the last ten minutes. Dr. Novikoff was one of my favorite professors because he managed to insert humor into the otherwise dry topic of biomedical materials.

I'd wanted to go with Carson to his appointment, but he'd been adamant that I go to class. It was a role reversal from when I'd had my concussion, but since I was behind because of that, I couldn't argue with him. I hated that he was at the appointment alone. He would most likely need surgery and a cast, then at least six to eight weeks of recovery time, and perhaps physical therapy after that. That was the best I could tell from my limited medical knowledge and what I'd learned online. He tried to act like it was no big deal, but I saw right through his charade. The injury had shaken him, but he refused to talk about it. He'd shut me out. That hurt, but I pushed the hurt aside because this wasn't about me.

Dr. Novikoff dismissed class, and I sighed. I'd been a complete waste of space for the past hour. Though I'd been physically present, my mind had been elsewhere. And my notebook page, which was normally full of notes at the end of a lecture, was blank.

As I walked out of the lecture hall, I called Carson, but it went to voice mail. *Damn it.* I had a copy of his schedule, so I knew where he should be if he was done with the doctor, but I seriously doubted he was in class. He had a hard enough time forcing himself to go to class under normal circumstances.

I was so distracted, I walked right into someone. I'd been holding my phone in front of me, and it banged painfully into my teeth as I collided with the person's chest. *Smooth, Becca.*

"Sorry," I said immediately. "My fault. I wasn't paying attention."

"I see that."

I looked up to see that it was Evan I had crashed into. I sighed with relief. At least it was someone I knew instead of a stranger. Evan already knew I was a spaz.

"Sorry," I said again.

"It was my fault, actually," Evan said. "I called your name and stepped in front of you to get your attention, but it didn't work. Obviously."

"I'm sorry." *You've apologized three times. I think he gets it.* "I'm a little distracted. Carson had an appointment with the doctor."

Evan winced. "His arm looked bad."

"Did you see him?" Maybe I was wrong, and Carson had come to campus.

He shook his head. "No, I meant on Saturday when it happened. It was obviously broken."

I frowned. "Really? You could see that?" I had been much closer than Evan, but I hadn't been able to determine that absolutely.

"They kept replaying it on the jumbotron."

"Oh." I'd been so focused on Carson on the field that I hadn't looked at the screen at all. I had been freaked out enough, so it was probably better I hadn't seen his broken arm blown up to the size of a bus on the screen. *Yikes.*

"He's tough, though," Evan said. "He'll bounce back."

"That's what everyone keeps saying." I was really sick of hearing it. No one knew him like I did. I wasn't worried about Carson physically because he was the toughest person I knew. But I couldn't help but remember the hollow expression that overtook him whenever he thought no one was watching. He was obviously putting on an act, and it ate at my insides that he felt like he had to do that with me. He'd built an unnecessary, impermeable wall between us.

Concern was all over Evan's face. "Is everything else okay?"

I pasted on the same smile Carson had been wearing the last two days every time someone looked his way. He wouldn't want me discussing his injury with anyone, not even Evan. "You know me. Just worrying."

He gave me a strange look. "I do know you, and it's not like you to worry unless there's something to worry about."

And there it was—reassurance that I wasn't worrying about nothing because Evan was right. Despite my hysterical response when Carson first got injured, I wasn't prone to overreacting.

Though it sounded dramatic, I couldn't help but think that when Carson broke his arm, something inside him broke too.

CHAPTER 22

Becca

I WENT STRAIGHT to Carson's house after my last class. Though he had texted me eventually, his text consisted of only two words: *Surgery tomorrow.* At least the doctors weren't prolonging it. The sooner he could get on the road to recovery, the sooner he could get back to feeling like himself.

When I let myself into his townhouse, he was lying on the couch on his back, staring at the ceiling and looking miserable. My heart clenched when I saw him. I propped myself on the edge of the couch, next to him. "Hey."

His dull eyes shifted to me. "Hey."

"So, surgery tomorrow?" I tried to sound upbeat, like surgery was a good thing. Considering the circumstances, it was. This was just a bump in the road that he needed to get past. "I assume it's in Roanoke." At his nod, I continued. "What time?"

"Nine."

I grimaced. "That's early, but better to get it over with, right? We'll have to leave by seven."

His gaze shifted back to the ceiling. "I asked Jake to drive me."

"But..." I was at a loss for words. It had never occurred to me that he would ask someone else to take him to the surgery. I searched his face, trying to read him, but he was expressionless. "I can take you. Jake doesn't need to miss class."

"Neither do you."

Again, I peered at his face, trying to find answers, but his expression gave nothing away. Neither did his monotone. Both were massive warning signs—Carson was usually animated and full of life.

"I'm all caught up. It's fine." I didn't bother to point out that I would be so consumed with worry, I wouldn't be able to pay attention in class anyway.

"I don't want you there."

His blunt words were a blow to my heart. A month ago, I would have bet my life on me being the only person he would want with him at a time like that. What had changed? *Our relationship.* That shouldn't matter, though. If anything, that should make him lean on me more. But instead, he was pushing me away.

I wanted to demand an explanation, but I reminded myself that this wasn't about me. Even though it hurt that he hadn't turned to me in his time of need, my feelings weren't important as long as he got the help he needed. At least that was what I tried to tell myself. It was hard to believe that statement when he was tearing my heart to shreds.

"Okay." I tried to keep my tone light. "If that's what you want, but let me know if you change your mind."

"I won't."

I flinched then tried to play it off by running my hands through my hair. He wasn't thinking straight, but when he recovered and thought back on this, he would feel bad about how he'd acted. Everyone handled stressful situations differently, so I wasn't going to give him shit about it while he was still in the middle of it.

"Do you want me to stay over tonight?" In the last month, I hadn't had to ask that question because the answer was always yes. But now I didn't know what was going through his mind. I barely recognized him.

"No."

I looked down at my lap and picked at my fingernails, trying to keep the tears out of my eyes. "Okay." I leaned down to press a kiss to his lips, and his mouth met mine with a desperate hunger for a brief moment before he turned away.

Not knowing what to make of it, I stood. "Rest up. I'll see you tomorrow."

He didn't say anything, so I let myself out.

***

Carson

JAKE KNOCKED ON my door at a quarter to seven the next morning. He looked like hell, like the only thing keeping his eyelids peeled open was the coffee he had clutched in his hand. I hadn't eaten or drunk anything since midnight, and at this ungodly hour, the rich smell of the caffeinated beverage made me nearly delirious.

"Are you ready?"

Shoving my keys in my pocket, I stepped out onto the porch and closed the door behind me. "Yeah."

The outpatient surgery center was about an hour away. The traffic on I-81 was always unpredictable, so considering it was rush hour, we wanted to give ourselves plenty of time.

Once in the truck, Jake secured his phone in the holder on the dash.

"Do you need the address?" I asked him.

"No, I got it. And before I forget, give me Becca's number."

"What? Why?"

Jake finished typing in the address and hit Go on the GPS. "Because you're not going to be in any shape to text her when you come out of surgery, and if she's anything like Rachel, she'll want to know the second you're out. I'm surprised she isn't taking you."

Scowling, I stared out the window as Jake backed out of the parking space. "She's got more important things to do," I muttered.

Jake let out a low whistle. "Ouch. That's harsh."

It took me a second to realize he thought I was repeating her words. I should've let it go, but I didn't want him to think she was an asshole. "She wanted to come, but I told her not to."

"So instead, you drag my ass out of bed? Nice." Jake glanced over at me. "And why the hell would you tell her that anyway? She sure as hell would be a better nurse than I am."

"She's better off not having to do that." The words were out of my mouth before I could stop them. *Damn it.* The early hour and lack of caffeine were getting to me. I didn't expect Jake to understand. He was a goddamn saint who'd taken legal guardianship over his three younger siblings. I was sure that balanced out any asshole tendencies he might have. I couldn't say I had a similar thing going for me.

Jake blew out a breath. "What's going on, man?"

"Nothing."

"Did Becca do something to piss you off?"

"No."

A few seconds passed. "Okay, so then are you the one being the asshole?"

It was exactly the opposite. I *was* thinking of her. I was *always* thinking of her, which was how I'd gotten her into this mess. I'd known I wasn't worthy of her, but I'd been selfish. It wasn't fair to her to keep her trapped with someone like me. While no one would ever be good enough for her, there were a hell of a lot of guys who would be better for her. We never should have ventured out of the friend zone because now I didn't know if we would be able to go back. I would lose all of her.

Feeling sorry for myself, I leaned my forehead against the window. The Zizzos had been such an important part of my life ever since Roman and I ended up on the same kickball team at recess in grade school. I couldn't imagine my life without them, but I guessed I would soon be living that reality. And I had no one to blame but myself.

Jake sighed heavily. "I take your silence to mean you *are* the one being the asshole."

"Leave it alone, Jake. You don't know what you're talking about."

"Yeah, because you won't tell me what's going on."

I stayed silent. Jake should know me well enough to know I wasn't going to cry on his shoulder or some shit. But he just couldn't seem to drop it.

He looked over at me. "You were one of the only people who didn't give up on me when my parents died. I'll always owe you for that, and I hope to God you'll never be in a situation like that. But looking at you now, it seems like you're fucking up, and you're doing stupid shit you're going to regret. So as a friend, I'm trying to point it out to you."

Even though anger formed in the pit of my stomach, I knew he meant well. The trouble was he had my best interests at heart instead of Becca's. "I'll keep it in mind." I scrubbed my left hand over my face. It was funny how quickly I'd adapted to not using my right arm. "God, this fucking sucks. The timing couldn't be worse."

"Sure, it could," Jake said easily. "It could have happened in August." When he noticed my scowl, he laughed. "Rachel's positivity is rubbing off on me."

"Well, you keep that shit to yourself."

He shrugged. "It's not so bad. It's kind of nice, actually. Now if I was in your shoes, I wouldn't be so positive."

"Hypocrite," I muttered.

"You had a good season last year. And the first part of this season was great too. I only have the first part of this season to rely on for the draft. Don't worry, man. You're still good."

I sure as hell hoped so because I didn't have a plan B.

***

Becca

I GOT A text from an unknown number around ten a.m., telling me that Carson was out of surgery and everything went well. I assumed it was Jake, and I appreciated that he thought to contact me. I hadn't expected to hear from Carson at all, and I guessed I technically still hadn't.

Sighing, I tried to pay attention to the lecture. But just like the previous day, it was pointless. Knowing Carson's surgery had gone well was only part of the puzzle. His injury had unleashed something inside him that a cast wouldn't help. Apparently, I couldn't help him either. Or at least he didn't want me to, which was even more troubling.

I didn't get it. Before we'd gotten together, I'd considered Carson my family here on campus. I'd thought he felt the same, but maybe I was wrong.

No, I'm not wrong. Carson loved me—I knew he did. This was uncharted territory, and frankly, I would have been happier if I'd never had to chart it.

After lunch, I decided to blow off my afternoon classes, which was a first for me. But I needed to check on Carson. Hopefully whatever stick had been up his ass had been dislodged, and he would let me help him like he'd helped me after I'd been hurt.

I left campus and stopped at the store to pick up a few get-well presents, then I headed to Carson's. When I walked up to his front door, I could hear the TV, which was an improvement. He usually had it on in the background, so that was a sign that he was getting back to normal. I let myself in but stopped myself before calling out when I saw him asleep on the couch.

I knelt next to him, surveying the dark-blue cast on his arm. I wondered if he got to pick the color. My gaze traveled to his face. He hadn't shaved since before the game, so the stubble on his cheeks had gotten so long, it was the beginning of a beard. He let it grow sometimes, like that one no-shave November our freshman year that had stretched into March. By the time he shaved, he'd looked like a mountain man. *Still sexy as hell, though.*

Though he normally looked peaceful while he slept, now his expression was twisted, as if what plagued him in life was also bothering him in his dreams. Not able to stop myself, I put my hand on his cheek, wishing I could help him, wishing he would let me try.

His eyes fluttered open, and I cringed. "Sorry," I said softly. "I came by to see how you are."

He looked around in confusion. "What time is it?"

"Two. Look, I got you something." I fished around in my shopping bag and pulled out a pack of black Sharpies. I grinned. "Now everyone can sign your cast. Hopefully the black will show up on the blue. Maybe I should get silver."

"You have class." He still seemed out of it, making me feel terrible for waking him up. I wondered if he was in pain from the surgery. Regardless, rest was the best medicine.

"Do you want me to help you upstairs?" I asked. "You'll sleep better there."

"I don't want your help."

I should have been used to his harsh words after the last few days, but I would never get used to this bitter, unfeeling Carson who fired off words that cut me. I wanted to believe we could get through anything, but with every inch he pushed me away, another shard was shoved into my heart, pushing it closer to breaking.

Wrapping my arms around myself, I stood and went to the other side of the room. I didn't want to do this now, but I couldn't take it. "Why are you pushing me away? Why won't you let me be here for you?"

"It's for your own good."

I spun to face him. "Excuse me?" For the first time, the pity I felt for him was replaced with anger. Who the hell was he to tell me what was good for me when he didn't even know what was good for himself? He was falling apart before my eyes.

He covered his face with his hand, and I wanted to rip that hand away. The least he could do was look at me when he was tearing me to shreds. "You know I'm no good for you."

I didn't know that, not at all, but he'd said it so factually that he no doubt believed it. I didn't understand why that had become his truth. Because when he held me, when he kissed me, he was nothing but good for me.

"Why do you keep saying that?" I demanded, no longer willing to let him believe his own lies. "You make me happy, and I love you."

"But you shouldn't."

Now he was really starting to piss me off, which generally happened whenever someone tried to tell me what I should and shouldn't do. I had never taken his shit when I was a kid, and I wasn't going to take it now. I shoved my hurt aside. "Why are you being like this?"

He swung his legs over the side of the couch, coming up to a sitting position. It was all I could do not to rush over to steady him. It was unnecessary, though. He could certainly manage basic movements with an injured arm. It was just that I wanted to do something, *anything*, to help him.

"I never should have let us get together. It was a mistake."

I gasped as his words forced themselves into my heart and detonated. "What?"

"I have nothing to offer you."

I don't want anything from you. But I didn't say that because I knew that wasn't what he wanted to hear. Anyway, that wasn't exactly true. I wanted him to love me. That was all I had ever wanted. "Of course you do."

He took a shaky breath and met my gaze. "I did, but now I can't guarantee that anymore."

"What are you talking about?"

"I'm not smart like you, or brave like Roman, or ambitious like my father. Did you know that I'm not going to graduate?"

I shook my head. I didn't understand what this had to do with anything.

"I never planned to graduate. I only did the minimum required to remain eligible. I wouldn't have even declared a major if they hadn't made me."

"Why are you telling me this?" I hated how shaky my voice sounded.

"I never told you that because I knew you would think less of me."

I opened my mouth to object, but the words wouldn't come. Truthfully, I didn't know how I would have reacted if he'd told me that bit of information under other circumstances. I would have been disappointed, but that wasn't the same as thinking less of him. Or maybe it was. But I wouldn't apologize for wanting him to live up to his potential. That was what a person was supposed to want for people she cared about.

"I was one hundred percent sure I'd end up being a professional athlete." He hung his head. "But now I just don't know."

I circled back to the words that had crushed my heart. "What does any of this have to do with us being a mistake? I can't believe you would think that, because being with you is the best thing to ever happen to me." I had laid my heart bare, hoping he wouldn't use my words as ammo against me. I couldn't believe I even had to worry about that.

"I knew I wasn't good enough for you, but I ignored it. This injury forced me to face facts, though. You're better off without me because you're everything, and I'm... I'm nothing." He choked out the last word.

I stepped toward him, wanting to take him in my arms. He'd hurt me, but he was hurting too, and that was so much worse. "You're not nothing." When I reached for him, he moved away, not letting me touch him. "You're everything to me."

He wouldn't meet my gaze. "I have nothing to offer you."

Goddamn him. I forced my hurt away, allowing my anger to surface again. Why did he think he needed to *give* me something? I had no idea what that even meant.

"You have you."

"You deserve more."

I stared at him. How could he think that? He treated me like I was the most precious thing in the world. He cared for me, looked after me. He *loved* me. I didn't need anything else.

He'd always been self-deprecating when it came to his academics, but it had spread to his entire existence. I didn't understand because Carson had always oozed confidence. But the last few weeks... My thoughts trailed off as it hit me.

Being with Carson might have been the best thing that had ever happened to me, but the converse wasn't true. For whatever twisted reason, being with me had caused him to question his worth. I thought back to the night I came home after my failed date with Blake. From the beginning, Carson had told me he didn't deserve me, and it had only grown from there. I'd brushed his comments off, not realizing how deeply they'd taken root in him, not realizing that he'd been poisoned by them.

But I knew him well enough to know there was nothing I could say to change his thoughts. Deep down, I also knew that would only be slapping a Band-Aid on a gaping, festering wound.

Until he accepted himself, he couldn't be with me. And that was something I couldn't help him with. It was a paradox, really. Maybe later, I would laugh about the absurdity of it. But now the final shard had been shoved so deeply into my heart that it was on the cusp of breaking.

Though I knew it was fruitless, I needed to throw a Hail Mary. "What if your love is enough for me, Carson? That's all I want from you."

His left hand clenched into a fist at his side, and his expression grew even more pained. "You deserve more. I can't let you settle for me."

I squeezed my eyes shut and willed myself to keep breathing as my heart broke. I'd loved Carson as a boy, and I loved the man he'd become, the man who stood before me. But I couldn't be with him, not like this. Anyway, he wasn't giving me much of a choice.

But I would give him one. "I love you, Carson, but I can't wait for you forever. I've already spent half my life waiting for you. I hope you'll stop believing the lies you've been telling yourself. If you do, you know where to find me."

Then I turned and walked out the door, using all the strength I had not to look back.

CHAPTER 23

Becca

NICOLE PUT HER hand on her hip and eyed me. "What do you mean you're not going to the game? You always go to the games."

I was suddenly regretting talking her into going with me to the middle school's robotics club meeting. I'd wanted to check it out myself before I asked WIE members to donate their time. I was blown away. The kids were so smart that they'd already taught me a few things about programming. At first, I'd felt awkward because, as a volunteer, I was supposed to be helping them, but it didn't take me long to realize that they liked showing off what they knew.

But Nicole was seriously driving me crazy.

"I told you," I muttered. "Carson and I aren't together anymore. I don't want to go."

She sighed. "I wish you'd tell me what happened."

Shaking my head, I tried to swallow the lump in my throat. "I don't want to talk about it. It just makes it worse." My cure for heartache was staying busy. That meant attending every WIE study hall and volunteering at the middle school. Hell, I'd even run some lines from *Othello* with Lucy. *Yeah, I was that desperate.* In related news, if a career in the biomedical field didn't work out, at least I knew theater wasn't an option. *Thanks, Lucy.* Maybe now she would finally stop asking me to rehearse with her.

"Boys! *Boys!*" Miss Hinchey yelled, giving a pair of kids a stern look. "Robot components are not swords. Please keep the make-believe out of the technology lab, okay?"

A group of girls snickered, and the two boys in question turned bright red. They returned what looked like metal arms to the workstation. *Peer pressure at its best.*

"But we always go to the games together," Nicole whined. "It won't be the same."

I sighed. Nicole was awesome, except when she wasn't. "Evan will be there."

She pursed her lips. "Carson needs to apologize so you can go to the games again. You *love* going to the games."

I *did* love going to the games, but one of the main reasons was because I liked watching Carson play. He wouldn't be playing, but even if he were, I still didn't know if I would go. Trying to cut Carson out of my life had been nearly impossible before when we'd just been friends. Now that we'd been more than friends, I'd succeeded. But damn, it was so hard. Just last night, I'd had to stop myself from texting him to ask if he had any assignments he needed help with before I remembered we were no longer speaking.

I missed him. I missed him so much it hurt. But I loved him enough to let him go. I just hoped I survived it.

***

Carson

BEING SIDELINED FUCKING sucked, especially when all I wanted to do was hide behind closed doors and drink myself into a stupor until my damn arm was better. But I still cared about the team, and wallowing in my misery would hurt morale. Normally, I liked being known as the outgoing one, but now it was biting me in the ass.

I zipped up my VVU warm-up jacket to my chin and jealously watched my teammates suit up. Even though I wasn't playing, I was still going to carry the flag out of the tunnel. I supposed I should be grateful that the team thought highly enough of me that they wanted me to, but instead I felt like a fraud. It wasn't worth arguing about, though. So I would carry the damn flag, wave at the crowd, and play my fucking part. Apparently, I was a "fan favorite." *Fuck my life.*

Beside me, Jake adjusted his pads. "You okay?"

"Sure." I wasn't, and we both knew it, but there was nothing to be done about it. Besides, Jake didn't need to worry about me. In my rare moments of not feeling like a pitiful jackass, I realized that what he'd said was right—he did have a lot more riding on this season than I did. Jake was a phenomenal receiver, but the shitty hand he'd been dealt in life meant he hadn't gotten to showcase that. I hoped he got an agent who could talk him into exploiting his situation as a human-interest story. ESPN and viewers would eat that shit up. I doubted Jake would go for it, though. It wasn't his style. But in the cutthroat world of professional sports, my view was that he should take advantage of everything he could.

"I'm glad you'll be out there," he said. "I know it sucks, but it wouldn't be the same without you."

"Thanks." I appreciated the sentiment, but he wouldn't see me during the game. My plan was to stay out of the way unless the crowd needed pumping up. Then I supposed I would trot myself out like a damn show pony. *Christ.* I was seriously questioning my past antics.

Coach Coyle walked in and gave his pregame non-speech, and then it was time to go. For the first time ever, my heart didn't pound and my chest didn't swell with pride as I ran out of the tunnel while "Enter Sandman" played and the fans jumped up and down, vibrating the stands.

I felt nothing.

***

SOMETHING THAT SUCKED worse than being sidelined was coming home afterward to an empty house. I'd fucked up beyond belief. I never should have given in to my feelings for Becca because there was no going back, and now I hadn't just lost a romantic relationship with her—I'd lost having her in my life at all. I hadn't even begun to process losing Roman as well. Thinking about the gaping hole in my life that the Zizzos had once filled was too much because I couldn't even think of Becca without a fierce ache overtaking my entire body.

It was my own damn fault. But she was better off without me. I'd underestimated her in my need to protect her, and if I was honest with myself, "protecting" her had been self-serving. I hadn't wanted to see her with anyone else. Now, though, I realized that Becca was smart enough not to date a jackass, and if she was momentarily fooled, she would kick him to the curb soon enough... just like she'd done with me.

I'd pushed her to the breaking point because our history had blinded her to seeing the truth about me. The thing was that although she was better off without me, I was not better off without her. Nowhere close. But that was my problem.

My phone rang, and I reached for it, thinking it was Jake. He'd wanted me to come out to Bleakers, but I'd declined, which was a first for me. I wasn't big on drinking alone, but I could not deal with Rachel's well-meaning twenty questions or with seeing my friends happy with their girls while I was fucking miserable. Yeah, I'm a self-centered asshole.

For a fleeting second, I wondered if maybe it would be better to go out. I could easily find a girl to go home with to help me forget Becca. But the thought of being physical with another girl after being with Becca turned my stomach. With Becca, I'd experienced love. Everything else would be a cheap substitute.

I blinked in surprise at the caller ID on my phone. *Why the hell is Chelsea calling?*

"When were you going to tell us you got injured?" she barked at me as soon as I picked up.

Nice to talk to you, too, Chelsea. Sometimes my sister could be just like my mother.

"Eventually." Truthfully, it hadn't occurred to me to make a special call to my family. I figured I would tell them the next time I talked to them, whenever that was.

On the other end of the line, Chelsea sighed. "I wished you would have texted at least. It was crappy finding out you were injured by watching your game and seeing you on the sideline."

Huh. I'd had no idea she watched the games. "Sorry."

"And thanks for the engagement card, by the way."

"What engagement card?"

"*Exactly.*"

What the hell was wrong with her tonight? "Uh, congratulations, I guess." Then I thought about it for a second and got pissed at her hypocrisy. "It's not like you called to let me know the happy news. I found out from Stacey. I didn't even know you were dating the guy. What's his name?"

"Don't be petty."

' "I'm not. I seriously can't remember his name." *Does that make me even more of a prick?*

"John."

That's right. John Henneman III, heir to the Henneman political dynasty.

"Well, I hope you and John will be happy."

She ignored my glib comment. "Just to give you a heads-up, once Mom finds out you're not playing, she's going to want you to come to the engagement party."

"Doesn't it bother you that she's using you like that?" Maybe it was a callous question, but I wasn't feeling up to putting the energy into being tactful.

"That's not what's it's about." She paused. "Well, not completely. She's happy for me."

I snorted. "Of course she is. It's a foot in the door with the Hennemans."

"I suppose that's a side benefit." At least she admitted it.

"Why are you marrying him?"

"What do you mean?" She sounded genuinely confused.

"I don't know. It just seems... convenient."

"Are you insinuating that I'm marrying John to help Mom's career?"

I could tell by her tone that she was irritated, but she had to know that was what people might think. *Or maybe I'm the only one who thinks that.* "Not only hers. Maybe your own too."

"That's low, Carson." She actually sounded hurt, and for a moment, I felt like an asshole, but I shook it off. My suspicions weren't all that outrageous.

"Like I said, I didn't even know you were dating the guy until Stacey told me you were engaged."

"It was pretty quick," she admitted. "But we've been friends since the first week of law school. Over the summer, things changed. When you know, you know. To answer your question, I'm marrying him because I love him. We're a lot alike. We have similar goals and ambitions." The warmth in her voice when she talked about him told me she wasn't lying.

"Then I'm happy for you, Chelsea. Really." I tried to sound sincere.

"Usually people sound a little more upbeat when they say things like that."

I ran a hand over my face. "Sorry. Things are a bit fucked up for me right now with football and... everything." No way in hell was I telling her about what had happened between Becca and me.

"Why don't you go home for a weekend? Get away from Bleaksburg for a few days. It might help."

"You've got to be joking. Hanging out with Mom and Dad isn't going to help my mood."

"They're not as bad as you make them out to be."

"Easy for you to say." Chelsea was the golden child, and I was the disappointment. Those roles had been assigned early on, and so far, we'd fulfilled them.

"You and Mom and Dad are just complete opposites. You don't understand each other—that's all. That doesn't mean they aren't proud of you."

"Bullshit."

"When is the last time you went to Dad's office?"

"Years. I have no reason to go there."

"Then you have no idea that he has a framed poster-sized picture of you in your VVU uniform in the foyer, right where everyone can see it. It's the only personal thing he has in the whole damn office. It doesn't fit with the decor at all, and Denise had a fit, but he insisted on putting it up."

Denise was his Stacey—she kept track of all the little things so he could focus on his business empire. While I liked Stacey, Denise was kind of a bitch.

"Why would he do that?"

Chelsea let out an exasperated sigh. "Because he's proud of you, you dipshit."

I took a minute to process what she'd said. Both of my parents were guarded with their thoughts and emotions, which had been hard for me growing up because I was the exact opposite—I was an open book. Sometimes, I seriously thought I'd been born into the wrong family. Or maybe I'd been switched at birth.

"You know," I said thoughtfully, "when you get in the courtroom, you're going to be in contempt if you don't watch your mouth." About the only thing Chelsea and I had in common was our potty mouths.

"Yeah, yeah," she muttered. "Just so you know, I don't expect you to come to the engagement party, even if you're not playing in a game. I know it's not your scene, and I know how loyal you are to your team."

"Thanks. That... that means a lot." I couldn't believe I was getting choked up talking to my sister. She wasn't as cold as our parents, but she and I had never been warm and fuzzy together.

"You can meet John another time. He's a fan."

"Really?"

"Yeah. He's a huge football fan in general. He collects shit, like jerseys and game balls." She paused. "I need to go, but the next time you have big news, like a season-ending injury, let me know, okay?"

"Same goes for you with your engagement."

"You got it. And also, just so you know, you've got a pass for the engagement party, but you better get your ass to the wedding."

I grinned, the first real smile since I got injured. "I wouldn't miss it."

CHAPTER 24

Becca

I CURSED AS we came up on another two-mile backup then looked guiltily at my passenger. Rayowa was a first-year engineering student from Nigeria. She'd started attending the WIE study halls last month, and when I'd learned that she planned to check herself into a hotel while the dorms were closed for fall break, I invited her to come home with me. Thanksgiving at my house was always a hodgepodge of people. My mom made room at our table for anyone who didn't have somewhere to go for the holiday. She affectionately referred to them as "strays," which was probably offensive, but no one seemed to mind.

"Sorry about all this traffic," I said.

Rayowa shook her head. "It is not your fault."

The younger girl was polite, but she was super quiet. I couldn't tell whether she was shy or simply not much of a talker. Either way, it made conversation difficult. She didn't seem to mind the silence, though, and to be honest, that was what I preferred right now as well.

I hadn't talked to Carson in over a month. I'd seen him once on campus, and the sight of him had stopped me in my tracks. I'd stared at him across the distance, trying to figure out from his appearance everything I'd been wondering.

Has he gotten his appetite back?

Is his arm healing properly?

Is he keeping up with his assignments?

Does he miss me?

Does he still love me?

When he'd turned in my direction, I had nearly run into a tree in my haste to scurry out of sight. But I couldn't face him, not when the last two questions were still the first and last things on my mind every day, not when I was barely holding myself together. I'd told Carson to come find me once he got himself sorted out. I never actually thought it would take him this long or that he might never come back. It had been a calculated risk, but I'd thought the odds were in my favor.

I guess the joke is on me.

I stood by what I'd said to him, though. Our relationship was no good for either of us if being with me caused him to degrade himself. I didn't fall in love with the Carson who hated himself. I fell in love with the confident Carson who was loyal, caring, and wore his heart on his sleeve. I'd been too wrapped up in the euphoria of finally being with him that I'd been blind to the change until it was too late.

Being with him for even that short time had been everything. Too bad I realized too late that not having Carson in my life at all was so much worse than being his friend and having to hide my feelings. Now we couldn't go back.

Several hours later, we finally made it to my house. Rayowa stood aside while I hugged my parents and my mom fussed over me. Then I introduced them, and my mother hugged Rayowa like she'd known the girl her whole life. The affection seemed to make Rayowa uncomfortable. Luckily, since Roman couldn't make it home for Thanksgiving, she would have a room to herself, so she would be able to hide if my family got to be too much for her over the next week. *Which is inevitable.*

After I got Rayowa settled, I planted myself at the kitchen counter while my mother finished making dinner. "How many will be at Thanksgiving this year?"

"Um..." She did some mental calculations. "Eleven? I think. It could change. It's still several days away."

"Wow," I said. "That's a lot."

She shrugged. "We've had that many before."

"I assume Mr. and Mrs. Meserve are coming?" They were an elderly couple from down the street. Though they had children and grandchildren, their family didn't live nearby and rarely came to visit.

"Of course. Mr. Meserve can't drive anymore. Did I tell you that? It about broke his heart when he failed the driving test, but it's for the best. He's a danger to himself and others."

"That's too bad. Are they looking at moving into assisted living or anything?"

My mom should her head. "Healthwise, they're actually in pretty good shape. It's just his eyesight that's bad. And she hasn't had her license for years. Driving makes her nervous. Anyway, I'm trying to teach them how to use Uber and Lyft."

I smirked at the thought. "How's that going?" My mother gave me a dry look, and I laughed. "That well, huh?"

"At least they can have groceries delivered."

"True." I inhaled the scent of the pasta sauce that was simmering on the stove. "That smells good. When will it be ready?"

"Not for another hour or two," she said apologetically. "I got a late start on it. So if you're hungry, have a snack. I stocked up on all your favorites."

I grinned. It was good to be home. I got up and walked to the fridge. Inside, I found my favorite flavors of yogurt, fresh strawberries that were already washed and sliced, and cheese sticks. I grabbed a strawberry Greek yogurt and shut the fridge. A picture that had been tacked onto the front of the fridge fluttered to the floor, so I leaned down to pick it up. When I flipped it over, my breath caught in my throat as I looked at the image of Roman and Carson in their high school JV football uniforms. Both were covered in mud, and their arms were flung around one another. Even at the awkward age of fourteen, it was obvious that both Roman and Carson were going to be handsome, especially Carson. He was nearly six inches taller than Roman in the picture, and he had the devilish look in his eyes that had been a constant in his high school years. That was probably right around the time that my puppy love for Carson had started turning into something deeper, something more real. I'd only been thirteen, but it hadn't mattered. I'd already known.

I clipped the picture back on the fridge and scanned the other ones. Most were of Roman and me, which was to be expected, but Carson was in a good number of them too. He was part of my past and, up until recently, a big part of my present. I'd hoped he would be an important part of my future. But with each day that passed without my hearing from him, I had to accept the truth—his time in my life might be done.

***

Carson

THIS WAS THE first Thanksgiving I'd been home since I started at VVU. We always had a game the Saturday following the holiday, and since there were no classes, the coaches used the week to double down on practice. Since I couldn't practice, I had the week free. Jake had invited me to his place for Thanksgiving, but since Chelsea texted and told me she would be home, I decided to make the trip too. But I arrived on Wednesday and was leaving on Friday—I wasn't crazy enough to stay the whole week. Besides, I wanted to get back to campus for Saturday's game. My backup, Hunter Ramsey, was a freshman who had planned to redshirt. That plan had gotten shot on account of my injury, though. I had fallen into a mentor role with him, something I'd never expected to be doing.

There was a bang on my childhood-bedroom door. "Get your ass out of bed!" Chelsea yelled. "Get dressed and come run with me."

Shit. I was usually all for working out, but I'd planned to spend most of the day in bed, playing Xbox and watching YouTube—basically anything to distract me from the fact that the Zizzos' house was just a few short miles away. That was about the distance from my place to Becca's apartment in Bleaksburg, but the college town was small—everything was only a few miles away. I was more acutely aware of the proximity here in Maryland. I wondered how much of a zoo it was at her house on account of the strays. The thought made me smile. I used to think of myself as one of Mrs. Zizzo's strays.

Bang, bang! "Get your ass out of bed!"

"Fuck, Chelsea!" I yelled back. Then realizing that cursing at her wasn't likely to yield positive results, I tried a different tactic. "Do you want to play Xbox?"

Her response was hysterical laughter. "Be downstairs in five minutes."

I sighed. Chelsea was a runner. She'd run track in high school and had even made it to the state championship. But she wasn't one of those sensible sprinters. No, she was a long-distance runner. In her undergrad years, she'd started running marathons—twenty-six hellish miles of running at a time. I was no stranger to running, but that was a bit much.

But for whatever reason, she'd decided I was going with her, so she wasn't going to take no for an answer. My sister had always been pushy, even as a kid. She almost always got her way.

I yanked open the dresser drawer to search for something suitable to wear in the brisk air. I hadn't planned on exercising outside, so I didn't bring my Under Armour. I found a lone compression shirt that had seen better days. It was about a size too small, but since it was old, the elasticity wasn't what it should have been. I would have to make it work.

When I came downstairs, Chelsea was waiting by the front door, peering at her sports watch. "Twelve seconds to spare. Nice work." She eyed me. "Nice belly shirt too."

I tugged it down and zipped up my jacket. "Shut up."

"Did you stretch?"

"When would I have had time to do that?"

She sighed. "Well, hurry up and get to it, then."

"Don't bitch at me. I wanted to be playing Xbox right now."

"Don't be a pansy."

I had no retort for that because after the first few miles, I was most definitely going to be a pansy. I could already feel the shin splints forming.

After a few moments of stretching, we took off. She set a steady pace that I had no trouble keeping up with. *For now.* I doubted I would feel the same in ten miles. But I wasn't going to ask her how far she intended to go. The first rule of being a Fleck was to never show weakness.

Despite the fact that I was sick and tired of running by the fifth mile, I had to admit that it felt good to be exercising outside in the fresh air instead of cooped up in a gym. Our father ran five miles every day, but to the best of my knowledge, it was always in our home gym rather than outside. I tended to stay indoors for workouts too. Maybe I should change that.

Chelsea led us down back roads and into a park. We ran straight through that, and she surprised me by going off the trail. *What the hell? Is she trying to twist an ankle?* I slowed my pace over the rough terrain, and she got ahead of me. Looking over her shoulder at me, she grinned then hopped a chain-link fence.

She's fucking crazy. I had no idea what she was up to, but she seemed to know what she was doing, so I followed her, scaling the fence more easily than she had. She was waiting for me on the other side of the brush at the edge of a parking lot.

I leaned down and rested my hands on my knees. "What the hell, Chelsea?"

"Come on." She didn't give me my much-needed breather. But instead of running, she walked through the parking lot to the front of the building. It took me a second to realize we were at Fleck Holdings headquarters since I'd never approached it from that direction. I glanced at the front row of parking. My father's Mercedes was in the space marked for the CEO. *Figures.* He never took a day off, not even on Christmas, though he did compromise and work from home that day.

"What are we doing here?" I asked.

"I want you to see something."

Again, I followed her lead because it wasn't worth arguing with her. Besides, like an idiot, I hadn't brought my phone. While I knew the way home on the interstate, I wasn't confident I would be able to find my way back the way Chelsea had taken us.

She led me into the elevator and punched the button for the fourteenth floor, which was the lowest of the five floors Fleck Holdings occupied in the building. Outside the main entrance to the company headquarters, she unzipped her running belt and pulled out a key then used it to gain access to the office.

"Why do you have that?"

"Dad always has a few spares in his home office. I took one." She gripped my shoulders and turned me ninety degrees. "Look."

I came face to face with myself. Chelsea hadn't been exaggerating when she'd said the picture of me in my VVU uniform was poster-size. She also hadn't been lying about it ruining the decor. But there I was.

Huh. I felt... I didn't know what I felt. *Numb.* It didn't make sense to me why he would have this here. He'd never shown more than a passing interest in my football career.

Chelsea pointed at another part of the wall. "These are new. They weren't here the last time I was here."

Multiple small pictures were framed, and they were all stills of me—yelling after I'd scored a touchdown, running with the ball, evading a tackle, jumping into the fans sitting behind the end zone. I could identify almost every game they were from, and a lot of those games hadn't been televised.

"Where did he get these?"

She shrugged. "You'll have to ask him."

"I still don't understand."

Sighing, she put her arm around my shoulders. "I already told you. Mom and Dad are different. They're like puzzles. They're proud of you, but they'll never tell you. You have to read between the lines."

I thought back to the obnoxiously large gift basket that had shown up on my doorstep a few days after I'd talked to Chelsea. It had contained fancy cheeses, meats, and crackers, plus dried fruit and wine—the kinds of things my mom liked to serve at her functions. The card had simply read "Get well soon," with no signature. I'd known who it was from, though. That was all I'd gotten—no phone call, no text, just a ridiculous gift basket filled with things I didn't even like.

"That's kind of messed up, don't you think?"

"I never said it wasn't."

I stared at the internal elevator that would take us up to my dad's office. While he was at work, Becca's dad was most likely planted on the couch with a beer in his hand, waiting for the football game to start. That was *if* he didn't have duty. When Officer Zizzo worked on holidays, it was because the community needed him to, not because he wanted to. I wondered if he'd started sneaking into the kitchen to steal bits of food. That drove Becca's mom crazy, but he still did it. I could picture the scene at the Zizzo house as clearly as if I were there. I wished I were there.

Yet my father was at his office. It wasn't like he had a reason to sneak into the kitchen to steal food, though. My mother always had Thanksgiving catered. She was most likely working in her home office as well.

"I wish they were different," I said. *I wish they were like the Zizzos.*

"But they're not." Chelsea's tone was matter of fact. "And the sooner you accept them for who they are, the better off you'll be." Her words were likely true, but it wasn't so simple.

"I don't know if I can."

"They accept you."

I snorted. "Bullshit." I gestured to the wall of photos. "Is this your proof?"

"That's about as much proof as you're ever going to get. I'm showing you this because I used to be bitter like you, and—"

"I'm not bitter." Yet I could hear the bitterness in my own voice.

"Now it's my turn to call bullshit on that one. You are so bitter, it's seeping out of your pores."

I scoffed, but I couldn't deny it.

"I'm not going to lie. Mom and Dad probably wanted you to follow in their footsteps. They're probably disappointed that you didn't. But that doesn't mean they aren't proud of the path you have taken. Because that, right there?" She gestured to the pictures. "That's pretty fucking awesome. Lawyers are a dime a dozen. Do you think Dad's going to make a wall for me? Hell no. But you're living a dream."

"Maybe not for much longer."

"So what? Then you'll do something else."

I turned to face her. "Like what, Chelsea?"

"Hell if I know. I don't know you anymore. You're more like our parents than you realize. You've shut me out, which is a total Fleck move."

"No, I..." But I trailed off because I guessed I had. I couldn't remember the last time I'd talked to my sister before her recent call. I'd more or less written her off because she reminded me of my parents—she reminded me that I wasn't what they wanted me to be. She was everything I wasn't.

Taking me by surprise, she wrapped her arms around me. "You're the only brother I'm ever going to have, and even though we're very different, I love you. More importantly, I *like* you. I know you're hurting right now, and even though you won't tell me what's going on, I know it's more than just this injury."

When she released me, I couldn't meet her gaze. She was throwing some deep shit at me, and it was totally unexpected but also really needed. Maybe I wasn't as alone as I thought. "Thanks. I, um, I love you too. I'll try to be better."

"Do that. Or else I'll make you run a marathon with me." She smiled. "Don't beat yourself up. I only recently figured out how to navigate my relationship with Mom and Dad. I thought I'd save you a few years of frustration by telling you."

"I doubt I would have figured it out on my own."

"Maybe. Good thing you have me." Her eyes took on a mischievous look. "Ready to run back?"

My sister was trying to kill me.

CHAPTER 25

Carson

I ADJUSTED MY tie in the mirror. Although I might not have packed running clothes, I had packed dress clothes. Like everything else in my family, Thanksgiving was a production. Even though it would just be the four of us, my mother insisted we all dress for the occasion.

Personally, I thought sweatpants were more appropriate attire for a holiday that was centered around eating. But no one had asked me. No one in my family ever did.

When I got to the dining room, my parents and Chelsea were already there. Though Chelsea claimed to understand my parents, it appeared that understanding included wine—a *lot* of wine. She smiled tightly at me and raised her glass. After yesterday, I understood my sister so much more than I ever did before, and for the first time, I wondered if being the golden child was as much of a burden as being the fuckup.

My mother smiled brightly, using what I considered her politician smile. Hell, it was the only smile we ever saw these days. Though, to be fair, I wasn't around much.

"Should we get started?" she asked. "It's exactly two o'clock."

"Of course," my father said.

We took our places at the table, and my mother presented my father with a carving knife. "Would you do the honors?"

He smiled at her. "This looks lovely, Marie."

She looked pleased. "Thank you."

I wondered what she was so pleased about. She hadn't done a damn thing to prepare this meal other than place an order, and Stacey had probably taken care of that.

"Before I cut into this beautiful bird," my father said, "I just want to say how nice it is to have the whole Fleck family here. Things are changing. Soon Chelsea will have a new name, and Carson will be at the mercy of wherever the draft sends him. This might be the last time it's just the four of us, so on this day of Thanksgiving, I wanted to say I am thankful for you all."

Holding back a snort, I stared at him. That was a total corporate speech, the kind he might give to his employees. But then I caught Chelsea's eye, and I remembered everything we'd talked about. I was finding fault because I was looking for it. In this situation, I was the one being the asshole. How many disparaging thoughts had I had about my parents in just the last few minutes? *Too many.* And it wasn't right. If I wanted them to accept me, I should do the same.

My mother squeezed my father's hand. "That was wonderful, Charles." She tilted her face up for a kiss, and my father planted the obligatory peck on her lips. It was a total show. But their hands remained clasped, and he brushed his thumb over her hand, lingering before he turned his attention back to the turkey.

They love each other. Despite their self-centered, egotistical tendencies, they loved one another. *Holy fuck.* It shouldn't have been so surprising, but it was. I'd always assumed my parents stayed together because it was mutually beneficial for them. I'd never thought love had anything to do with it.

"Carson," my mother said to me, "we missed you at the engagement party. There were a lot of people I wanted to introduce you to."

"I'm sorry I couldn't make it." I tried to sound sincere, even though I would have rather been anywhere but there. "But my team is my priority."

She held my gaze for a moment. "I understand that. Loyalty is an admirable trait."

I remembered Chelsea's words from yesterday—that was as close to a compliment as I would get from her. But knowing what I now knew, I was going to try to accept it for what it was and have it be enough.

Dinner consisted of more polite conversation, and though I failed a lot of the time, I tried not to look at everything my parents said through a cynical lens. I was only a tiny step closer to understanding them, but that one step had already made a huge difference because it made me realize that the problem was partially my perception of them. The revelation was mind-blowing.

Once we'd cleared the dishes and put them in the kitchen for the housekeeper to take care of the next day, we returned to the table for pie, coffee, and more polite conversation.

My mother looked at me over the rim of her mug. "Will you be rushing off to the Zizzos for a second meal now?" Her question wasn't surprising considering I'd ridden my bike over there to do exactly that every year since I was twelve, but I was a little surprised she'd remembered.

"No, I..." I looked down, and the blue of my cast caught my eye. It was bare. Though Becca had bought me markers, I hadn't done anything with them. It had been kind of a silly thought to have people sign my cast considering I was nearly twenty-two, but that wasn't why she'd done it. She'd wanted to cheer me up, and instead I'd pushed her away. Pain seized my heart as her words from another time sounded in my mind.

You're the one who's hurting me, Carson.

This time, I couldn't deny it. I'd hurt her and for no reason. Well, no good reason anyway. My damn insecurities were no excuse for hurting the only woman I'd ever loved—the only woman I *would* ever love.

I'm such an idiot. I'd done some pretty stupid shit in my life, but this was a next-level fuckup.

Becca's voice sounded in my mind again. *You know where to find me.*

Hell yeah, I did. My chair screeched backward on the hardwood floor as I stood. "Sorry, Mom. Sorry, Dad. I gotta go." On my way past my sister, I leaned down to kiss her cheek. "You're the best."

Then I raced out the front door.

***

Becca

"NO, MRS. MESERVE," I said gently, my patience wearing thin. "That's not Nia. Remember? I introduced you to Rayowa. She goes to VVU with me."

"Oh." The older woman nodded, but I could tell by the confused look in her eyes that what I'd said hadn't registered. Dementia had taken root in Mrs. Meserve since the last time I saw her.

I turned to Rayowa, who was seated on my other side at the table. "Sorry. She gets confused easily."

"It's okay," Rayowa said. "She reminds me of my great-grandmother. She could never keep me and my sisters straight, and lately she has been calling us by our mother and aunts' names."

I was grateful Rayowa was taking it in stride. It seemed that every time I looked up, Mrs. Meserve was talking to her as if she were Nia, the little girl who used to live next door. The real Nia was now in her thirties and a mother of three.

Across the table, my dad and my great-uncle Howie on my mother's side were arguing loudly about baseball, and it sounded like Uncle Howie had just insulted my father's beloved Orioles. *Lord help us.* Good thing we had a police officer present. *Oh, wait. He's the one screaming at the dinner table.* I winced as some four-letter words floated through the air.

"Sorry," I told Rayowa. "Thanksgiving at my house is a bit chaotic."

She smiled. "I like it. It's interesting. My family is quiet. Boring."

"Quiet isn't boring. Quiet is peaceful."

Rayowa laughed. "If you say so."

My mother started clearing the dishes, which wasn't hard. Since we used paper plates, all she had to do was scoop them into the trash can. I would have gotten up to help her, but somehow, I'd ended up in the worst seat at the table, crammed in the corner with the grandfather clock so close to my chair, I couldn't even scoot back. I seriously didn't know if I would be able to fit pie in my stomach with the table pressed up against my belly like it was. *Too bad we no longer set up a dreaded kids' table.*

The doorbell rang, but its sound was barely audible over the din of the chatter.

"Dad!" I said, but he waved me off as he continued to argue with Uncle Howie. My mother was in the kitchen, and I was trapped. I suddenly couldn't remember why I had been looking forward to this event. I normally embraced the chaos, but since my split with Carson was still wreaking havoc on my thoughts and emotions, I yearned for quiet.

Across from me, Andy laughed. He was a buddy of Roman's from boot camp who was stationed in Maryland. He stood. "I'll get it."

I smiled gratefully. "Thanks."

A moment later, he returned to the dining room, followed by Carson.

My breath caught. Carson wore a short-sleeve button-down shirt with a tie, which would have looked ridiculous on almost anyone but him. I vaguely remembered that Thanksgiving at his house was more formal, and he wouldn't have been able to fit a long-sleeve shirt over his cast. But I hadn't even known he was in town. Of course, how would I? We hadn't spoken in over a month.

My heart pounded, and my mouth grew dry. He was as handsome as ever, maybe even more so than I remembered. I tried to read his expression, but my heart interrupted my thoughts as it beat to a steady, chanted rhythm of *He's here. He's here. He's here.*

Why was he there?

His eyes locked on me. "Becca, can I talk to you?"

I swallowed, hoping to God he'd come to his senses and realized what I'd known all along—that he was worth more love than I could possibly give him. I tried to stand, and my chair thudded against the clock, pushing me back to a seated position. I would need to slide out without pushing the chair back, but I couldn't do that with the row of people on either side of me. *Damn it.*

"I'm sorry. I can't..."

Carson's expression grew determined. "Then I'll say what I need to right here in front of everyone."

My entire body stilled. *Oh God.*

My dad and Uncle Howie paused in their argument, and my dad noticed that Carson was there. *Great observation skills, Dad.* In his defense, he'd had more than a few beers, and he was off duty.

"Carson!" he said. "Are you here for pie?"

No, he's here for me. God, I hoped I was right, that the risk I'd taken had paid off. More importantly than us being together, though, I hoped he was okay with himself again, that he'd exorcised the demons that had taken him over.

"No, sir," he said, his eyes not leaving mine. "I'm here because I'm in love with your daughter."

My mouth parted, and I sucked in air, suddenly finding it hard to breathe. Everyone around me gasped, and their heads swiveled to look at me. I wanted to wrap my arms around him, to feel his heartbeat against my own, and to tell him I'd never stopped loving him, that I would always love him. But I was trapped in my chair.

"Carson, I—"

"No, let me finish," he cut me off. "I fu—messed up. I've got issues, and I let them get in the way of us, in the way of the best thing that ever happened to me." He drew in a ragged breath. "But I love you, and I'm not going to stop loving you even if you won't have me back. I loved you before I even knew I did."

My chin quivered, and I put my hands over my eyes. Taking a few deep breaths, I willed the tears to recede. When I'd let Carson go, I'd wanted nothing more than for him to come to this realization. All I wanted to do was go to him, but I was stuck behind this damn table while the dinner guests watched our exchange like it was a TV drama.

And he wasn't finished. "I know I have some work to do on myself, but I want to be with you, Becca. I want that more than anything I've ever wanted before. I'll give you everything that I am. I only hope that's enough for you."

The damn tears disobeyed my will and spilled onto my cheeks.

Carson's expression turned pained and took on a broken look. "I'm sorry, Becca. I don't ever want to make you cry. I'll go." He turned.

"No, wait!" I called out. He spun slowly, and I took a deep breath. There were so many things I wanted to say to him. But damn it, only one thing came to mind. "You had me at hello."

He blinked then blinked again as his brow furrowed. "Did you... Did you just *Jerry Maguire* me?"

Laughing and crying at the same time, I nodded. "Yes, you idiot."

"Then why are you crying?"

I tried to push away from the table again and failed. "I'm crying because I'm frustrated that I'm stuck between the table and this stupid clock. I can't get to you."

"Everybody move!" my mom commanded from where she'd been watching in the kitchen doorway. "Let her out."

There was a mad scramble as people shifted in our small dining room. But they didn't move fast enough, because as soon as I could shimmy out from behind the table, Carson lifted me over the rest of the chairs.

I wrapped myself around him. "I love you so much. You really did have me at hello."

He chuckled. "I didn't actually say hello."

I pulled back and arched a brow. "Then I guess you'd better say it."

He grinned, his eyes taking on a mischievous gleam. "Hello."

EPILOGUE

Carson

IT TURNED OUT Roman's buddy Andy filmed the whole spectacle at Thanksgiving and sent the clip to Roman. I was never going to live that down in this lifetime or the next. I didn't give a shit, though. Roman hadn't found the one yet, so he didn't understand. But when he did, payback was waiting. I was just so grateful he would still be around for me to hassle him when the time came.

I parked in front of Becca's apartment and trotted up the stairs to get her. My girl was finally twenty-one. We were going on a bar crawl, but she didn't know me as well as she thought she did if she thought that would be sufficient to celebrate her birthday.

She opened the door, wearing all black—tight pants, a form-fitting, low-cut shirt, and tall boots.

I eyed her appreciatively. "Are you sure I can't convince you to stay in?"

Grinning, she tossed her hair over her shoulder. "Tempting, but Nicole would hunt me down. She's been waiting for my twenty-first for forever. Let me grab my coat."

Becca thought I was taking her out for dinner to lay down a solid foundation in her stomach for the copious amount of alcohol people were going to be shoving at her. That was partly true—I was definitely going to make sure she got fed before the heavy drinking started. She hadn't seemed too keen on the idea of getting plastered, though—the night of the nipple-pinching incident was still too fresh in her mind—so I might have to resume my old guard-dog duties. Except instead of fending off guys hitting on her, I would have to fend off well-meaning friends from buying her shots. I would let her decide, though.

Once we were in the Jeep, Becca shivered and put her hands in front of the heat vent. Winters in Bleaksburg were brutal. "Can you tell me where you're taking me now?"

That part was tricky since I was no good at subterfuge. "I got a reservation at Flavio's. I hope that's okay." I relaxed as the lie rolled easily off my tongue.

"Anywhere is okay as long as it's with you." Her smile was so genuine, it made my heart skip a beat. She would be with me, but she would also be with fifty of her other friends. I hoped that was okay, but I couldn't ask her now. That was kind of the point of a surprise party.

My phone rang, right on schedule. I answered it using the speakerphone in the car. "Carson, oh my God," Rachel said. "Can you come to Bleakers? Like now?"

I glanced over at Becca. "It's not really a good time."

"Please, Carson. Jake got in a fight. The bouncer called the cops." She was supposed to sound panicked, but instead she sounded like a high-pitched chipmunk.

"We'll be right there," Becca said before I could answer. "Just stay calm."

"Okay, thanks." Rachel disconnected.

"I'm sorry," I said. "Let me call Wyatt and see—"

"No." Becca shook her head. "Your friend needs you. We can be late to dinner."

I sighed, trying to hide my joy at the fact that this was going exactly as planned. When Rachel had suggested a fake emergency as a ploy to get Becca to Bleakers, I hadn't been convinced it would work. I guessed she'd known what she was talking about.

"Thanks for understanding," I said. "I'll make it up to you."

"Don't worry about it. I just hope Jake is okay. It's not like him to get in a fight."

"No, it's not," I agreed. We hadn't been able to come up with a better lie, though.

We found parking and walked to Bleakers. Rachel was waiting for us out front. "They're letting him wait for the cops in the private room. Management has the other guy in the office."

Becca released my hand so she could hug Rachel. "We'll figure this out." Rachel grinned at me over Becca's shoulder then quickly wiped the smile off her face when Becca broke off the embrace.

Rachel led the way to the private room, which was dark. When she pushed aside the curtain over the doorway, the lights flicked on.

"Surprise!"

Becca stumbled backward against my chest as she was faced with all her friends and then some—Nicole, Evan, her other engineering friends, Blake, Lucy, Jake, Wyatt, Katie, and a lot of other people I didn't know. I'd enlisted Nicole and Lucy's help for the invite list.

I steadied Becca and leaned down to whisper in her ear. "Happy birthday. You really didn't think a bar crawl was all I had planned, did you?"

She spun to face me, her eyes wide. "You tricked me."

I nodded solemnly. "I did."

She pressed her lips to mine. "Thank you. This is awesome."

"It's just the beginning."

She raised her eyebrows for a moment before a knowing smile stretched across her face. She understood what I meant—it was *our* beginning. And it was fucking awesome.

About the Author

 Jessica lives in Virginia with her college-sweetheart husband, two rambunctious sons, and two rowdy but lovable rescue dogs. Since her house is overflowing with testosterone, it's a good thing she has a healthy appreciation for Marvel movies, Nerf guns, and football.

To learn more about Jessica, visit her website jessicaruddick.com. Connect with her on Twitter at @JessicaMRuddick or on Facebook at facebook.com/AuthorJessicaRuddick.

Other Books by Jessica Ruddick

Virginia Valley University
In the Pocket
Fair Catch
False Start

The Elemental Saga
Undefined (Book One)
Untamed (Book Two)
Unleashed (Book Three)
Unveiled (Book Four)

The Legacy Series
Birthright (Book One)
Retribution (Book Two)
Sacrifice (Book Three)
Redemption (Book Four)

The Love on Campus Series
Letting Go
Wanting More

Made in the USA
Middletown, DE
13 March 2021